THE HINDU WAY

ALSO BY SHASHI THAROOR

NON-FICTION

The Paradoxical Prime Minister: Narendra Modi and His India
Why I Am a Hindu
An Era of Darkness: The British Empire in India
India Shastra: Reflections on the Nation in Our Time
India: the Future is Now (ed.)
Pax Indica: India and the World of the 21st Century
Shadows Across the Playing Field: 60 Years of India-Pakistan Cricket (with Shahryar Khan)
India (with Ferrante Ferranti)
The Elephant, the Tiger, and the Cell Phone: Reflections on India in the 21st Century
Bookless in Baghdad
Nehru: The Invention of India
Kerala: God's Own Country (with M. F. Husain)
India: From Midnight to the Millennium and Beyond
Reasons of State

FICTION

Riot
The Five Dollar Smile and Other Stories
Show Business
The Great Indian Novel

Ganesh, the author's ishta devata

From the author's puja room

THE
HINDU
WAY

An Introduction to Hinduism

SHASHI THAROOR

ALEPH

ALEPH

ALEPH BOOK COMPANY
An independent publishing firm
promoted by Rupa Publications India

First published in India in 2019
by Aleph Book Company
7/16 Ansari Road, Daryaganj
New Delhi 110 002

ISBN: 978-93-88292-85-6

1 3 5 7 9 10 8 6 4 2

For sale in the Indian subcontinent only

Printed by Parksons Graphics Pvt. Ltd., Mumbai.

For Eliseo Kailash Calderon Tharoor
inheritor of many bloodlines
may his interest in books and ideas only grow with time!

Samudra Manthan or the primordial churning of the ocean

What thing I am I do not know.
I wander secluded, burdened by my mind.
When the first-born of Truth has come to me
I receive a share in that self-same Word.
—*Rig Veda*, I.164.37

May we not anger you, O God, in our worship
By praise that is unworthy or by scanty tribute.
—*Rig Veda*, II.33.4

May He delight in these my words.
—*Rig Veda*, I.25.18

Brahma on his vahana (or vehicle)—Hansa, a swan

CONTENTS

*A wooden sculpture of Ganesh—the elephant-headed Hindu deity
who is considered the remover of obstacles*

PROLOGUE

I decided to publish this book following the tremendous positive response its parent, *Why I Am a Hindu*, received from readers. Many of them felt that some of the sections of that book served as an accessible introduction to the fundamentals of the faith I profess, but were unhappy that I then digressed into an analysis of the Hindutva ideology and the politics of the Hindutva movement. Many said to me that were it not for the political sections of the book, they would have found in my volume the perfect introduction to Hinduism that they would have wished to share with all those not especially conversant with the faith, including their expatriate relatives, non-Indians, irreligious, young non-practitioners in Hindu families and any others interested in Hinduism but not in the politics surrounding it.

Why I Am a Hindu was indeed intended to contrast the Hinduism I grew up with, professed and practised with the narrow-minded faith of the Hindutvavadis, so I make no apologies for its broader theme and focus. But the demands of many readers for a book on 'Hinduism without the politics of Hindutva' was not an unreasonable one. So many readers, of varying backgrounds and ages, came up to me to say that my description of their faith had given them a sense of recognition and dawning self-realization; they felt I had expressed what they intimately felt but had been unable to put words to. It is this sense of appreciation that prompted me to take a second look at Hinduism. I've taken these readers at their word and persuaded my publishers to put out a richly illustrated edition that reproduces some of the sections of the previous book along with a couple of new and revised chapters.

As I write in the prologue of *Why I Am a Hindu*, my work on Hinduism exists for two main reasons. The first was to try and understand for myself, and for whoever else was interested, the extraordinary wisdom and virtues of the faith I have lived for over six decades, a faith that I have tried to absorb through beliefs and practices handed down to me by my father and others, my own observations, as well as an extensive reading of the scriptures in translation and numerous scholarly treatises. The second reason I wrote this book was to show that the intolerant and often violent forms of Hindutva that began to impose themselves on the public consciousness of Indians in the 1980s went against the spirit of Hinduism, that most plural, inclusive, eclectic and expansive of faiths. While that theme has been omitted from this volume, it animates my faith. The Hinduism I expound is not the Hinduism of those who in recent years have conducted mob-lynchings, 'cow vigilantism' and the occasional murder of non-Hindus.

I am neither a Sanskritist nor a scholar of Hinduism and did not set out to write a scholarly exposition of the religion. Mine is a layman's view of Hinduism, and my exposition seeks to give the reader an overview of the faith as I understand it, as well as accessible summaries of its main features. As will be apparent, I have relied on some

Vishnu puja

of its greatest teachers and adepts to explain its essence. My narrative weaves between personal witness and an attentive reading of the relevant scriptures and academic texts. I seek to bring together ideas of Hinduism from ancient texts, their development by many thinkers, and the practices and the challenges of Hindutva ideology. My approach is to present both the ancient texts of Hinduism and the modern beliefs of Hindutva descriptively and on their own terms, rather than through the theoretical approaches of historians, theologians and social scientists. In this way I seek to arrive at what I hope the reader will find is a lucid and reflective account of one of the world's oldest and greatest faiths and its contemporary existence.

But I do not pretend to offer a comprehensive view of Hinduism: that would go well beyond the space and scope of this book. Instead, I describe aspects of Hindu thought that matter to me, question practices I am less enthusiastic about, outline Hinduism's capacity to grow and reform and be revitalized for subsequent generations, outline the history of Hinduism in India and provide a feeling for what being Hindu means in a multi-religious country. In the process I devote as much space to anecdotes from the faith as I do to its timeless metaphysics. But this is what makes it, as its subtitle indicates, an 'Introduction to Hinduism' and no more than that.

Hinduism is uniquely difficult to encapsulate for various reasons: no single founder or prophet, no organized church, no single holy book, and so on; the faith is almost Wikipedia-like in the authorial diversity of its scriptures and tenets. The metaphors used by scholars to describe Hinduism have ranged from the banyan tree and the jungle to a kaleidoscope and even a pan of lasagne. One scholar has pointed out that 'Hinduism' can stand for a civilization as 'Hellenism' does, and also for a faith as 'Judaism' does; political ideologues in the mid-twentieth century insisted it also stood for a 'race' of people embraced by its beliefs. But isn't it also true that our Indian understanding of what 'religion' means has been so drastically affected by colonization, secularization, modernity and interaction with global currents, that our own way of conceptualizing our native conglomeration of tradition, belief and faith is irretrievably lost?

I cannot be sure, and yet I would argue it does

The Hindu Trinity: Brahma, Vishnu and Shiva

not matter. Some might suggest that this book is an exercise in attempting to fit something unwieldy and unclassifiable into terms an English-speaking, twenty-first-century reader can understand. Would what we call today 'Hinduism' be recognized by the ancient sage Yajnavalkya or even by Adi Shankara who reinterpreted the same faith nearly 2,000 years later? In essence, can today's Hinduism be divorced from the journeys that this aggregate of faiths took over three millennia of enquiry and exploration, resistance to assault and creative reform? Is it even possible, a thoughtful friend asks me, to think of Hinduism as 'pristine' and thus implicitly to say 'I am Hindu' without acknowledging that what one means is not some eternal category of belief but a set of self-descriptors that is contingent on history?

Some may well suggest that my portrayal of Hinduism means that I too have joined those who seek to 'tame' this most unruly of belief systems. Critics allege that the Indian secular liberals want to do just that to Hinduism because they cannot understand religious belief, while the Hindutvavadis want to do so because they cannot control too diverse a set of beliefs. Both sets of attempts result in an effort to 'homogenize' Hinduism for various ends. But the quotidian practices of Hindus involve intense prayer and meditation as well as fierce and bloody rituals, slavish devotion to gurus as well as philosophically abstruse speculations—a range of conduct that has little respect for a writer's need to describe religious phenomena in coherent terms.

As a Hindu, I write of my own faith, and confess that I am incapable of the detachment that one might find in conventional scholarly studies of Hinduism. Rather, mine is an engaged view of the religion, from within its confines, if something so capacious can be seen as confining at all. Though I have read a great deal of Western academic work on Hinduism, I do not partake of the hypercritical views of some twentieth-century Indologists, whose Orientalist gaze upon Hinduism, based perhaps understandably on modern notions of egalitarianism, rationalism and social justice, has sparked hysterical accusations of Hinduphobia. While I do not go as far myself in rejecting their right to express such views, I fear that some Western writing on Hinduism has paradoxically provoked a backlash that has driven many Hindus into the arms of radicals. Despite the flaws in some of its practices, my admiration for and pride in Hinduism outweighs my critical concerns, and I make no apology for this.

This book could not have been written without the help of numerous people who have been kind enough to comment on various drafts of the text. My former aide and associate, Manu S. Pillai, a gifted historian himself, offered me useful guidance, as did my 'sister from another womb', Dr Nanditha Krishna of the Indian Council of Historical Research, who has authored several books herself on various aspects of Hinduism. (She has asked me to point out that she agrees with my depiction of Hinduism but not with my rejection of Hindutva.) My thanks to Nanditha for allowing me to use her translation of the Nasadiya Sukta (the Creation Hymn). Keerthik Sasidharan, an intellectual moonlighting as a banker, raised a number of the questions I have summarized in this prologue and offered other insights into the faith. Devdutt Pattanaik, undoubtedly India's most popular interpreter of Hinduism, came up with a number of pertinent suggestions on *Why I Am a Hindu*, the book from which this book has been carved out. Prof Sheeba Thattil's research was invaluable in assembling vast amounts of material on Hinduism, including several works now out of print. I would like to thank Dr Karan Singh for allowing me to use his translation of Mirabai's poem. As always, family played a vital part. My son Kanishk Tharoor, and my niece Dr Ragini Tharoor Srinivasan, read the manuscript attentively and offered invaluable suggestions and criticisms. Ragini's searching comments and criticisms were especially helpful in making me think through my own assumptions and arguments, and I am most grateful. My sisters, Shobha and Smita, offered thoughts on an early draft and have remained strongly supportive throughout.

As always, my publisher, David Davidar, and his editorial colleague, Simar Puneet, have been superb guides in the process of bringing this book from gestation to publication. Simar's diligence and meticulous reading, and her marvellously inventive and exhaustive photo research, as well as Rosemary Sebastian Tharakan's thorough fact-checking, have ensured that my manuscript is as error-free as possible. David's intelligence, vision and humanity have accompanied me through many of my books, and while his exacting deadlines in the midst of more mundane preoccupations have sometimes exhausted me, they have kept me focused on the work that is now before you. His role has helped shape this final product, and to him I offer a special word of thanks.

While many minds have therefore contributed to the contents of this volume, the final responsibility for the arguments and interpretations in this book rests with me. If, after reading this book, Hindu and non-Hindu alike come away with a new appreciation of the faith I cherish, and the challenges it is currently dealing with in contemporary India, *The Hindu Way*, like its parent, *Why I Am a Hindu*, would have served its purpose.

Shashi Tharoor
New Delhi
July 2019

SECTION ONE

~

MY HINDUISM

*Ganesh with his two wives, Siddhi and Buddhi,
surrounded by his attendants*

Saraswati, the goddess of knowledge,
music, art, wisdom and learning

MY HINDUISM

Why am I a Hindu?

The obvious answer to this question is, of course, that it's because I was born one. Most people have little choice about the faith they grow up with: it was selected for them at birth, by the accident of geography and their parents' cultural moorings. The overwhelming majority of Hindus in the world were born Hindu. A small handful, inspired by marriage, migration or philosophical conviction, have adopted the faith, usually by a process of 'conversion' unknown to most Hindus. Unlike that small minority, I was never anything else: I was born a Hindu, grew up as one, and have considered myself one all my life.

But what does being a Hindu mean? Many of us began having to interrogate ourselves in the late 1980s, when the world media first began to speak and write of 'Hindu fundamentalism'. This was odd, because we knew of Hinduism as a religion without fundamentals: no founder or prophet, no organized church, no compulsory beliefs or

3

rites of worship, no uniform conception of the 'good life', no single sacred book.

My Hinduism was a lived faith; it was a Hinduism of experience and upbringing, a Hinduism of observation and conversation, not one anchored in deep religious study (though of course the two are not mutually exclusive). I knew few mantras, just a few snatches of a couple of hymns and practically no Sanskrit: my knowledge of Hindu sacred texts and philosophies came entirely from reading them in English translation. (When I went to a temple, I prayed in an odd combination of English, Sanskrit and my 'mother tongue' Malayalam, instinctively convinced that an omniscient God would naturally be multilingual.)

As a student of history I had always been curious about ancient Indian traditions and beliefs, and I had amassed a rather decent collection of books on the subject of Hindu thought, including multiple translations of the Bhagavad Gita. I had also been a passionate follower of the thoughts and speeches of Swami Vivekananda (as will be apparent in what follows). I had read widely in English about my faith, absorbing the wisdom of Dr Sarvepalli Radhakrishnan and Ananda Coomaraswamy, learning about the lives of such notable figures as Swami Vivekananda, Ramakrishna Paramahamsa and Paramahansa Yogananda, and delving into a variety of scholarly studies, from the old classics by A. L. Basham and R. C. Zaehner to the brilliantly interpretative translations and exegeses of Raimon Panikkar and Dr Karan Singh. From these, and others, notably my own father, I had acquired a set of personal convictions that made up 'my' Hinduism. But was that enough, and what did it amount to in the face of a violent new assertion of Hinduness in a form I could not recognize as bearing any relation to my own faith?

Swami Vivekananda

DEFINING HINDUISM

The first challenge, of course, was definitional. The name 'Hindu' itself denotes something less, and more, than a set of theological beliefs. In many languages, French and Persian amongst them, the word for 'Indian' is 'Hindu'. Originally, *Hindu* simply meant the people beyond the river Sindhu, or Indus. But the Indus is now in Islamic Pakistan; and to make matters worse, the word 'Hindu' did not exist in any Indian language till its use by foreigners gave Indians a term for self-definition. Hindus, in other words, call themselves by a label that they didn't invent themselves in any of their own languages, but adopted cheerfully when others began to refer to them by that word. (Of course, many prefer a different term altogether—Sanatana Dharma, or eternal faith, which we will discuss later.)

'Hinduism' is thus the name that foreigners first applied to what they saw as the indigenous religion of India. It embraces an eclectic range of doctrines and practices, from pantheism to agnosticism and from faith in reincarnation to belief in the caste system. But none of these constitutes an obligatory credo for a Hindu: there are none. We have no compulsory dogmas.

This is, of course, rather unusual. A Catholic is a Catholic because he believes Jesus was the Son of God who sacrificed himself for Man; a Catholic believes in the Immaculate Conception and the Virgin Birth, offers confession, genuflects in church and is guided by the Pope and a celibate priesthood. A Muslim must believe that there is no God but Allah and that Muhammad is His Prophet. A Jew cherishes his Torah or Pentateuch and his Talmud; a Parsi worships at a Fire Temple; a Sikh honours the teachings of the Guru Granth Sahib above all else. There is no Hindu equivalent to any of these beliefs. There are simply no binding requirements to being a Hindu. Not even a belief in God.

I grew up in a Hindu household. Our home always had a prayer-room, where paintings and portraits of assorted divinities jostled for shelf- and wall-space with fading photographs of departed ancestors, all stained by ash scattered from the incense burned daily by my devout parents. I have written before of how my earliest experiences of piety came from watching my father at prayer. Every morning, after his bath, my father would stand in front of the prayer-room wrapped in his towel, his wet hair still uncombed, and chant his Sanskrit mantras. But he never obliged me to join him; he exemplified the Hindu idea that religion is an intensely personal matter, that prayer is between you and whatever image of your Maker you choose to worship. In the Hindu way, I was to find my own truth.

MY TRUTH

I think I have. I am a believer, despite a brief period of schoolboy atheism (of the kind that comes with the discovery of rationality and goes with an acknowledgement of its limitations). And I am happy to describe myself as a believing Hindu: not just because it is the faith into which I was born, but for a string of other reasons, though faith requires no reason.

One reason is cultural: as a Hindu I belong to a faith that expresses the ancient genius of my own people. I am proud of the history of my faith in my own land: of the travels of Adi Shankara, who journeyed from the southernmost tip of the country to Kashmir in the north, Gujarat in the west and Odisha in the east, debating spiritual scholars everywhere, preaching his beliefs, establishing his mutths. I am reaffirmed in this atavistic allegiance by the Harvard scholar Diana Eck writing of the 'sacred geography' of India, 'knit together by countless tracks of pilgrimage'. The great philosopher-president of India, Dr Sarvepalli Radhakrishnan, wrote of Hindus as 'a distinct cultural unit, with a common history, a common literature, and a common civilization'. In reiterating my allegiance to Hinduism, I am consciously laying claim to this geography and history, its literature and civilization, identifying myself as an heir (one among a billion heirs) to a venerable tradition that stretches back into time immemorial. I fully accept that many of my friends, compatriots and fellow-Hindus feel no similar need, and that there are Hindus who are not (or are no longer) Indian, but I am comfortable with this 'cultural' and 'geographical' Hinduism that anchors me to my ancestral past.

Adi Shankara statue in Santa Cruz, California

But another 'reason' for my belief in Hinduism is, for lack of a better phrase, its intellectual 'fit': I am more comfortable with the tenets of Hinduism than I would be with those of the other faiths of which I know. I have long thought of myself as liberal, not merely in the political sense of the term, or even in relation to principles of economics, but as an attitude to life. To accept people as one finds them, to allow them to be and become what they choose, and to encourage them to do whatever they like (so long as it does not harm others) is my natural instinct. Rigid and censorious beliefs have never appealed to my temperament. In matters of religion, too, I found my liberal instincts reinforced by the faith in which I was brought up. Hinduism is, in many ways, predicated on the idea that the eternal wisdom of the ages and of divinity cannot be confined to a single sacred book; we have many, and we can delve into each to find our own truth (or truths). As a Hindu I can claim adherence to a religion without an established church or priestly papacy, a religion whose rituals and customs I am free to reject, a religion that does not oblige me to demonstrate my faith by any visible sign, by subsuming my identity in any collectivity, not even by a specific day or time or frequency of worship. (There is no Hindu Pope, no Hindu Vatican, no Hindu catechism, not even a Hindu Sunday.) As a Hindu I follow a faith that offers a veritable smorgasbord of options to the worshipper of divinities to adore and to pray to, of rituals to observe (or not), of customs and practices to honour (or not), of fasts to keep (or not). As a Hindu I subscribe to a creed that is free of the restrictive dogmas of holy writ, one that refuses to be shackled to the limitations of a single volume of holy revelation.

A Hindu can be astika or nastika: the terms are said to relate more to orthopraxy (action) rather than orthodoxy (belief), but action proceeds from a set of convictions. As an astika he can accept the sacredness of the Vedas, the existence of atman (the soul) and belief in God, or he can reject one or more of these credos and still be Hindu, an adherent of the nastika variant of Hindu philosophy. As an astika Hindu he can subscribe to any of the six major schools of philosophy, the Shad Darshanas (which I describe later); as a nastika Hindu he can declare allegiance to one of five schools, including Buddhism and Jainism, which after arising as reform movements against the ritualistic Hinduism of their day, were practically re-absorbed into the parent faith (though their adherents may not see it that way). Or the nastika can attach himself to the materialist Charvaka School, whose followers denounced most religious practices and devoted themselves to wealth and profit. The palette of options available is as colourful as the most inventive artist's.

At the same time, as a Hindu, I appreciate the fact that Hinduism professes no false certitudes. Its capacity to express wonder at Creation and simultaneously scepticism about the omniscience of the Creator are unique to Hinduism. Both are captured beautifully in this verse from the 3,500-year-old *Rig Veda*, the Nasadiya Sukta or Creation Hymn:

Then there was neither non-existence nor existence,
Then there was neither space, nor the sky beyond.
What covered it? Where was it? What sheltered it?
Was there water, in depths unfathomed?

Then there was neither death nor immortality
Nor was there then the division between night and day.
That One breathed, breathlessly and self-sustaining.
There was that One then, and there was no other.

In the beginning there was only darkness, veiled in darkness,
In profound darkness, a water without light.
All that existed then was void and formless.
That One arose at last, born of the power of heat.

In the beginning arose desire,
That primal seed, born of the mind.
The sages who searched their hearts with wisdom,
Discovered the link of the existent to the non-existent.

And they stretched their cord of vision across the void,
What was above? What was below?
Then seeds were sown and mighty power arose,
Below was strength, Above was impulse.

Who really knows? And who can say?
Whence did it all come? And how did creation happen?
The gods themselves are later than creation,
So who knows truly whence this great creation sprang?

Who knows whence this creation had its origin?

He, whether He fashioned it or whether He did not,
He, who surveys it all from the highest heaven,
He knows—or maybe even He does not know.

—*Rig Veda*, X.129

Rishi Bharadwaja, whom Rama, Sita and
Lakshmana spent time with during their exile

'Maybe even He does not know!' I love a faith that raises such a fundamental question about no less a Supreme Being than the Creator of the Universe Himself. Maybe He does not know, indeed. Who are we mere mortals to claim a knowledge of which even He cannot be certain?

Hindu thought also makes a virtue out of the unknowability of God. There is a marvellous story in the Upanishads about a sage who is asked to define the nature of God; the wise man, normally loquacious, falls silent. He is pressed by his disciples for an answer, and he replies that that *was* his answer, for the Absolute is silence; the mystery of the divine reality cannot be reduced to words or speech. Neither thought nor words can suffice: 'It is not understood by those who understand it,' says the *Kena Upanishad*, 'it is understood by those who do not understand it.' The final words of the Upanishads are 'neti, neti'—'not this, not this'— signifying the unspeakability of the Absolute. For many sages, their consciousness of the Divine is untranslatable to others, for those who have not attained the same realization cannot grasp it through word or sign: it is 'that of which nothing can be said'.

And while I am, paradoxically, listing my 'reasons' for a faith beyond understanding, let me cite the clincher: above all, as a Hindu, I belong to the only major religion in the world that does not claim to be the only true religion. I find it immensely congenial to be able to face my fellow human beings of other faiths without being burdened by the conviction that I am embarked upon a 'true path' that they have missed. This dogma lies at the core of the 'Semitic faiths', Christianity, Islam, and Judaism. 'I am the Way, the Truth and the Life; no man cometh unto the Father [God], but by me' (John 14:6), says the Bible; 'There is no God but Allah, and Muhammad is His Prophet', declares the Quran, denying unbelievers all possibility of redemption, let alone of salvation or paradise. Hinduism asserts that all ways of belief are equally valid, and Hindus readily venerate the saints, and the sacred objects, of other faiths. I am proud that I can honour the sanctity of other faiths without feeling I am betraying my own.

After all, as the philosopher Raimon Panikkar put it so brilliantly in his *The Vedic Experience*, 'It is precisely faith that makes thinking possible, for faith offers the unthought ground out of which thinking can emerge. It is faith that makes moral and other decisions possible, opening to us the horizon against which our actions become meaningful.' As a Hindu I seek meaning in my actions within the context of my religious beliefs.

✿

A FAITH WITHOUT DOGMA

And yet, Hinduism is a civilization, not a dogma. There is no such thing as a Hindu heresy. Hinduism is a faith that allows each believer to stretch his or her imagination to a personal notion of the creative godhead of divinity. Hinduism is also a faith that uniquely does not have any notion of heresy in it: you cannot be a Hindu heretic because there is no standard set of dogmas from which you can deviate that make you a heretic. Indeed, not even what one might think of as the most basic tenet of any religion—a belief in the existence of God—is a pre-requisite in Hinduism. As I have noted, an important branch of Hindu philosophy, the Charvaka School, goes so far as to embrace atheism within the Hindu philosophical framework.

The Charvakas were an interesting example of the intellectual heterodoxy of ancient Hinduism. Not only were they unabashedly materialist, but they challenged the most cherished assumptions of the astikas. The sage Madhvacharya summarized the Charvaka School in his *Sarvadarsana Sangraha* as arguing that 'there is no heaven, no final liberation, no soul (which continues to exist) in another world, nor any ceremonies of castes or orders which are productive of future reward'. The Charvakas were in fact contemptuous of holy men and their practices: 'The Agnihotra sacrifice, the three Vedas, the mendicant's triple staff (tridanda), and the practice of smearing oneself with ashes, are only means of livelihood ordained by the creator for men who have neither understanding nor energy.' And they were also scathing about the theological claims of astika philosophers: 'If [it be true that] an animal slaughtered at the Jyotistoma sacrifice is [in consequence] exalted to heaven', they asked, 'why does the worshipper not immolate his own father?'

Hinduism, in other words, incorporates almost all forms of belief and worship within it; there is no need to choose some or reject others. Mahatma Gandhi famously appreciated this quality of Hinduism: 'Its freedom from dogma makes a forcible appeal to me,' he wrote, 'inasmuch as it gives the votary the largest scope for self-expression.' It is therefore a timeless faith, populated by ideas at once ancient and modern, hosting texts, philosophies, belief systems and schools of thought that do not necessarily all agree with each other. But none has ever been rejected by some supreme authority as beyond the pale; there is no such authority in Hinduism. There can be no Hindu Inquisition because there is neither an exacting theology that everyone must subscribe to as holy writ, nor an exalted authority empowered to appoint an Inquisitor. Hindu thought is like a vast library in which no book ever goes out of print; even if the religious ideas a specific volume contains have not been read, enunciated or followed in centuries, the book remains available to be dipped into, to be revised and reprinted with new annotations or a new commentary whenever a reader feels the need for it. In many cases the thoughts it contains may have been modified by or adapted to other ideas that may have arisen in response; in most, it's simply there, to be referred to, used or ignored as Hindus see fit.

Inevitably, though, the question 'who is a Hindu?' has been asked, and equally inevitably, political figures have entered the definitional fray. 'Lokmanya' Bal Gangadhar Tilak suggested, in a meeting of the Sanatana Dharma Sabha, that 'a Hindu is he who believes that the Vedas contain self-evident and axiomatic truths', thus seeking to create a religious identity, based on sacred texts, that would be eligible for special consideration from a British colonial regime that had already extended recognition to Muslims (as members of a defined religious community following the dictates of the Quran). Two decades later Mahatma Gandhi added to Tilak's basic view, writing that Hindus are people who believe in the Vedas, the Upanishads, the multiple Hindu scriptures, the various incarnations of God, rebirth or reincarnation, varna (caste) and ashrama (the four stages of life, which I describe later), and veneration and protection of the cow, and do not express disbelief in idol worship. This is a rather long and contentious list, since many Hindus (myself included) do not subscribe to some of these requirements and do not consider themselves any less Hindu for not doing so. The foundational theorist of the political philosophy of Hindutva, V. D. Savarkar, asserted in the 1920s that one could be a Hindu even if one did not recognize the religious authority of the Vedas. To him, the various religious disputes within Hindu religious thought—between monism and pantheism, between Dvaita and Advaita, between the Vedas and the Upanishads and even including agnosticism and atheism— were irrelevant to the issue of Hindu identity. Savarkar saw 'Hindu-ness' or Hindutva as opposed to 'Hinduism' as a uniting cultural construct that underlay the identity of all those who belong to 'Bharatvarsha', the ancient land of India. Unsurprisingly, then, India's first prime minister, Jawaharlal Nehru, observed that 'being a Hindu means all things to all men'. British civil servant and historian Sir Alfred Lyall described Hinduism as a 'tangled jungle' full of paradoxes and contradictions, 'a religious chaos' spread all over India, difficult to comprehend and define. No wonder Dr Sarvepalli Radhakrishnan began his celebrated 1926 Upton Lectures on Hinduism by asking of his own faith: 'Is it a museum of beliefs, a medley of rites, or a mere map, a geographical expression?'.

As I have argued, one corollary of this eclecticism is the willingness of Hindus to accept other faiths and modes of worship—indeed often embrace them for themselves. It is quite common for Hindus to show reverence to the religious places of other faiths, and to carry relics or sacred objects of other faiths. History is replete with accounts of Hindus thronging Sufi dargahs, Sikh gurudwaras and Christian shrines (notably the Basilica of Our Lady of Good Health in Velankanni town in Tamil Nadu, which has been described as the 'Lourdes of the East', or Mount Mary Church in Mumbai's Bandra) with the same reverence they might express in their own temples. My late father was a devout Hindu who prayed faithfully twice a day, after his baths. He regularly went on pilgrimages to all the major temples and religious sites in our land. When a fire engulfed the Guruvayur Temple in November 1970, he led a fund-raising drive in Bombay that saw much of his meagre savings diverted to the rebuilding of that shrine. Yet, when a Catholic friend—his life insurance agent, who had made a trip to the Vatican—presented him with an amulet of the Virgin Mary that had personally been blessed by the Pope, he accepted it with reverence and carried it around with him for years. That is the Hinduism most Hindus know: a faith that accords respect and even reverence to the sanctified beliefs of others.

This inclination to revere the Divine, whatever its source, is a notable Hindu trait, reflecting a traditional unwillingness to succumb to doctrinal absolutism. In his historic speech at Chicago's Parliament of the World's Religions on 11 September 1893, Swami Vivekananda spoke of Hinduism as teaching the world not just tolerance but acceptance.

Large gopuram at the Thanjavur temple, circa 1860–1889

The Swami believed that Hinduism, with its openness, its respect for variety, its acceptance of all other faiths, was one religion that should be able to spread its influence without threatening others. At the Chicago Parliament, he articulated the liberal humanism that lies at the heart of his (and my) creed: 'I am proud to belong to a religion which has taught the world both tolerance and universal acceptance. We believe not only in universal toleration, but we accept all religions as true.' He went on to quote a hymn, the Shiva Mahimna Stotram, which he remembered from his formative years at school: 'As the different streams having their sources in different places all mingle their water in the sea, so, O Lord, the different paths which men take through different tendencies, various though they appear, crooked or straight, all lead to Thee...the wonderful doctrine preached in the [Bhagavad] Gita echoes the same idea, saying: "Whosoever comes to Me, through whatsoever form, I reach him; all men are struggling through paths which in the end lead to me".'

This was a profoundly important idea, and central to the philosophy Vivekananda was preaching. Tolerance, after all, implies that you have the truth, but will generously indulge another who does not; you will, in an act of tolerance, allow him the right to be wrong. Acceptance, on the other hand, implies that you have a truth but the other person may also have a truth; that you accept his truth and respect it, while expecting him to respect (and accept) your truth in turn. This practice of acceptance of difference—the idea that other ways of being and believing are equally valid—is central to Hinduism and the basis for India's democratic culture.

'I challenge the world to find,' Vivekananda proudly declared in a different speech in Chicago, 'throughout the whole system of Sanskrit philosophy, any such expression as that the Hindu alone will be saved and not others. Says Vyasa, "We find perfect men even beyond the pale of our caste and creed".'

One of Hinduism's great strengths—though there are some who see this as a weakness—is its lack of prescriptive tenets. The faith assumes that different people require different pathways to the Ultimate; even within Hinduism, there is no desire to require the same things of all people, it being accepted that people of different spiritual and intellectual attainments will employ different routes in seeking the Divine.

❀

Shiva, Vishnu and Brahma adoring Kali

MULTIPLE DIVINITIES

As a result, Hindus allow themselves to worship the divine in multiple forms; the 333 million gods of legend (some versions say 33 million, 300 million and 330 million: even here we are flexible!) are in fact merely a reflection of the infinite aspects of divinity. While other faiths tend to personify the idea of God, seeing Him in anthropomorphic terms as a man-like Being, the Hindu idea of God is both simpler and more complicated. God, to the Hindu, is everywhere, a presence and an absence, within us and outside us. God transcends both time and space. God has no beginning and no end, but equally has no shape and no form. God can therefore be imagined in a myriad ways, and in all conceivable shapes and forms, since there is nowhere that God is not, and nowhere that God cannot be. The highest form of God is the Brahman, the Absolute, the universal soul that suffuses all creation.

As a verse in the *Maitreya Upanishad* puts it:

In the beginning everything was Brahman. He was one, and infinite; infinite in the East, infinite in the South, infinite in the West, infinite in the North, above and below and everywhere infinite. East and the other regions do not exist for him, nor across, nor below, nor above. The Highest Self is not to be fixed, he is unlimited, unborn, not to be reasoned about, not to be conceived. He is like the ether (everywhere), and at the destruction of the universe, he alone is awake. Then from that ether he wakes all this world, which consists of thought only, and by him alone is all this meditated on, and in him it is dissolved. His is that luminous form which shines in the sun, and the manifold light in the smokeless fire, and the fire in the stomach which consumes the food. Thus it is said:

'He who is in the fire, and he who is in the heart, and he who is in the sun, they are one and the same.'

One of the most famous dialogues in Hindu philosophy, from the *Chandogya Upanishad*, relates to a discussion between a rishi and his son about the existence of God. The young man, Svetaketu, asks his father, Uddalaka Aruni, how he could demonstrate that God exists when there was no visible proof of God's existence. In the typical Hindu manner of instruction, Uddalaka asks his son to fetch a fruit from the banyan tree and cut it open. Inside the fruit, the son finds a small seed. The father asks him to break it apart and see what there is in it; but the seed is all there is. Uddalaka tells his son that all he can see is a small seed; yet something exists in that seed that is so powerful that an immense banyan tree can grow out of it. Similarly, God is not visible, but exists, and the world has grown out of God.

The son is only partly persuaded, so the father asks him

to mix salt and water in a bowl. Now, he tells Svetaketu, taste the water and the salt in different parts of the bowl, and once you have done so, separate the salt from the water. The son does as instructed, and points out that the water in every part of the bowl tastes equally salty, and that once dissolved, the salt cannot be separated from the water. Aha, says Uddalaka: you find the salt all-pervasive in the bowl; so too is the universal spirit, which is all-pervasive in creation. When, at the end of our lives, we human beings merge with Brahman, we cannot be separated from it any more than the salt can from the water in your bowl.

Since God is everywhere and in everything, this all-pervasive Universal Spirit is nirguna, without qualities, without shape and without gender; Hindus cannot refer to nirguna Brahman as 'He' since God can be and is also 'She' and 'It'. The Vedas use the interrogative pronoun 'ka' (who?), or more precisely kasmai (to whom?) for the unknowable God. The impersonal pronoun often used in Sanskrit for God is 'tat', 'that' in English; in other words, that which exists. Hindu meditation begins with the words 'Om tat sat': Om, the primordial sound that encompasses past, present and future; tat, that which exists; sat, Truth. The *Chandogya Upanishad* tells the story of Svetaketu, who is taught metaphysics by his father in a series of lessons that each end with the statement 'Tat tvam asi'—'That you are'—that you are the same as the Brahman that pervades the cosmos.

As the Hiranyagarbha hymn in the *Rig Veda* asks:

O Father of the Earth, by fixed laws ruling
O Father of the Heavens, pray protect us,
O Father of the great and shining Waters!
What God shall we adore with our oblation?
—*Rig Veda*, I.121.9

But the sages realized that all this was rather abstruse, and would be difficult for the average human being to comprehend. The nirguna Brahman was a philosophical concept at the heart of Hinduism, but people needed to worship something they could imagine and visualize. Hence the idea of the saguna Brahman—the Absolute given form, qualities and attributes, also known as Ishvara or Bhagavan. Strictly speaking, Ishvara is the best translation of God in the Christian or Allah in the Muslim sense of these terms, since those faiths have no equivalent for God in the sense of Brahman. But the Hindu Ishvara takes multiple forms: there is the trinity of Brahma (the Creator), Vishnu (the Preserver) and Shiva or Mahesh (the Destroyer), all different manifestations of the God Principle, and their myriad manifestations, plus their avataras, consorts and companions, who may all be worshipped depending on the preferences of the devotee. The avatara doctrine—under which these gods manifested themselves in different, recognizable human-like forms, such as Rama or Krishna—also had the distinct advantage of permitting the worshipper to venerate a personal god without this involving any rupture with the mainstream corpus of Hindu thought, which emphasized the impersonal formless aspect of divinity and insisted on 'neti, neti'. The unknowable nirguna Brahman, after all, becomes all the more knowable when it takes human form as an avatara; the abstraction of Hindu philosophic thought becomes more accessible in the form of a recognizable figure. The idea of the avatara responded to the popular demand for devotion to personal gods, and to their recurrence in the life of the believer. As Krishna says in the Gita (4. 7-8): 'Whenever righteousness declines in the world and unrighteousness arises, I return to earth. For the deliverance of good, the destruction of evil and the re-establishment of dharma, I am reborn from time to time.'

Vishnu and his avatars

At the same time it is remarkable how the ten avataras of Vishnu, the Dasavataras, seemingly chart the course of human evolution two millennia before Darwin, starting with Matsya (the fish), and proceeding successively through Kurma (the tortoise), Varaha (the boar), and Narasimha (the half man-half lion) to more recognizable human forms, Vamana (the dwarf) and Parasurama (who wields a great axe), then perfect men who are worshipped as divine (Sri Rama and Sri Krishna), then the Buddha (an interesting inclusion, of which more later) and finally Kalki, who is yet to be born, a brilliant youth on a white steed with a devastating sword, encircled by flames, who represents the destruction of the world as we know it.

Shiva as Nataraja, the lord of dance

Some speak simplistically of the holy trinity of Brahma, Vishnu and Shiva as three separate gods, but all three are in fact three sides of one complex being: aspects of the uttama purusha, the perfect personality. There is a God who created the gods (and the demons): Prajapati, lord of all creatures. There are multiple further manifestations of the divine in popular Hindu iconography: a myriad gods and goddesses. This might well have resulted from the Vedic civilization's absorption of the tribal and folk deities it found being worshipped in India before its advance through the country; each local manifestation of a god or a goddess was included in the all-embracing Hindu pantheon, so that as Hinduism spread, it accommodated earlier forms of worship rather than overthrowing them. Similarly many tribes revered animals, but instead of disrespecting them, Hinduism absorbed the animals too, by making them the companions or vehicles (vahanas) of the gods. So Vedic gods found themselves riding a lion, mounting a peacock, reclining on a swan, or sitting on a bull. It was part of the agglomerative nature of Hinduism that it neither rejected nor dismissed the faiths it encountered, but sought to bring them into the fold in this way.

Hinduism, therefore, has given birth to a rich iconography, varying according to the specific divine form and further according to the role in which that divinity is depicted, whether at a peaceful moment or in an attack upon evil, for instance, or whether as 'Himself' or transformed for a specific purpose (Vishnu, for instance, became a half-man half-lion, Narasimha, to kill a demon who could not be killed by a human). While the iconography of Shiva, Vishnu and the 'remover of obstacles', the elephant-headed Ganesh, is well known, every depiction of Ishvara (in whichever form) involves certain symbolic images and attributes, and the images of these gods were configured to embody profound conceptions of the universe, from the subduing of ignorance and the defeat of evil to the harmonies of destruction and regeneration.

Thus Brahma, the Creator, is always shown with four heads, facing all four directions, as befits the creator of the universe; he holds the Vedas in his hand, a prayer-vessel beside him, and sits on a lotus, the favoured flower in Hindu iconography since it remains pure and unsoiled by the mud and dirt from which it emerges. His consort is Saraswati, goddess of learning and wisdom, who is always depicted holding the musical instrument the veena, symbolizing the music of the cosmos, the inner sound of Om from which the universe emerged. She has rosary beads in one hand to signify the importance of prayer and meditation, and palm leaf scrolls in another, to epitomize learning. She too sits on a lotus, but sometimes on a peacock, a symbol of the ego that should be suppressed in the pursuit of true knowledge, and her vahana or vehicle is the graceful swan.

Brahma is rarely worshipped—there are barely a handful of temples dedicated to him, the most remarkable at Pushkar in Rajasthan—but Saraswati is ubiquitous, widely honoured and portrayed, and there is a specific day devoted each year to her exaltation, Saraswati Puja, whereas there is none to Brahma. That she is merely a consort to one of the holy trinity is irrelevant to her importance. Hinduism cannot entirely be absolved of gender bias, but its reverence for the female principle in the godhead is exemplary.

No better example of this exists than the many manifestations of the goddess in the form of Shakti, which literally means strength—the power of the life-force that creates, nurtures, sustains and also destroys the world. The goddess is seen as a source of energy, without which the male aspect of the godhead would be ineffectual. This female energy takes many forms. As Saraswati, she embodies learning; as Lakshmi, wealth and prosperity. As Uma or Parvati, she is Shiva's gentle ardhangani, his half, as inseparable from the Lord as fire and heat, or purusha (the spirit) and prakriti (matter), are inseparable. As Kamakshi or Rajarajeshwari, she is the Great Mother. As Durga, she rides a tiger, bearing weapons to fight the eight evils of humankind—greed, hate, envy, contempt for others, passion, vanity, jealousy and illusion. In her most frightening form she is Kali, the

Goddess Saraswati, the goddess of knowledge, music, art, wisdom and learning

personification of time (kala), dark, angry and armed, weapons flailing, her body dripping with blood, wearing the skulls of her victims, sometimes holding aloft the severed head of one or grinding her foot into the prone body of another.

If that sounds macabre, there are fifty-one Shakti-peethas across India, each consecrated to a body part of Shiva's first wife, Sati, whose body was said to have been dismembered in fifty-one pieces by the flying Sudarshana Chakra weapon of Lord Vishnu. (Sati had killed herself during a fire sacrifice

Goddess Durga, the slayer of the buffalo demon

conducted by her father, and her disconsolate husband was carrying her body around in grief and mourning; Vishnu's act was intended to get Shiva to snap out of it. Sati was duly reincarnated as Parvati.) There are temples where the goddess retreats into seclusion for three days a month to menstruate, as in Chengannur in Kerala; others where Devi's footprint (on stone) alone is worshipped. My home state of Kerala overflows with temples to the goddess, often referred to simply as Devi or Bhagavathi (both of which simply mean the goddess), though the most popular form of Bhagavathi-worship is of the goddess as Bhadrakali, a form of Kali. One temple in Thiruvananthapuram, the Attukal Bhagavathi

Temple, is listed in the Guinness Book of World Records for the largest gathering of women in one place at one time: millions (2.5 million in 2009, a record that is broken every year, with 4.5 million reported in 2017) assemble each February for the Pongala, at which offerings are cooked and prepared for the goddess.

There is a marvellous Puranic story about the birth of Durga. It is said that a terrible buffalo-headed demon, Mahishasura, had succeeded in conquering all the gods (or devas) and established himself as the master of all creation. The gods, despairing in defeat, retreated to a conclave under Lord Indra to find a solution. They decided to pool their strengths, each contributing a particular weapon or personal attribute, and when they had made their contributions and due rituals had been conducted, a dazzling light engulfed the universe from which emerged a fierce female warrior, riding a snarling tiger, wielding a weapon in each of her eighteen arms. She engaged in furious and bloody battle with Mahishasura for nine days and nine nights, at the end of which she vanquished him. These nine days and nights are celebrated annually by Hindus as the nine-day Navaratri festival, which celebrates the defeat of terrible evil by the forces of good (though interestingly, some fringe groups have started to commemorate Mahishasura instead, claiming he is the symbol of the indigenous Adivasis vanquished by the 'civilizing' onslaught of the mainstream Hindus).

The various manifestations of Devi suggest that Hinduism took on board multiple goddess-worshipping cults; Kali seems to have been a pre-Vedic goddess converted by the Hindus into one more form of Shakti. Sometimes the same figures in Hindu texts have different genders: Vishnu famously adopted a female form for specific purposes. A female form of Ganesh, now little worshipped, was depicted as Vinayaki or Ganeshvari. In the Mahabharata, Arjuna becomes Arjuni (female) and Brihannala (of the third gender) without losing his masculine valour; indeed, the Madurai temple has sculptures of him in all three forms.

Similarly Hanuman, a monkey-god, was enlisted in the service of Lord Rama in the epic Ramayana; scholars see in his appearance the absorption of animist nature-worship into Vedic theism, and the accommodation of aboriginals into the Hindu fold. Characters depicted in the epics as animals with anthropomorphic characteristics may in fact have been Adivasis: Hanuman was perhaps the leader of a monkey-totem Adivasi tribe, Jatayu that of a vulture-totem tribe and Jambuvan of a tribe using bear totems.

Another interesting example is that of the god Jagannath in Odisha, famous for his ratha or chariot. It's a beautiful, elaborately carved wooden vehicle used for a sanctified purpose—to wheel an image of a deity worshipped by millions to a temple in full public view—but it has given its name to an awful English word, 'juggernaut'.

The word is a colonial mangling of Jagannath (Sanskrit for 'lord of the world'), a manifestation of the god Krishna. Legend has it that in ancient times, King Indradyumna chanced upon the corpse of Lord Krishna, who had been slain by a hunter, and was informed by the god Vishnu that he should make a wooden statue of the Lord and inter his bones in it. The great sage Vishwakarma, the architect of the gods, undertook the task on condition that he not be disturbed while carving the statue. When, after fifteen days, the impatient king went to enquire about the progress of the sculpture, the irritated sage abandoned it unfinished, without hands or feet. King Indradyumna prayed to Brahma, the Creator, who breathed life into the statue by giving it eyes and a soul, though He could do nothing about the stumps

Subhadra in the middle with her brothers
Lord Balabhadra (Balarama) and Lord Jagannath (Krishna)

where the deity's limbs should have been. This consecrated statue is worshipped at the Jagannath Temple in Puri, in the eastern state of Odisha.

The legend almost certainly masks a different story. As I have noted, as Hinduism spread through the subcontinent, it absorbed local animist and tribal faiths it encountered, by accommodating their images of worship into the Hindu pantheon. Jagannath was probably a tribal god who was reimagined, through this legend, as a manifestation of Krishna (himself an incarnation of Vishnu), his somewhat rough and limbless appearance explained through an elaborate story that fits within Hindu lore. One of the ways of ensuring the new deity's acceptance by the people was by parading Him four times a year in elaborate yatras on land and water, of which the most famous is the ratha-yatra, or chariot procession, in the month of Ashadha, according to the Hindu calendar (roughly mid-June to mid-July in the Gregorian). This is when the idol is wheeled to the temple in an enormous chariot as devotees line the streets in a frenzy, hailing the lord with chants and prayers and craning their necks for a glimpse of the deity seated in the chariot, followed by lesser chariots bearing statues of his brother Balarama and sister Subhadra.

How did the deity transported in this devotional procession become transmogrified into an English term for a relentless, remorseless, unstoppable force that destroys anything in its path? Orientalism began early, alas: four centuries before the British conquest of India began, falsely distorted tales about India were propagated in the fourteenth-century travelogue of Sir John Mandeville, who described the festival in his *Travels* and depicted Hindus throwing themselves under the wheels of the enormous Jagannath chariots as a religious sacrifice and being crushed to death. Hinduism, in fact, has no concept of such human sacrifice; if Sir John really saw a Hindu killed under the wheels of a chariot, it can only be because a poor devotee stumbled and fell accidentally upon the path in the tumult and the enormous chariot could not easily stop or turn on the narrow road. Still, the tale, the false image of the faith it portrayed, and the unfortunate associations of the word persisted. By the eighteenth century 'juggernaut' was in common use as a synonym for an irresistible and destructive force that demands total devotion or unforgiving sacrifice—the sense in which it pops up in the novels of Charlotte Brontë and Charles Dickens, and even Robert Louis Stevenson, who applied it to Dr Jekyll's foil, Mr Hyde. It was only Mark Twain, in his *Autobiography*, who described Juggernaut as the kindest of gods; and a look at the lovely model of an eighteenth-century ratha in the British Museum's collection shows you why, for such an exquisite piece of art would only have been used to transport a figure of reverence, not of fear. But alas, by then, the damage had been done.

But I digress. Hinduism did not stop with the absorption of earlier animist or tribal religions. It accepted the precepts of Mahavira, the founder of Jainism, treating his followers as a special sect of Hindus rather than as a separate faith.

When Buddhism sought to reform Hinduism, Hinduism turned around and sought to absorb it too, by including the Buddha as a reincarnation of Vishnu and his agnostic teachings as merely a nastika form of the mother faith. As a result Buddhism has hardly any strength or presence in the land of its birth, having been absorbed and overtaken by the religion it sought to challenge. Hinduism could well have tried the same with Christianity and Islam, too, had it been allowed to do so; but these faiths were not interested in being embraced by Hinduism, since they saw themselves as the revealed Truth rather than as one among multiple versions of truth.

Hinduism is also unusual in seeing God, Man and the universe as co-related. As the philosopher Raimon Panikkar has explained, in Hindu thought, God without Man is nothing, literally 'no-thing'; Man without God is just a 'thing', without meaning or larger purpose; and the universe without Man or God is 'any-thing', sheer unexisting chaos. In Panikkar's explanation, nothing separates Man from God; 'there is neither intermediary nor barrier between them'. So Hindu prayers mix the sacred with the profane: a Hindu can ask God for anything. Among the tens of thousands of sacred verses and hymns in the Hindu scriptures are a merchant's prayer for wealth, a bankrupt's plea to the divine to free him of debt, verses extolling the union of a man with a woman, and even the lament of a rueful (and luckless) gambler asking God to help him shake his addiction. Prayer and worship, for the Hindu, are thus not purely spiritual exercises: they enhance the quality of his life in the material world, in the here and now.

Hindus are often asked, during certain ritual prayers, to imagine their ishta-devta, their personal God, or rather that way of imagining the abstraction of the Absolute in an anthropomorphic form that most appeals to them. I pick Ganesh, or Ganapathi, as we prefer to call him in the South, myself, not because I believe God looks like Him, but because of the myriad aspects of the godhead, the ones He represents appeal most to me.

> *Om maha Ganapathe namaha,*
> *sarva vighna upashantaye,*
> *Om Ganeshaya namaha...*

Every morning, for longer than I can remember, I have begun my day with that prayer. I learned it without being fully aware what all the Sanskrit words meant, knowing only that I was invoking, like millions of Hindus around the world, the name of the great elephant-headed god to bless all my endeavours to come.

Ganesh sits impassively on my bedroom shelf, in my office, in my living-room and my dining-room, as well as my prayer alcove, in multiple forms of statuary, stone, metal and papier-mache. There is nothing incongruous about this; he is used to worse, appearing as he does on innumerable calendars, posters, trademarks and wedding invitation cards. Paunchy, long-trunked (though with one broken tusk), attired in whatever costume the artist fancies (from ascetic to astronaut), Ganesh, riding his way across Indian hearts on a rat, is arguably Hinduism's most popular divine figure.

Few auspicious occasions are embarked upon without first seeking Ganesh's blessing. His principal attribute in Hindu mythology—a quality that flows from both his wisdom and his strength—is as a remover of obstacles to

Lord Ganesh

the fulfilment of desires. No wonder everyone wants Ganesh on their side before launching any important project, from starting a factory to acquiring a wife. My own student-day courtship violated time-honoured Indian rules about caste, language, region, age and parental approval; but when we got married, my then wife-to-be and I had an embossed red Ganesh adorning the front of our wedding invitations.

I have since developed an even more personal connection to Ganesh. The great 2,000-year-old epic, the Mahabharata, was supposedly dictated by the sage Veda Vyasa to Ganesh himself; since then, many a writer has found it helpful to invoke Ganesh in his epigraph. When I recast the characters and episodes of the Mahabharata into a political satire on twentieth-century Indian history, *The Great Indian Novel* (1989), I had it dictated by a retired nationalist, Ved Vyas, to a secretary named Ganapathi, with a big nose and shrewd, intelligent eyes, who enters with elephantine tread, dragging an enormous trunk behind him. Such are the secular uses of Hindu divinity.

For in my Hinduism the godhead is not some remote and forbidding entity in the distant heavens. God is immediately accessible all around us, and He takes many forms for those who need to imagine Him in a more personalized fashion. The Hindu pantheon includes thousands of such figures, great and small. Ganesh is the chief of the ganas, or what some scholars call the 'inferior deities'. He is not part of the trinity of Brahma, Vishnu and Shiva, who are the principal Hindu gods, the three facets of the Ultimate First Cause. But he is the son of Shiva, or at least of Shiva's wife, Parvati (one theory is that she shaped him from the scurf of her own body, without paternal involvement).

As a writer I have always been interested in the kinds of stories a society tells about itself. So part of the appeal of Ganesh for me lies in the plethora of stories about how this most unflappable of deities lost his (original) head and acquired his unconventional appearance.

The most widely-held version is the one my grandmother told me when I was little, about the time that Parvati went to take a bath and asked her son to guard the door. Shiva arrived and wished to enter, but Ganesh would not let him in. Enraged by this effrontery, Shiva cut off the boy's head. Parvati, horrified, asked him to replace it, and Shiva obliged with the head of the first creature he could find, an elephant.

This was a salutary lesson in the perils of excessive obedience to your parents, though I don't think my grandmother intended me to take it that way. My mother, who always tried unsuccessfully to resist the temptation to boast about her children, had another version: a vain Parvati asked Shani (Saturn) to look at her perfect son, forgetting that Shani's gaze would reduce the boy's head to ashes. Once again, an elephant's was the head that came to hand.

Growing up in an India where loyalty seems all too often on sale to the highest bidder, I could not but be impressed by

Ganesh's rare quality of stubborn devotion to duty. However he may have lost his head, it was Ganesh's obduracy as a guard that, in my grandmother's telling, cost him a tusk. 'The powerful avatar Parasurama,' she recounted, as we little ones gathered round her at dusk, 'possessor of many a boon from Shiva, came to call on the Great Destroyer at his abode of Mount Kailash. Once again, Ganesh was at the door, and he refused to let the visitor disturb the sleeping Shiva. Parasurama, furious, tried to force his way in, but found Ganesh a determined opponent.' (My eyes widened in excitement at this part.) 'Ganesh picked Parasurama up with his long trunk, swung him round and round till he was dizzy and helpless, and threw him to the ground. When his head cleared, Parasurama flung his axe at the obstinate Ganesh. Now Ganesh could have easily avoided the axe, but he recognized the weapon as one of Shiva's. He could not insult his father by resisting his weapon. So he took the axe humbly upon his tusk.' Ever since, Ganesh has been depicted with only one full tusk, the other half-amputated by the axe.

The thrill of that story did not diminish for me when I learned the more prosaic version which says that Ganesh wore down one tusk to a stub by using it to write down the epic verse of the Mahabharata. For this reason, the missing tusk signifies knowledge. As I grew older, I learned of more such symbols associated with Ganesh. Scholars of Hinduism tell us that Ganesh's fat body represents the hugeness of the cosmos, its combination of man and pachyderm signifying the unity of the microcosm (man) with the macrocosm (depicted as an elephant). Some suggest it has the less esoteric purpose of demonstrating that appearances mean little, and that an outwardly unattractive form can hide internal spiritual beauty. In any case, his looks do not prevent Ganesh, in most popular depictions, from being

Dancing Ganesh, Karnataka,
sixteenth–seventeenth century

surrounded by beautiful women, including his twin wives,
Siddhi and Buddhi. Siddhi represents spiritual power and
Buddhi intellect; in some versions there is a third wife,
Riddhi, embodying prosperity (though she usually replaces
Buddhi—perhaps making the point that you can have either
brains or wealth but not both!) Further, Ganesh's trunk can
be curled into the symbol 'Om', the primal sound; and the
snake found coiled around his waist represents the force
of cosmic energy.

'But Ammamma,' I would ask my grandmother, 'why
does Ganesh ride a rat?' For in most of the pictures in our
prayer room, the deity is shown on this unusual mount.

Kartikeya, the god of war and brother to Ganesh

At the simplest level the sight of an elephantine god on a tiny mouse visually equates the importance of the greatest and smallest of God's creatures. And, as my grandmother explained, each animal is a symbol of Ganesh's capacities: 'like an elephant, he can crash through the jungle uprooting every impediment in his path, while like the rat he can burrow his way through the tightest of defences.' A god who thus combines the attributes of elephant, mouse and man can remove any obstacle confronting those who propitiate him. No wonder that many worship him as their principal deity, despite his formally more modest standing in the pantheon.

And what is the secret of his appeal to a twenty-first century urbanite like myself? As his unblinking gaze and broad brow suggest, Ganesh is an extremely intelligent god. When I was very young I heard the story of how Parvati asked her two sons, Ganesh and Kartikeya, to go around the world in a race. Kartikeya, the more vigorous and martial-minded of the two, set off at once, confident he would encircle the globe faster than his corpulent brother. Ganesh, after resting a while, took a few steps around his mother and sat down again. Parvati reminded him of her challenge. 'But you are my world,' Ganesh disarmingly replied, 'and I have gone around you.' Needless to say, he won the race—and my unqualified admiration.

So it is no surprise that Ganesh is worshipped in India with not just reverence but enthusiasm. Sometimes this can be carried to extremes, as when Ganesh devotees in Western India in the 1890s allowed the bubonic plague to take many lives rather than co-operate with a British campaign to exterminate the rats that carried it (for the rats were also, after all, Ganesh's mounts). Or when, in late September 1995, word spread around the world that statues of Ganesh had begun drinking milk. In some cases, statues of his divine parents, Shiva and Parvati, were also reported to be imbibing these liquid offerings, but Ganesh it was who took the elephant's share.

In India, the rationalists were quick to react. It was, they averred, a matter of simple physics. Molecules on the rough stone and marble surfaces of the statues had created a 'capillary action' which sucked in the droplets of milk. (*Om capillary actioneyeh namaha*?) These were not really absorbed into the statue but formed a thin layer of droplets on the surface which would be visible if the statue were dark. A team of government scientists proceeded to demonstrate this on television, placing green powder in the milk and showing a green stain spreading over the face of a white marble statue. Mass hysteria was alleged; Indian priests (who live off the offerings of devotees in the temples) were merely trying to whip up more custom, said some; it was all politics, said others, pointing to the need for the then-flagging Hindutva movement to attract the credulous to their credo. *The Pioneer* newspaper published a photograph of a spout emerging from the back of a temple from which milk poured into a bucket; the implication was that it was chicanery, not divine ingestion, that accounted for the disappearing milk in the temples. Still, millions of devotees who flocked to temples worldwide saw in the phenomenon a simple message from the heavens that the gods remained interested in the affairs of ordinary mortals.

But Hindus have always believed that to be the case; the 'milk miracle' merely reinforced an unstated assumption about the nature of the godhead. Our gods crowd the streets, smile or frown on us from the skies, jostle us for space on the buses; they are part of our daily lives, as intimate and personal as the towels in which we wrap ourselves after a bath. As Thiruvananthapuram's MP, I was struck by the fact that my constituency is the one place in the world where even the airport runway shuts down twice a year for a few hours so that Lord Padmanabhaswamy can be escorted on his usual traditional route across the airfield for His ritual seaside bath. And none in the city, of any faith, considers this remotely unusual.

So the intrusion of the gods into our lives through the milk-drinking episode is no great aberration. They are part of our lives anyway; we see ourselves in them, only idealized. My own affection is for Ganesh himself, a god who—overweight, long-nosed, broken-tusked and big-eared—cheerfully reflects our own physical imperfections. After all, a country with many seemingly insurmountable problems needs a god who can overcome obstacles.

*An idol of Ganesh being taken for immersion during
Ganesh Chaturthi in Mumbai*

When I was a child in Bombay, I was enraptured once a
year by the city's great Ganesh Chaturthi festival, in which
India's bustling commercial capital gives itself over to the
celebration of this many-talented deity. Hundreds of statues
of Ganesh are made, decorated and lovingly dressed; then
they are taken out across the busy city streets in teeming
processions of followers, who collectively number over a
million, before being floated out to sea in a triumphant
gesture of release. As a little boy I stood on the beach
watching the statues settle gradually into the water while the
streams of worshippers dispersed. It was sad to see the giant

elephant heads disappear beneath the waves, but I knew that Ganesh had not really left me. I would find him again, in my wall-calendars, on my mantelpiece, at the beginning of my books—and in the prayers with which I would resume my life the morning after the festival:

Om maha Ganapathe namaha,
sarva vighna upashantaye,
Om Ganeshaya namaha...

Om, I invoke the name of Ganapathi;
Remover of all obstacles,
Om, I invoke the name of Ganesh...

SECTION TWO

~

THE HINDU WAY

A calm and serene Lord Krishna with his animal companions

Krishna and Arjuna at the battle of Kurukshetra

chapter two

THE HINDU WAY

The sage Yajnavalkya was once asked to list the number of gods; it is said he began with the number 3,300 and ended by reducing them all to one—Brahman, the pervasive spirit of the cosmos that underlies all creation. The Upanishads say 'ekam sat vipra bahudha vadanti'. This was Swami Vivekananda's favourite phrase about spirituality: 'That which exists is One; the sages call It by various names.'

Hindus therefore understand that all worship of God reflects an effort to reach out to that which cannot be touched or seen; since God is, in that sense, literally unknowable, one may imagine Him/Her/It in any form, since each form may be just as valid as another and none can be guaranteed to be more accurate than the next one. The various forms of God in Hinduism, reducing the abstract to the specific visual form, reflect the limitations of the human imagination rather than any shapes within which the divine must be confined. Indeed, Hindu legends have the gods manifesting themselves in so many shapes and forms that the notion

Arjuna battles with the Kauravas at Kurukshetra

of one agreed image of God would be preposterous. Thus one can imagine God as a potbellied man with an elephant head, and also as a ten-armed woman with a beatific smile; and since both forms are equally valid to the worshipper, why not also imagine God as a bleeding man on a cross? All are acceptable to the Hindu; the reverence accorded to each representation of the unknowable God by worshippers of other faiths is enough to prompt similar respect from the Hindu. Acceptance is always the name of the game.

As I have remarked at the outset, the key to understanding

François Bernier

Hinduism is that it is one faith that claims no monopoly on the Truth. Hindus understand that theirs may not necessarily be the only path that leads to salvation; they are taught to respect all other paths that seek the Truth, knowing that these will vary depending on the circumstances of each individual's life, the culture in which they are born or live, their values and motivations. In the Gita, Lord Krishna says, 'Whosoever follows any faith and worships me under whatsoever denomination in whatsoever form with steadfastness, his faith I shall reinforce'. The acknowledgement of multiple paths to the ultimate truth of creation is implicit in the philosophical disputes and arguments that have marked the faith for millennia.

One consequence of this acceptance of difference is that it flies in the face of the certitudes most other religions assert. The French traveller François Bernier, on his well-documented journey through India in the seventeenth century, tried to introduce some Brahmins in 1671 to Christianity, and was startled by their response: 'They pretended not [that] their law was universal; that God had only made it for them, and it was, therefore, they could not receive a stranger into their religion: that they thought not our religion was therefore false, but that it might be it was good for us, and that God might have appointed several different ways to go to heaven; but they will not hear that our religion should be the general religion for the whole earth; and theirs a fable and pure device.'

We respect your truth, the Brahmins were saying; please respect ours.

Some scholars have described Hindus as henotheists, that is, people who worship their God but do not deny the existence of other gods. Every Hindu worships some god, but it may not be the same god worshipped by every other Hindu either. As Radhakrishnan puts it: 'God is more than the law that commands, the judge that condemns, the love that constrains, the father to whom we owe our being, or the mother with whom is bound up all that we can hope for or aspire to.' God is all that, and infinitely more.

This henotheistic attitude means, however, undifferentiated respect for all the various possible ways of worshipping God, whether Hindu or not. A Hindu can accept the worship of the Abrahamic God as another practice of the same kind as he sees pursued by other Hindus. For him, someone worshipping Christ is essentially no different from himself worshipping Vishnu or Shiva. The acceptance of difference starts here for the Hindu. This was why it was possible for a large community of Jews, the Bene Israel, after arriving on the shores of western India around the time of Christ, to practise their faith for centuries in rural Maharashtra without being seen by their Hindu neighbours as practitioners of a different religion; Hindus used to seeing various Hindus pursue their own modes of devotion found

*Vishnu resting on Ananta-Shesha, with
Lakshmi massaging his feet and Brahma in heaven*

nothing odd in a people with their own different practices,
assuming them to be just another kind of Hindu, until a
wandering rabbi from Jerusalem arrived in India centuries
later and identified them as the Jews they were.

It didn't matter to the Hindus around them. The
Haristuti has a prayer that says: 'May Vishnu, the ruler of
the three worlds, worshipped by the Shaivites as Shiva, by
the Vedantins as Brahman, by the Buddhists as the Buddha,
by the Naiyayikas as the chief agent, by the Jainas as the
liberated, by the ritualists as the principle of dharma,
may he grant our prayers.' This cheerful eclecticism was
the attitude that enabled Swami Vivekananda, concluding
the presentation of a paper at Chicago's Parliament of the
World's Religions in 1893, to call upon the blessings of 'He
who is the Brahman of the Hindus, the Ahura Mazda of
the Zoroastrians, the Buddha of the Buddhists, the Jehovah
of the Jews, and the Father in Heaven of the Christians.'

To him they were one and the same: 'That which exists is One; the sages call It by various names.'

❀

SEEING LIFE WHOLE

The British, who in their two centuries of imperial rule over India struggled to understand and come to terms with Hinduism, did a great deal to explore and debate its meanings as best they could. Some saw it, in E. M. Forster's notorious phrase, as 'a mystery and a muddle'; others tried to reduce it to terms they could relate to. Whether Hinduism was polytheistic or monotheistic was a question that agitated many British minds. After the Census of 1911, one senior British official concluded that 'the great majority of Hindus have a firm belief in one supreme God—Parameshwara, Ishvara or Narayana.' The chief British census official in India, Sir Herbert Risley, observed that 'these ideas are not the monopoly of the learned: they are shared in great measure by the man on the street.' An 'intelligent Hindu peasant', he claimed, not only was familiar with Hindu concepts like the paramatma (supreme soul), karma (loosely translatable as 'fate'), maya (illusion), mukti (salvation) and so on, but had 'a rough working theory of their bearing upon his own future'.

A few basic ideas were deeply ingrained into every Hindu, whether he lived up to them or not. Among these commonly-held beliefs were two four-fold divisions. The first was the organization of life into four stages, or ashramas: these were brahmacharya, the bachelor existence, a time to be spent learning and acquiring mastery over the essential disciplines needed to lead a meaningful life; then grihastha, the life of a householder, when one married, procreated, and assumed the responsibilities of family life; then vanaprastha, when one retired and retreated to the forest to lead a life of contemplation in harmony with nature; and finally, sannyas, the stage of renunciation of all worldly ties, at which one seeks one's ultimate merger with Brahman, the spirit suffusing the cosmos.

The four stages of life also related to the four ends of life, the Purusharthas, that every Hindu had to pursue: dharma, the moral code (discussed more fully later), artha, prosperity or material well-being, kama, desire for pleasure and gratification, and ultimately moksha, or the salvation that comes from ultimate self-realization, the fulfilment of which is the purpose of each individual life.

These stages and ends of life in Hinduism embraced an all-encompassing idea of human needs in a comprehensive vision. Every person needs to learn and to earn; to have sex, food and money; to love, to nurture, to assume responsibility; each individual also has a shared concern for the common good and an indefinable curiosity about the unseen, about that which can only be experienced and not understood through words. All of these urges coexist in all of us; they overlap and interact with each other; we pursue them systematically or randomly, or we stumble across them, but they are present in each of our lives in an interdependence of which we are barely conscious but which the Hindu rishis fully appreciated. The common expression 'mata, pita, guru, daivam' encapsulates the human journey—one is first, from birth, totally dependent on the mother, then exposed to the outer world by the father, then taught and guided by the guru, until one finally finds God.

The Hindu appreciation of life saw it whole, recognized the supreme ends of life and the stages needed to progress towards their achievement. It did not seek to suppress or

*A life-size sandstone sculpture of an apsara
(celestial dancer) from the Chandela period,
mid-eleventh century*

deny the normal lust for sex, wealth or possessions, but
sublimated these in a larger purpose. (Kama even has its own
shastra, Vatsyayana's *Kama Sutra*). Hinduism accommodated
the acknowledgement of worldly desires within the quest
for the eternal. As Radhakrishnan postulated, Hinduism
'binds together the kingdoms of earth and heaven'. Indeed,
it is no coincidence that Hindu gods are all married;
they are depicted with consorts, each of whom, like the
gods and goddesses themselves, have multiple aspects and
manifestations. It is a striking feature of Hinduism that our
gods can be susceptible to desire; they are depicted falling
for apsaras and seducing sages' wives. Lord Shiva even fell

for Vishnu in the transformed appearance of the ethereally beautiful Mohini. Prudery appears to have been imported into Hindu social attitudes only in reaction to the Muslim invasions and Victorian colonial rule.

Hindus pursue their quest for the eternal—the search for 'the light beyond the darkness'—through three types of activity: jnana or the quest for knowledge, not merely theoretical learning but in the form of realized experience which leads to wisdom; bhakti or devotion, expressed principally through prayer, fasting, temple rituals and sacrifice, but also through meditation and self-interrogation; and karma or action and service in the fulfilment of dharma. (Karma is a concept that is variously translated as action, fate or destiny, and causality; it means all three, though the meaning depends on the context in which the phrase is used.)

Bhakti is of course the most popular path, and the easiest for most people to pursue, since a capacity for worship comes inborn in all of us. Purists categorize Hindu worship in a taxonomy that runs like this: the most simple Hindus worship spirits and animist forces; the next level of ordinary Hindus worship their own ancestors, popular deities and gurus or godmen; the level above that worships incarnations like Rama, Krishna, or Buddha; above this level are those who worship a personal god, an ishta-devta; and highest of all are those Hindus who worship the Absolute, in the form of Brahman. Those who worship the ishta-devta or personal bhagavan (in other words those trying to reach Brahman through a divine intermediary) must settle for a somewhat lower place in the hierarchy of spiritual yearning than those who seek Brahman for itself, in the quest for ultimate self-realization. A verse from the *Kena Upanishad* captures some of the exquisite literary talents of the ancients along with the profundity of their philosophical enquiry:

Who sends the mind to wander afar? Who first drives life to start on its journey? Who impels us to utter these words? Who is the Spirit behind the eye and the ear?

It is the ear of the ear, the eye of the eye, and the Word of words, the mind of mind, and the life of life. Those who follow wisdom pass beyond and, on leaving this world, become immortal.

There the eye goes not, nor words, nor mind. We know not, we cannot understand, how he can be explained: He is above the known and he is above the unknown. Thus have we heard from the ancient sages who explained this truth to us.

What cannot be spoken with words, but that whereby words are spoken: Know that alone to be Brahman, the Spirit; and not what people here adore.

What cannot be thought with the mind, but that whereby the mind can think: Know that alone to be Brahman, the Spirit; and not what people here adore.

What cannot be seen with the eye, but that whereby the eye can see: Know that alone to be Brahman, the Spirit; and not what people here adore.

What cannot be heard with the ear, but that whereby the ear can hear: Know that alone to be Brahman, the Spirit; and not what people here adore.

What cannot be indrawn with breath, but that whereby breath is indrawn: Know that alone to be Brahman, the Spirit; and not what people here adore.

Into all of this, great variations and choices enter. Some critics have described Hinduism as animism tempered by philosophy, or mysticism leavened by metaphysics. They are not wholly right, but they are not wrong either. Ultimately, all such worship is merely a means to an end. Some look for God in nature, in forests and rivers, some in images of wood or stone, and some in the heavens; but the Hindu sage looks for God within, and finds Him in his own deeper self.

❀

THE BANYAN TREE OF HINDUISM

As a result of this openness and diversity, Hinduism is a typically Indian growth, a banyan tree. It spreads its branches far and wide, and these in turn sink back into the earth to take fresh root in the welcoming soil. In the shade of the vast canopy of this capacious banyan tree, sustained by multiple roots and several trunks, a great variety of flora and fauna, thought and action, flourishes.

The multiplicity of places of worship in India gives Hindus plenty of choice, and affords religious-minded temple-goers opportunities for extensive pilgrimages. Most Hindu families embark on these quite often; for some, the only holidays they undertake are to temple towns, to worship at the shrine of a powerful deity. While some pilgrimages, especially to well-established temple towns, take on the characteristics of a religious holiday, others can be quite arduous. The annual yatra to the ice-cave at Amarnath in Kashmir involves a major trek; that of Mount Kailash and Lake Manasarovar in Tibet, renowned as the abode of Shiva, has cost the lives of many of who have attempted it across the narrow and treacherous Himalayan passes. Pilgrimages to Kedarnath and Badrinath, and to the sources of the Ganga and the Yamuna at Gangotri and Yamunotri respectively, are other Himalayan journeys that are not for the weak or faint-hearted. Other religious trips are to sites where large numbers of Hindus gather for a special occasion: from the Thrissur Pooram, an annual festival which involves the largest processional of

Lake Manasarovar

caparisoned elephants in the world (usually up to a hundred pachyderms decked up to the hilt), to the ratha-yatra at the Jagannath Temple in Puri, Odisha and the Kumbh Melas described below. Utsavas (religious festivals, from the Sanskrit 'ut', to let go or remove, and 'sava', worldly sorrows, hence an occasion to release one's burdens or cares) abound across the country. Regional festivals witness throngs of worshippers in different parts of the country on different occasions at fixed times of the year—Bengalis celebrating Durga Puja, Maharashtrians Ganesh Chaturthi, the Ram Leela across north India, Onam in Kerala, Pongal in Tamil Nadu. Holi, the festival of colours, is famously the most fun-filled of all utsavas, while an occasion like Makar Sankranti, marking the transit of the sun into the Makara rashi in Hindu astrology, is observed with due solemnity. The largest crowds gather during the Kumbha Melas that take place every twelve years in Haridwar, Allahabad (Prayag), Nasik, and Ujjain: the Allahabad Kumbh, at the confluence of the Ganga and the Yamuna, is an extraordinary sight, attracting some twenty million people each time.

Sometimes a pilgrimage may consist of a regular visit to one favourite temple: the Kerala political leader K. Karunakaran travelled to the fabled Krishna temple in Guruvayur on the first of every month (according to the Malayalam calendar) throughout his long life, and thousands do the same to the hilltop shrine to Ayyappa at Sabarimalai, or to Balaji at Tirumalai. Sometimes it is to a particular area where many temples abound: the temples to the nine planets at Kumbakonam, for instance. But quite often it can be an extensive circuit, such as the one my family undertook by car across southern India when I was fourteen, a three-week journey that enabled us to pray at Tirupati, Madurai (whose famed Meenakshi Temple, dedicated to a warrior queen who became a consort of Shiva, boasts 33,000 sculptures), Thanjavur, Kanchipuram, Palani, Rameswaram and innumerable smaller towns in Tamil Nadu and Kerala, halting at each place just to worship at the principal temple, and moving on to the next one. My parents found this profoundly satisfying; for their children, it was all a bit of an adventure, though we learned a little about Hinduism at each stop.

The striking thing to a young boy during this journey was the remarkable variety of these places of worship, the differences in their architectural styles and physical appearances, the different manifestations of god being worshipped at different temples, the variety of rituals and the behaviour of the priests, the different materials offered as prasadam to the gods, and the idiosyncratic practices associated with each shrine, most famously the shaving of the head at the Venkatachalapathi Temple in Tirumalai, Tirupati (Andhra Pradesh), the richest temple in the country, where my fourteen-year-old locks were duly shorn as an offering to Lord Balaji.

Sri Venkatachalapathi Temple at Tirupati

The Hindu acceptance of variety goes much farther than this, however. Foreigners sometimes politely ask if Hinduism requires vegetarianism or abjures alcohol, and are puzzled when different Hindus give them different answers to the question. Versions of the faith come with their own prescriptions and proscriptions; but there is no universal requirement. There are Hindus, particularly Vaishnavas in the north, who recoil in horror at the very thought of consuming meat and others who will not touch even garlic or onion (considered tamasik foods by purists), while there are Hindus who eat all of these and would consider it mildly uncivilized not to do so. Goats are routinely sacrificed at the Kalighat Temple in Kolkata and other animals at Kali temples across the land, but most Hindu religious occasions are marked by ostentatious vegetarianism. My children's mother is half-Bengali, half-Kashmiri, descended from a long line of carnivorous Brahmins on both sides who were alternately horrified and mournful about my vegetarianism (some tried to excuse it on the grounds that I must be a 'Vaishnava', a worshipper of Vishnu, though I was too eclectic to be so typecast and had actually been named for Shiva, having been born on Maha Shivaratri. But then in Tamil, the word for vegetarian is 'shaiva'. Go figure!). We brought up our sons to 'eat everything', but their mixed genetic inheritance prevailed: one twin took to meat-eating with relish, while the other, at age seven, with no persuasion whatsoever from his father, turned staunchly vegetarian.

Alcohol offers its own contradictions. There is a strain of prohibition in some aspects of Hindu thought, but this coexists with the use of alcohol in some religious rituals (such as at the Kal Bhairava temples) and indeed with the routine habit, of some sannyasis, of consuming marijuana and other hallucinogens in the pursuit of spiritual experiences. In the Vedas, soma (or som-ras) was a favourite beverage of the Vedic deities, and much alcohol flowed during religious ceremonies and sacrifices; in the *Rig Veda,* Mandala IV, Hymn 18, the god Indra is said to have drunk three lakes of soma to fortify himself before slaying the dragon Vritra, who had imprisoned all the waters of the world. The Mahabharata is replete with details of alcohol consumed by those who are worshipped as incarnations of Vishnu. In Puranic mythology, there is a Hindu goddess of wine, Varuni, who emerged from the primordial Churning of the Ocean, the Samudra Manthan, as one of fourteen 'ratnas' bestowed upon the world, including the moon. Sanskrit literature, including the poetry and plays of Kalidasa, India's greatest literary figure (even though only a fraction of his sublime work has survived), is replete with references to intoxicating drinks. Yet other texts also offer Dharmashastric objections to Brahmins consuming liquor, and Brahminical Hinduism has tended to disapprove of alcohol consumption.

There is doctrinal variety, as well. Those Hindus who are steeped in the Upanishads and the Bhagavad Gita, suffused with a sense of Brahman (the Ultimate Reality underlying all phenomena) pervading the cosmos and debating its unity with atman (the Universal Soul also present in each of us) would consider themselves monotheists; the 'common man', innocent of such texts, might think of the multiple deities he sees around him as different gods, and have no difficulty with being considered a polytheist. The truth is that it doesn't matter. These are all equally valid ways of being a Hindu.

This pervasive multiplicity of practices and beliefs makes it difficult to conceptualize Hinduism as one might other religions. As a term of description, indeed, 'Hindu' implies no monolithic identity; to speak of the 'Hindu community' as one might the 'Muslim ummah' is contestable, since Muslims are bound to each other by credos, convictions and rules of which Hindus are innocent. The absence of standard practices and belief systems, and the absence of ecclesiastical hierarchies and universal religious institutions, adds to the difficulty. When Christians disagree amongst each other, they disagree with reference to the interpretation of one single book, the Bible, whose teachings remain the fountainhead of their faith. The same is true of Muslims, though the room for interpretation is less, since the Quran is seen as the revealed word of God, though the Hadith offers more room for discussion. Hinduism has no such handy volume; when Hindus seek guidance, it is rarely to textual authority that they turn (though often to spiritual guides or gurus, whose knowledge, at least in theory, may be derived from their understanding of various scriptures).

In recent times, the Bhagavad Gita has become the equivalent of a 'sacred book' for the Hindus, due to its frequent use by twentieth-century gurus such as Swami Chinmayananda and political leaders like Mahatma Gandhi. The Gita subsumes the ideals of the Vedas and

Indra, King of Gods, riding his elephant Airavata

Upanishads in the words of the popular deity Krishna, and its exhortation to do one's duty irrespective of the consequences has been cited as an inspiration by various figures on the world stage, from Turkish Prime Minister Bulent Ecevit to justify his country's invasion of Cyprus, to the present author reflecting on his failed run for the Secretary-Generalship of the United Nations.

But Hinduism cannot be reduced to the Bhagavad Gita, or any single holy book. Dr Radhakrishnan put it best: to him, Hinduism is 'not a definite dogmatic creed, but a vast, complex, but subtly unified mass of spiritual thought and realization.' The spiritual leader Dada Vaswani calls Hinduism variously 'a fellowship of faiths', 'a federation of philosophies', and 'a league of religions'. Note the plural in that last word.

Indeed, the writer Rutvij Merchant adapted a phrase of mine to make the point. I had written in my book *India: From Midnight to the Millennium*, that any truism about India can be immediately contradicted by another truism about India. He observed that 'Hinduism appears to be very much like India; an essential paradox, as any attempt at a truism about Hinduism can be immediately contradicted by another truism about Hinduism.' Remarking that there are as many Hinduisms as there are adherents, he goes on to add: 'Interestingly, Shashi Tharoor's statement about India "that the singular thing about the country is that you can only speak about it in the plural", applies to Hinduism perfectly; if religion is seen as a technology that can be leveraged to grow spiritually and eventually achieve union with the Supreme, there appears to be no uniformity or synchronization to the Hindu way; indeed the term "the Hindu way" is in itself a fallacy as there is no one Hindu way.'

Merchant interestingly defines a Hindu as one who is an ardent seeker of Truth: 'An individual who strives to actively discern the existence of the objective Reality otherwise termed as God and attain Him if convinced of His existence, using means that are inherently subjective and dependent on the individual's own proclivities, beliefs and values, is a Hindu.' This definition of Hinduism, if it can be called that—since it could apply to almost anyone of any culture or religious faith—emphasizes the individualist nature of the quest for truth, the role of reasoning in the process, and the ultimate yearning for God (whether one uses that term or speaks of the soul's merger with Brahman, the idea is the same).

Some Hindus reject the term 'Hindu' altogether as a description of their faith, preferring to speak of 'Brahmanism', though this is used by some Dalits and others as a term of abuse against the Brahmins who have dominated the faith. But in its origins, the expression refers to the ideal of attaining the Brahman, the Universal Spirit that suffuses the cosmos. Many use the Sanskrit-Hindi phrase, 'Sanatana Dharma', or 'eternal faith' (though 'faith', as I explain shortly, is an inadequate translation of 'dharma'). Sanatana is eternal in the sense that it refers to a dharma that is old and new at the same time, ever–present and ever-evolving. In Hinduism, there is no difficulty in accepting that some aspects of dharma will be rendered irrelevant over the aeons and that other ideas, innovations and reforms will be infused into the faith and rejuvenate it. The essence of dharma, however, remains unchanged throughout eternity.

The Hindu concept of time is very different from Western ideas. In Hindu thought, the world has no beginning and no end, but only experiences endless repetitive cycles of time in four yugas (aeons or ages): Satya Yuga, the age of truth, Treta Yuga, Dvapara Yuga and Kali Yuga (the age of destruction and untruth, the one in which we are all living now). Each Kali Yuga ends with a great flood (pralaya) that destroys the world, only to start afresh with a new Satya Yuga. Some Hindus argue that Vaishnavites and Shaivites differ in their perception of time; after all, Vishnu is reincarnated in various avatars, while Shiva simply 'is'. Vaishnavites, in this reading, are constantly changing through time, while Shaivites are focused on the

*Goddess Durga, in her most ferocious form,
as Kali. She is wearing a mundamala, a
garland of severed heads*

annihilation of the self. Though the distinction is interesting,
both sets of Hindus relate to time very differently from
followers of other faiths, whose temporal existence on this
earth culminates, after death, in paradise or hellfire.

I mentioned earlier that dharma is often translated as
faith, and that this is an inadequate translation. The concept
of dharma is much broader, embracing an entire system of
social ethics covering law-abiding conduct. Indeed, in an
afterword to my book *The Great Indian Novel* in 1989, I
listed a whole series of meanings that have been ascribed to
the term 'dharma', an untranslatable Sanskrit term that is,
nonetheless, breezily defined as an unitalicized entry in many

an English dictionary. (The *Chambers Twentieth-Century Dictionary*, for example, defines it as 'the righteousness that underlies the law'.) A passable effort, to be sure, but no one-word translation in English ('faith', 'religion', 'law'), can convey the full range of meaning implicit in the term. 'English has no equivalent for dharma,' writes P. Lal, defining dharma as 'code of good conduct, pattern of noble living, religious rules and observance'. Nanditha Krishna, author of several popular books on various aspects of Hinduism, translates dharma as 'law of righteousness'. In his book *The Speaking Tree*, Richard Lannoy actually defines dharma in nine different ways in different contexts. These include moral law, spiritual order, sacred law, righteousness, and even the sweeping 'the totality of social, ethical and spiritual harmony.' Indeed, dharma in its classic sense embraces the total cosmic responsibility of both God and Man. My late friend Ansar Hussain Khan, author of the polemical *The Rediscovery of India*, suggested that dharma is most simply defined as 'that by which we live'.

The word dharma is formed from the Sanskrit root 'dhr', to hold; dharma is therefore that which holds a person or object and maintains it in existence; it is the law that governs its being. To live according to dharma is to be in consonance with the truth of things. A moral life, for a Hindu, is a life lived in accordance with his dharma, which in turn must be in conformity with the absolute truth that encompasses the universe.

❦

A POLYCENTRIC FAITH

Hinduism is a polycentric faith. Since it admits multiple centres of belief and practice, there is no single structure of theological authority or liturgical power. When there is no centre, there is no periphery either; Sanatana Dharma is inclusive, since there is no basis for excluding any belief. Radhakrishnan argues that Hindu tolerance is not indifference: Hindus understand that not all self-declared truths are of equal value. Still, they are all welcome in that gigantic buffet table of spiritual options the Hindu feels empowered to dip into. Of course, the flip side of the coin is that Hindus tend not to see non-Hindu religious traditions as 'other'; and in particular, they do not see them as challenging or putting into doubt Hindu beliefs and practices, which after all are timeless and eternal.

Unlike Hinduism, however, as we have seen, the Semitic (or Abrahamic) faiths believe themselves to be of divine origin. The True Faith was revealed by God to Abraham and was therefore beyond contestation, even if its three major variants, Judaism, Christianity and Islam (in order of appearance!) relied on different texts; and in Muslim belief, God revealed Himself further to Muhammad, who became the definitive Prophet of His word. Since the word of God cannot be false, all three Semitic religions came to revolve around ideas of absolute truth; they were the only way to reach God, and those who chose other paths were doomed to hellfire or damnation. Many saw it as their duty to show the absolute truth they had found to those who were still in darkness but unaware of the error of their ways. If you resisted their truth, you were wrong and if you were unwilling to correct yourself, you must be either misguided, evil or blind—the only possible explanations for those unable or unwilling to see the truth laid before them by these 'revealed' religions. For this reason it was permissible, for some 'true believers', to convert you to the 'right' path by force or inducement.

Sanatana Dharma, however, saw its adherents engaged

in a permanent quest for truth, which was not something revealed from on high by God or a prophet, but something that had to be searched for by prayer, meditation, good conduct and experience, and could well be attained only at the very end of one's life, if at all. Religion is, after all, experience; ideally, it is an experience of God. The *Svetashvatara Upanishad* says: 'God, the maker of All, the great spirit ever seated in the hearts of creatures, is fashioned by the heart, the understanding and the will. They who know that become immortal.' The heart, the understanding and the will each play their part; all are indispensable. This also means that religious experience is personal experience; self-realization will vary from individual to individual. After all, the Divine, as Radhakrishnan argued, reveals itself to men within the framework of their intimate perceptions and prejudices. The Western faiths look outward to the heavens for their revealed truths; the Hindu looks within himself.

A Hindu could live his faith at one or more of several levels: the quotidian, with its temple rituals, religious observances, social customs and good deeds (the path of religious performance); the spiritual, with extensive prayer, meditation, worship of and service to a deity, penance and austerities (the path of devotion); and the intellectual, with a serious study of philosophy and theology (the path of knowledge). Most Hindus never get beyond the first stage; their Hinduism is a religion of temple visits, fasts to favourite gods, the observance of specific festivals according to the tradition in their geographic regions. But even for the others, who demand more from (and look for more in) their faith, their quest for the truth, their enquiry into the mysteries of Creation, would not end with a blinding flash of realization from the pages of a sacred book. After all, unlike the Bible, the Dialogues of the Buddha, and the Quran, all the unchallengeable principal texts of their religions, even the Vedas are merely the first in a substantial corpus of scriptural works.

It is also true that in a religion as vast, capacious and evolving as Hinduism, there is much in the religious texts that contradict themselves, and each scholar can find scriptural justification for a point of view diametrically opposed to that of another scholar, also with his own scriptural justification. Take, for example, the place of women in Hindu society, which has undoubtedly undergone much transformation, for better and for worse. The *Manusmriti*, the epics and the dicta of Yajnavalkya contain much material that is bloodcurdlingly misogynist in relegating women to a place of inferiority in relation to men. Bhishma in the Anushasana Parva of the Mahabharata declares: 'Women have one eternal duty in this world: dependence upon and obedient service to their husbands.' And yet this is the faith that regarded wives as ardhangini, half of the whole, and sahadharmini, the partner of the man in the fulfilment of dharma. The sage Sayana, in his commentary on the *Rig Veda*, wrote 'The wife and the husband, being the equal halves of one substance, are equal in every respect; both should join and take equal part in all work, religious and secular.' A warrior queen like Kaikeyi strode on to the battlefield alongside her husband. Swami Vivekananda pointed out with pride that some of the most exalted rishis of the Hindu faith, the most learned and respected authorities on the scriptures, are women. (Twenty-one of the original rishikas to whom the Vedas were revealed were women: the names of Gargi and Maitreyi today adorn colleges in Delhi University; Vishavara, Ghosha and Apala were also prominent seers.) Adi Shankara, in a theological debate with his famous critic Madana Mishra, appointed as the judge between them the latter's learned wife Sarasavani. Even Manu declared, 'where women are honoured, there the gods rejoice, but where they are not honoured, there all rituals are useless.' Of the 210 Shiva-worshipping Lingayat saints, thirty-five are women. In other words, there is authority for different approaches in the ancient texts; the Hindu is invited to take his pick. If the Hindu chooses wrongly, or unwisely, among the opinions offered to him, it is not Hinduism's fault.

The Hindu understands that all scripture requires interpretation, and cannot be taken literally. In particular, there has long been an acknowledgement that what is laid down in ancient texts may not necessarily have been what was, or is, practised in the faith. The strong position held by the polyandrous, property-owning Nair women in Kerala's matrilineal society, the honoured position of Rajput women, who killed themselves en masse after their husbands fell on the battlefield, and the reverence accorded to women mystics like Mirabai and social reformers like Savitribai Phule, show Hinduism as accepting of women as figures of authority and respect. The fact that the *Manusmriti* says something does not preclude the possibility that throughout the ages, it was honoured in the breach.

Hinduism offers the believer much to choose from: what you choose to follow is your Hinduism, while others might find scriptural justification for a contrary view. Hindu philosophy testifies to the extent to which reasoned debate amongst the believers—in dialogue with but not restrictively bound by their scriptures—has allowed Hindu religious philosophers throughout history to reform themselves and their faith.

❧

MANY SACRED BOOKS

As I have asserted, Hinduism has not one sacred book, but several, both complementary and

Veda Vyasa

contradictory to each other. The Hindu scriptures are commonly divided into Srutis, Smritis, Itihasas, Puranas, Agamas and Darshanas.

The Srutis are that which has been heard or revealed. The four Vedas—*Rig Veda*, *Sama Veda*, *Yajur Veda* and *Atharva Veda*—are Sruti, having been revealed to, or heard by, the rishis, codified by the sage Veda Vyasa and passed down through generations of disciples. But they are not revealed texts in the Christian or Muslim senses of the term; the rishi is a Mantra-Drashta, a seer of mantra or thought; the thought is not his own, but he 'hears' or 'sees' it. It is interesting that the Sanksrit word for philosophy is darshana, literally 'seeing': the perception of the seer is as important in Hinduism as his intellectual enquiry. In this, too, Hindu philosophy differs considerably from its Western counterparts.

*A depiction of Pashupati, lord of the beasts, on the Gundenstrup
cauldron, dating to mid-second century* BCE

In fact the *Rig Veda* is estimated to have taken perhaps
half a millennium to attain its corpus of 10,552 mantras in
verse, and in the course of these five centuries at least fifty
poet-rishis had a hand in its composition. Their sacredness
comes from their divine inspiration and sustained quality, not
from having been handed down fully composed by God like
the Quran. The story is no different with the later Vedas;
the four Vedas are believed to have been created between
1500 BCE and 500 BCE, a period of several thousand years.
In that period we see enormous evolution from the nomadic
faith of the *Rig Veda*, in which animal sacrifices, including
those of cattle, were offered to the gods and the healthy
scepticism in some of its verses, to the evidence in the later
Vedas of adjustment to new social realities, such as the *Yajur
Veda*'s references to new gods, clearly taken into Hinduism
from prevailing local faiths—including Pashupati, lord of the
beasts, and Aushadi, lord of medicinal herbs.

Similarly the 108 Upanishads, which distil the essence of

the Vedic philosophy, are also Sruti. They were also written over centuries: it is believed that the first eight go back to the period between the eighth century BCE to the fourth century BCE, congruent with the Age of the Buddha. The next three Upanishads are post-Buddhist and date from 300 BCE to 200 CE, whereas the remaining 97 Upanishads belong to the Puranic period—from the second century CE to the tenth century CE. The chronological gap between the earliest verses of the *Rig Veda* and the bulk of the Upanishads was greater than the time that separates us today from the life of Jesus Christ. An entire Upanishad (the *Mandukya Upanishad*) is devoted to the primal sound, Om. In the reckoning of many Hindus, the Upa-Vedas, or subsidiary vedas, include *Ayurveda*, the science of wellness, *Dhanurveda*, the science of weapons and the rules of warfare, *Gandharva Veda*, the science of the performing arts (including the classic text on music, dance and theatre, the *Natya Shastra*) and the *Arthashastra*, the treatise on statecraft that in many respects anticipated Machiavelli's *The Prince* by nearly two millennia. The Vedangas, the explanatory 'limbs' of the Vedas, deal with such matters as grammar, phonetics, etymology, the art of poetry, the science of rituals and (in the famous *Jyotisha Vedanga*) the subjects of astronomy and astrology. All these again are the product of centuries of writing and reflection.

The Smritis are that which is remembered; they are composed by human beings without any specific divine inspiration and passed on to guide ordinary people in the conduct of their lives and the performance of their spiritual and worldly duties. The eighteen Smritis, written down largely over the five centuries between 300 BCE and 200 CE, are often referred to as the Dharmashastras, since they explicate how dharma must be observed, and these are seen as practices that must change with time and place. The Smritis describe the daily life of individuals, prescribing rituals and rules which vary according to each varna or social class and are collectively known as varna-ashrama-dharma. The Smritis also lay down the rules of governance, known as Raj Dharma, and adumbrate the earliest ideas of what may be considered a Hindu constitutional order, headed by a king.

Since the Smritis are purely man-made and mutable, Hinduism does not aver that laws laid down a millennium ago must be followed to the letter today. The foundational laws of Yajnavalkya and the Code of Manu, often cited as the source of 'Hindu law', are Smriti; no Hindu seriously argues that they must be observed to the letter today. (Indeed, it is debatable whether they were strictly followed even in the times in which they were propounded.) Indeed, the Smritis were not all internally consistent:

> A profusion of arguments! The Smritis differ among themselves.
> No one's opinion is final or conclusive.
> The essence of dharma is hidden and elusive.
> The right path is the path followed by great men.
> —Yaksha Prashna, Sloka 114

The Itihasas, the epics, respond to the human need for instruction through story: the profound philosophical enquiries of the Srutis and the Smritis are more easily digested by the common people in the form of parables and epic narratives (which in turn easily lend themselves to theatrical form, dance and music, all the better to communicate their message to the masses). Itihas. literally means 'the way it was' and many take the epics literally, though they have been embroidered with mystical and fantastic elements, and it is quite probable that divinity was ascribed to their principal personages only in

Valmiki writing the Ramayana

later retellings. Their principal purpose remains to impart the values of the Dharmashastras in story form. The Ramayana tells the story of a kingly figure, Rama, who upholds both his personal dharma and his raja dharma: in the earliest versions he was not portrayed as a god, but as an ideal man devoted to upholding truth. Indeed there is impressive evidence for the historicity of Rama in Valmiki's text, which is replete with astonishingly accurate geographical, botanical and zoological details about his journey from Ayodhya to Lanka and back. He makes enormous sacrifices in his personal life, including giving up his beloved wife, in order to fulfil his dharma. The Mahabharata was told and retold, with countless interpolations and additions, till about 400 CE; it incorporates the classic poem, the Bhagavad Gita, the Song of the Lord, which distils the essence of the Upanishads and to many Hindus is the core religious text of their faith.

The two great Hindu epics, the Ramayana and the Mahabharata, tell stirring stories accompanied by digressive meditations on values, morals and principles. They are polycentric and fundamental texts about such key issues in society as what constitutes ethical conduct; how a just society is made and sustained; and the duties and obligations of kings, counsellors, warriors, women and sages. They deal with great moral dilemmas and issues of right conduct, justice and fidelity, violence and redemption; they give voice to a range of actors and concerns; they provide models for social and political action; and because they are told and retold as stories, they have embedded themselves in the popular consciousness of Hindus. The Ramayana, the epic tale of an exiled prince's conquest of the demon kingdom where his wife is held hostage, is a stirring saga, intimately familiar to all Indians and most Southeast Asians. Lord Rama's ultimate triumph and his return to rule his own kingdom as a just and benevolent king is the archetypal story of the victory of good over evil; yet in many of its episodes, including what becomes of his queen, there are complex moral dilemmas unveiled that do not lend themselves to simplistic interpretations.

The Mahabharata deals much more with adharma: it is a tale of the real world, one whose heroes have feet of clay, whose stories have ambiguous ends, whose events range from great feats of honour and valour to dubious compromises, broken promises, dishonourable battles, expedient lies, dispensable morality. It asks profound questions about the nature of dharma: Yudhishthira says 'dharma is subtle' and each episode in the epic appears to be a case study of

Hanuman in the presence of Lord Rama and Sita

what this means—is dharma derived from the shastras, from precedents, from nyay, from niti? Is it determined by caste or gender? The Mahabharata offers much ground for reflection on weighty ethical and moral dilemmas. When the low-born Ekalavya becomes a master archer by eavesdropping

THE HINDU WAY

on lessons offered by Dronacharya to his caste betters, the teacher asks for the boy's thumb in tribute, which would destroy his ability to practise what he has learned. When Draupadi, wife of the Pandavas, is 'lost' in a wager in a fixed game of dice, she questions the right of her husband to stake her and the propriety of the winners to seize her. By raising these questions, the epic obliges Hindus to interrogate themselves about their beliefs. The Mahabharata has come to stand for so much in the popular consciousness of Indians: the issues the epic raises, as well as the values it seeks to promote, are central to an understanding of what makes India India. Its characters and personages still march triumphantly in Indian minds, its myths and legends still inspire the Indian imagination, its events still speak to Indians with a contemporary resonance.

While the Ramayana (composed from around the 200 BCE to perhaps 200 CE) and the Mahabharata (said to be composed between about 400 BCE and 400 CE, after some eight centuries of retellings and interpolations) are the two best-known epics whose core story (and many subsidiary tales) are widely known to practically every Indian, the Itihasas also include the *Yogavasishtha*, stories and fables imparted by the sage Vasishtha to Lord Rama, and the *Harivamsha*, which tells stories of creation and of the origins of Lord Krishna. When the Ramayana and the Mahabharata were retold in the vernacular languages, they acquired immense popularity and impact. The Kamban Ramayana in Tamil in the twelfth century CE, and Tulsidas's *Ramcharitmanas* in Awadhi in the sixteenth century, exalted Rama to his present place in the Hindu pantheon.

The Mahabharata incorporated the Bhagavad Gita, the Song of the Lord, an extraordinary, inspirational and profoundly philosophical text which addresses in powerful and poetic language a basic conundrum of human existence: what

Kamban, who wrote the Ramayana in Tamil

human beings should do when they are pulled in contradictory directions by equally important but incompatible obligations. We are all faced in life with having to make hard choices; the Gita presents us with the searingly hard choice confronting the heroic warrior Arjuna, who finds himself on the battlefield, about to go to war, in the name of a just cause, whose triumph will involve the killing of several members of his own family. His duty and his moral commitment to one side of the battle stands against his love for his own kith and kin, whose blood he must shed, and that too in violation of the universal moral duty not to take life. But if, for this reason, he refuses to fight, his absence from the battlefield could allow the forces of unrighteousness to prevail; it would mean the victory of those who have committed wrongs, and it would violate his own duty and obligation as a warrior to deploy his martial skills in fulfilment of his duty and in defence of the right. Arjuna confesses his agonizing dilemma to Lord Krishna, whose counsel makes up the bulk of the Gita. Perform your dharma, Krishna tells Arjuna: do your duty regardless of the outcome. The right action in conformity with your dharma is your only obligation; its consequences, even its success or failure, should have nothing to do with the moral motivation for your action. Your own feelings, or prospects of reward, are irrelevant to the need to act. Krishna's philosophical advice is essentially to do what is right regardless of the consequences. Implicit is an acknowledgement that doing the right thing is not always easy, that it can cause pain and grief to others, even others one loves or is bound to. But the path of dharma, leading a life of good conduct—what a Westerner might call a moral life—is a complicated and ambiguous task, not to be reduced to simple calculations of defeat or failure, life or death, reward or punishment. Armed with this advice, and with Krishna as his charioteer, Arjuna goes forth to sanguinary battle, and prevails, leaving the battlefield littered with the blood-soaked bodies of his own cousins.

The Gita is an amazing text, full of wisdom and philosophical reason, but also a call for action, an exhortation to fulfil one's duty with conviction and courage. It has probably inspired more commentaries per line of text than any other work in the vast canons of Hinduism. Swami Vivekananda and Mahatma Gandhi swore by it; each found different aspects of its poetic brilliance and profundity to live by.

The eighteen Puranas (composed roughly between

The Prachetas paying homage to Shiva,
from a Bhagavata Purana series.

250 CE and 1000 CE) convey the truths of the Vedas and the Dharmashastras in short stories as well, and have formed the basis of religious education in rural India for millennia. They differ from the Itihasas since they do not comprise a grand epic narrative but several different stories featuring non-recurrent characters. The moral code conveyed through Puranic stories is still the basis for Hindu ethics, and the characters in many Puranic tales have come to epitomize the virtues of faith, chastity, obedience, loyalty, constancy, generosity and so on. Their names are often cited, whether in conversation or even political discourse, as emblematic of those virtues: Prahalada, the faithful believer, Savitri, the devoted wife, Dhruva, the constant, Harishchandra, the truthful, and so on. The Puranas also tell the stories of the ten incarnations of Vishnu; and the *Srimad Bhagavatam*, or *Bhagavata Purana*, focusing on the life and times of Lord Krishna, is still recited in temples and homes across India.

The Puranas mark a significant development in Hinduism,

with a much greater emphasis on the worship of Gods in human form, unlike the earlier Vedic faith; where the latter had relied on rituals and sacrifices in which homams (prayer rituals around a fire), usually involving the fire god Agni, played a major role, the Puranic practice principally involved idol-worship and pujas. (It is suggested that while the Vedic era saw only the worship of a formless and imageless God, the conduct of rituals and the propitiation of the river and mountain and tree gods of local tribes, all of which were 'portable' and not confined to a fixed spot, it was the arrival of the Greeks under Alexander in the fourth century BCE that brought into India the idea of permanent temples enshrining stone images of heroes and gods.) Again, while the Hinduism of the Vedas emerged from mantras and rituals, including elaborate sacrifices, the Puranas promoted their values entirely on the basis of myths and stories. By developing the concept of the saguna Brahman to go with the exalted idea of the nirguna Brahman, the Puranic faith integrated the Vedic religion into the daily worship of ordinary people. Using the seductive power of maya (illusion), the nirguna Brahman of the Vedas took the form of saguna Brahman or Ishvara, the creator of prakriti, the natural world and the God or Bhagavan of all human beings. Vishnu and Shiva were recognized as Ishvaras; the followers of the former, the Vaishnavas, worshipped Him in several avatars, while the followers of Shiva, the Shaivites, confined their worship to Shiva alone, though in several aspects (the dancing Nataraja, the powerfully symbolic lingam), and his immediate family (his consort Parvati, his sons Ganesh or Vinayaka, and Skanda or Murugan). Puranic Hinduism witnessed the absorption (even 'Sanskritization') of the existing local cultures and the adoption of their deities and heroes into Hindu mythology; it is in the Puranic age that both Vaishnavites and Shaivites

Agni, the god of fire

accepted idol worship, which was earlier absent from the
Vedic faith. The Puranas offered a bridge between the Vedic
religion and local folkways, between highbrow philosophers
and vernacular cultures, assimilating both in a narrative of
inclusive ethics. It is in the Puranas that much of what we
today understand by popular Hinduism is anchored.

Not quite fitting into any of these categories is another
magnificent work of early Hinduism, authored in the South
by Thiruvalluvar (born around 300 CE) whose *Thirukkural*,
a collection of 1,330 couplets or kurals containing profound
aphorisms and imparting moral lessons, has been called by
some 'the Veda of the Tamils'.

Thiruvalluvar, the author of the Thirukkural

By the sixth century CE India and Hinduism had a rich mythology, a corpus of elaborate rites and rituals, extraordinary heroic poetry, a well-developed system of popular ethics, an evolving religious architecture and a spiritual literature for the masses. It also had non-religious texts of universal significance, notably the fables of the *Panchatantra*, which imparted practical advice on worldly matters (and on the foibles of human character) in the form of entertaining tales featuring both humans and animals. There is cynicism, including about kings and political leaders; violence, often unfortunate; and humour, sometimes at the expense of the vainglorious. 'We are told quite frankly,' observes the historian Upinder Singh, 'that conventional virtues can lead to ruin. Truthfulness, kindness, and helpfulness to others lead to disaster. The idea of self-sacrifice (even feigned) is mocked. Cunning, quick thinking, and hard-headedness are valorized. The only social relationship that is celebrated is friendship, and even that does not emerge unscathed.'

With idol worship came temple construction, a feature of Hinduism only since the fifth century CE, and reaching its apogee in the magnificent Chola temples of the eleventh to the thirteenth centuries, many of which are still in use today. The 108 Agamas lay down the disciplines and doctrines for the worship of specific deities, notably Shiva, Vishnu and Shakti, which in turn have given birth to cults focused on each of these manifestations of the divine. They also specify the rules for constructing temples in honour of each of these, and for observing related rituals and rites. They are meticulously detailed, ranging from the ablutions to be performed by the worshipper to the adornments on the idol, the timing and order of prayers and so on, and also replete with devotional songs and verses. However, most people worship daily in the privacy of their own homes: instead of idols consecrated in temples, they have portable idols installed in an alcove or puja-room. This practice is sanctified in the *Srimad Bhagavatam* or *Bhagavata Purana* (Part 11, Chapter 27, Sloka 12), which specifies that eight types of material engender permissible forms of idol worship: stone, wood, metal, clay, sand, crystal, a drawing or even just a mental image. Some of the prominent temples were located on the banks of sacred rivers—notably the Ganga, Yamuna, Narmada, Godavari, Krishna, and Kaveri—whose flowing waters were said to have cleansing properties that could purify those who immersed themselves in them. The Kumbh Mela at the confluence of the Ganga and the Yamuna attracts hundreds of thousands of worshippers even today.

The Darshanas are the texts of the six principal schools of

Devotees at the Kumbh Mela

Hindu philosophy, drawing from many and are unabashedly intellectual and abstrusely academic in nature. The six (the Shad Darshanas) include three lesser-known schools of Hindu philosophy: the Nyaya School, which emphasizes logic and debate; the Vaisheshika School, which sees the universe as made up of countless atoms, each with its own distinctive quality; and the Mimamsa School, which emphasizes the role of sacrifice and ritual in seeking salvation (some scholars describe the Vedic religion as Mimamsa Hinduism to distinguish it from the Puranic Hinduism of later years). A fourth, the Yoga School, is better known around the world for its physical practices, but in fact principally focuses on the control of the mind, the breath and the body as the means to attaining the divine samadhi. The central debate in Hindu philosophy is, however, between the two other schools, the oldest, the Sankhya School (so old that it is mentioned in the Mahabharata), based on reasoning, which argues the case for dualism or Dvaita (the idea that there is a clear distinction between spirit and matter, between the divine and the worldly) and the newest (founded just over a millennium ago), the Vedanta School, which rejects dualism (Advaita) and sees spirit and matter as essentially one. Vedanta, or 'the end of the Vedas', has, thanks to the initial efforts of Adi Shankara and the nineteenth-century preaching of Swami Vivekananda, become the principal school of Hindu philosophy today, as well as the most influential internationally, and is discussed more fully in chapter six.

Hindus trust the Vedas but most do not see them as immune to analysis or criticism; it has been axiomatic in Hinduism that what was valuable to our forefathers might be valuable to us today, but each generation is allowed to enquire into its own spiritual patrimony. The Vedas have a sanctified place in the Hindu consciousness, but the Upanishads, the Puranas, the epics, and other works of spiritual and philosophical enquiry are also counted among our most basic scriptures. The three prasthanas or divisions of the Vedanta—the Upanishads, the *Brahma Sutras* (555 aphoristic verses attributed to Badarayana and written down some time between 450 BCE and 200 CE, which summarize the spiritual and philosophical ideas in the Upanishads) and the Bhagavad Gita—correspond roughly, according to Hindu philosophers, with the three stages of faith, knowledge and discipline. Each has value; each can be understood and practised alone or in combination with the others.

That said, as we have seen, Hindus, unlike Muslims and Christians, do not see their religious texts as claiming to embody the ultimate truth. Indeed, it would be a problem if they did, because then different texts would offer contradictory truths and men might be obliged to fight each other to demonstrate the superiority of their truth. Instead, a work of scripture is, to a Hindu, a means of self-realization; the words, and the insights they contain, are devices through which a diligent Hindu approaches self-transformation. A religious text is a breach in the fog of ignorance that enshrouds the human mind. Allow its insights, the magic of its words, the music of its mantras, to penetrate through the fog, and a transformation might follow. The transformation is not merely in understanding the words of the text as in an Abrahamic holy book, but in opening the mind to new possibilities—including the possibility that the literal claims of the text might be false. The purpose of the religious text is to enter the mind of the reader and help constitute the self.

As Swami Vivekananda put it: 'To the Westerners their religious books have been inspired, while with us our books have been expired; breath-like they came, the breath of God, out of the hearts of sages they sprang, the mantra-drashtas.'

Given this attitude to the Hindu holy texts, the Sanatana Dharma's attitude to the Bible, the Torah or the Quran is the same. Hindus do not look for the literal meanings of these holy books; and since they do not read them literally, they do not argue over them literally either. The Hindu has historically refused to pick a fight over the meaning of other people's religious texts; since they cannot literally be true, to the Hindu, they can either help in self-realization or not, but they are not worth quarrelling about. You say your holy book is the word of God? Fine; if it helps you understand your true self, if it opens your mind's eyes to the ultimate truth of Creation and helps you merge your soul into the cosmos, it will have served its purpose. Ah, you say, that's not what your holy book is supposed to do? What use is it to you then? Come, let me read it; perhaps it will help open my eyes.

This approach to theological disputation left the honest Christian missionary in colonial times somewhat confused.

Samudra Manthan, through which all of creation came into being

THE HINDU LIFE EXPERIENCE

As a result, Hinduism occupies a unique place among the world's faiths. In it, as Dr Radhakrishnan explained: 'Intellect is subordinated to intuition, dogma to experience, outer expression to inward realization. Religion is not the acceptance of academic abstractions or the celebration of ceremonies, but a kind of life or experience. It is insight into the nature of reality (darshana) or experience of reality (anubhava).' Hindus dislike people being drafted into truth-armies firing cannons of certitudes; their instinct is to remain sceptical, open, questioning. Reason and intuition must go together. Blind belief in dogma is absent in Hinduism; all spiritual teachings are subject to disputation, and perceptions must be tested through logical thought. The Hindu sacred texts 'are not so much dogmatic dicta as transcripts from life.'

This is all very well, one might say, but what of the vast majority of Hindus, who have not read most of these sacred texts, who are unaware of the glorious capaciousness of their faith, who are inured to theological heterodoxy and scriptural eclecticism? What of those who only know Hinduism as a cultural identity, who go to their temples to pray to their ishta-devta (their favourite gods) when they are in trouble or distress, who observe fasts for specific deities, celebrate joyously the major festivals in their area and are conscious of their difference from those who practise other faiths? Is the Hinduism I am describing their Hinduism too?

I would claim it is. Because ultimately the nature of any religious faith is not determined by its scholars, theologians and scriptural exegetes. It is precisely the ordinary believer, the worshipper who is indifferent to theories about his faith but believes in God and values his religion as his way of reaching his hands out to his Maker, who demonstrates the essence of his faith in his own practice of it. In Hinduism, there is an understandable tendency to see the faith through its remarkable Sanskrit scriptural and philosophical writings. But just as important to the practice of Hinduism are the non-Sanskritic, oral, vernacular and regional traditions of worship and ritual, which are indispensable to the way the faith is experienced in different parts of the country. And it is precisely because Hinduism has been practised in a certain way for millennia that it has survived as long as it has with its essential nature unchanged, even as it has faced the vicissitudes of reformist movements like Buddhism and Jainism, military assaults from Muslim invaders, conquest and Islamic rule, the conversion activity of Christian missionaries, reformist challenges like those of Ramananda, Chaitanya and Kabir (of whom later), syncretic movements like Sikhism and the Brahmo Samaj and attempts at conversion of its adherents to other faiths. Every Hindu may not be conscious of the finer points of his faith, but he has been raised in the tradition of its assumptions and doctrines, even when

Diwali, the festival of lights

these have not been explained to him. His Hinduism may be a Hinduism of habit rather than a Hinduism of learning, but it is a lived Hinduism for all that.

These 'habits' vary enormously from place to place, caste to caste, and community to community. In South India it is entirely common to see celebrations and practices completely unfamiliar to a north Indian, and vice-versa. The Thaipusam festival, taking place in the Tamil month of Thai, in which devotees carry ceremonial offerings on wooden planks called kavadis and many pierce themselves through the body and march in excruciating processionals to demonstrate their devotion to Lord Murugan, is unknown in other parts of India. Pongal is a huge festival in Tamil Nadu and southern Kerala but a north Indian Hindu will have no clue what it signifies. While Diwali, the Festival of Lights, has over the years become, in popular perception, the standout Hindu festival, it is observed fairly modestly in the south; in Kerala, on the other hand, the festival of Onam is celebrated with enormous gaiety and piety unlike in the north, where it is not celebrated at all.

Onam, in fact, offers another striking example of Hindu diversity. It celebrates the annual return to earth of the asura King Mahabali, a wise and benevolent monarch under whose egalitarian rule the people of Kerala flourished in mythical times. The gods, jealous of his overweening power and popularity, sent Lord Vishnu to earth in the form of a Brahmin dwarf, Vamana, who asked the king for as much land as he could cover in three steps. The king, surprised by the modesty of his request, granted his wish; whereupon the dwarf grew to his celestial size as the Lord. With one step he covered the earth, with his second the heavens; and when he had nowhere left to place his third step, he turned to the king to fulfil his promise. King Mahabali humbly offered his own head; Lord Vishnu placed his foot on the monarch's head, driving the king through the ground into the netherworld. Onam commemorates Mahabali's annual return to earth to see how his people are getting on; rather like Santa Claus, he is largely portrayed as a jolly, rotund figure happy to see his subjects enjoying a good time, and Onam is an occasion for holiday cheer, gift-giving and enormous feasts. As I have noted, it is, however, not celebrated by north Indian Hindus, who instead observe, the day before Onam, a minor festival called Vamana Puja in which they worship Vishnu in the form of a dwarf. A Malayalam tweet by a north Indian politician, Amit Shah, the BJP minister, wishing Keralites well on the occasion of Vamana Puja, caused great offence to its intended audience, since it was portrayed as celebrating the ill-treatment of the popular local king vanquished by Vamana!

As a result of its huge diversity, and the multiple folk

religious practices it has absorbed over the millennia, mainstream Hinduism abounds in festivals. There is no day in the calendar which is not associated with some auspicious occasion, or dedicated to a specific god, or assigned to a particular religious practice. The importance and significance of each day will again vary depending on which part of India one is in, and which community one belongs to. In the national capital, Delhi, it is entirely possible to see Punjabis celebrating Lohri while Bengalis go about their business, Biharis enveloped in Chhath Puja while Maharashtrians remain ignorant of it and Malayalis in Onam holiday spirit while northerners are just gearing themselves up for Diwali.

Rituals are undoubtedly a precious part of religious practice for most Hindus. Some are conducted by priests in arcane Sanskrit while the devotee, having paid his fee, stands with hands folded and listens in incomprehension. (There is a distinction in many scriptural texts between the priest who performs the ritual and the yajamana or the person for whom it is performed, whose only role consists of offering a dakshina or gratuity to the priest.) Some— particularly the rituals associated with birth and naming, the first feeding of grain to a baby, the first instruction in the alphabet, and of course marriage, death and cremation—are full of inescapable meaning for every participant and bind the worshipper to his faith, family and community. Most often the rituals require a visit to a temple; sometimes they are performed at home. My sisters, who live abroad, do not go as often to temples as our mother, who lives in India, though they strive to keep up certain religious traditions and practices even in foreign lands. But they tell me that they are deeply comforted by the knowledge that on every special occasion in their family, our mother is going to an ancient temple to pray for them, to seek the Lord's blessings for their families, and to distribute alms to the poor in their name. In turn, whether in damp London or sunny California, they remember to light a lamp at dusk in their prayer-rooms, as Hindus have done for centuries.

Hindu rituals almost always require a priest, in most parts of India; however my own community, the Nairs of Kerala, dispenses with the services of a priest on the occasion of marriage, seeing it as a social contract to be performed under the guidance of family elders in the presence of large numbers of usually well-fed witnesses, which would be enough to seal a marriage in the eyes of the world. The eyes of a representative of God they consider much less important; whereas in the north, it would be unthinkable not to have a priest officiating—indeed the wedding might well be considered null and void if a priest didn't turn up to conduct it.

Given this dislike of priestly intermediaries in my gene pool, it is no wonder that as a young boy I asked my father why it was necessary to go to temples. If God is everywhere, I reasoned, isn't He (or She) at home, at school, at work? Why do we need to go to a temple to find Her? My father patiently explained that while God is everywhere, He was especially powerful in certain places, especially those where He had manifested himself through the spontaneous appearance of an idol (as in the Krishna idol in Guruvayur) or other miracles. Such places then became sanctified by the devotions of millions of worshippers over hundreds of years, and thus acquired even more religious significance. It was a self-perpetuating phenomenon: a temple became famous because of something associated with it, usually a legend involving the deity in question, then worshippers came and testified to its powers, saying their prayers at that place had been answered by the Goddess, for instance, and then more worshippers came and the more devotion

*Every evening as dusk descends, priests perform Ganga Aarti
by the banks of River Ganga, offering prayers*

the temple attracted, the more were the stories of miracles
and blessings accruing from worship there, and the more
people kept coming...

On that south Indian pilgrimage when I was fourteen, I
also found myself asking my father about the behaviour of
some of the priests at the more famous temples, who openly
stuck out their hands for more money after performing the
rituals my father had already paid for. He looked somewhat
embarrassed at first, then replied softly but firmly that
priests had to live too. They were performing a service to
us devotees, but they had families they were responsible for,

children they had to educate, and it was only fair they asked for help from the people on whose behalf they had interceded with God. After all, they had what today we would call 'domain knowledge'; they knew the scriptures, had mastered the mantras and could recite the appropriate ones with the required fluency. Why shouldn't they be rewarded for their expertise?

This left my teenage mind only partly mollified, and I have not been as enthusiastic a temple-goer as my parents, especially since I rationalized that praying in the privacy of my own home would be just as effective, as long as my heart was pure and my thoughts clear. I maintain an eclectic prayer-alcove in my home, where dozens of pictures, idols and relics of Hindu deities—including a print that reproduces one of my parents' religious pictures, that I saw my father pray before every day as I grew up—all compete for my reverential attention daily.

Still, the passion of other worshippers keeps drawing me back to temples, especially in my constituency, Thiruvananthapuram, which is blessed with more places of worship per square kilometre than any other metropolis in India, and where friends, colleagues and party workers insist on accompanying me, praying for me and promising assorted divinities that I will perform certain rituals in fulfilment of their undertakings. (I have, as a result, been weighed against bananas, coconuts and salt because *they* had sworn that I would be: this is a powerful incentive against weight-loss, since the heavier I was, the more the temples in question benefited from donations of those items). But I am not complaining. I find peace in the temples, and a strengthening of my ties to those who have accompanied me there, as if we have shared something indefinable in that common space where hope and need combine in supplication to the Divine.

Some have seen in Hinduism a selfish religion, a collection of individuals praying for themselves, with no equivalent of the Muslim Friday prayer or the Sunday Christian Mass with its service and sermon uniting a community in worship. Philosophically, after all, the most important claim the Upanishads make is that the essence of each individual is also the essence of all things; the human self, the atman, and the cosmic reality, Brahman, are essentially the same. This leads to the view that one only needs to look within to find divinity; one has no need of fellow worshippers or collective sermonizing. Hindu religious practice is essentially contemplative, as the seeker turns his gaze inwards in quest of real awareness. The *Mundaka Upanishad* (II.2.3) offers a marvellous metaphor: the Imperishable is the target for the seeker, the Upanishads are his bow, constant meditation is his arrow, and the string of the bow is drawn with his mind filled with Brahman. Because of this interiority, some Hindu critics see Hinduism as lacking the unity that strengthens other faiths and helps them to negotiate the modern world and social pressures better. Its focus on self-realization rather than collective advancement, they say, might allow plenty of room for philosophical thought, but none for collective action. To such critics, this prevents Hindus from constituting a defined 'community' that can withstand external pressures.

The *Atharva Veda* points out that the quest for awareness, the search for answers, the journey towards self-realization, never ceases:

> How does the wind not cease to blow?
> How does the mind take no repose?

Why do the waters, seeking to reach the truth,
Never at any time cease to flow?
                                    —*Atharva Veda*, X.7.37

And yet this process is not purely self-centred individualism, since the real self one discovers in this profound quest is the same self as everyone else's. Self-realization leads ultimately to merging one's soul into the collective Brahman. So when one goes to a temple to worship, one is finding a common sanctified space to help one travel to the same destination as every other worshipper.

SECTION THREE

~

QUESTIONING HINDU CUSTOMS

Lord Murugan (also known as Kartikeya), brother of Lord Ganesh, is the god of war and victory. Seen here astride his mount, the peacock.

Matsya is the fish avatar of Vishnu. Often listed as the first of the Dashavatars (ten avatars) of Lord Vishnu, Matsya is described to have rescued the first man, Manu, from a great deluge. In the Matsya avatar, Lord Vishnu is depicted as half-man, half-fish, seen here cradling four infants, representing the four Vedas.

chapter three

QUESTIONING HINDU CUSTOMS

Some of Thiruvananthapuram's old temples, especially the eleventh-century Sree Padmanabhaswamy Kshetram, recently revealed to be one of the richest temples in the world because of all the treasures deposited there by the triumphant Travancore maharajas of yore, are truly beautiful. This is where Vishnu, is worshipped as Padmanabha, lying on the great serpent Ananta as he floats on the vast Ocean of Milk, the Kshir Sagar. It is in this posture that he is so revered that the kings of the Travancore kingdom called themselves 'Padmanabhadasa', servants of Padmanabha, and ruled in his name rather than in their own—a curious inversion of the concept of the divine right of kings, since here it was the kingly right of the divine.

If many temples are beautiful, though, not all old Hindu practices sanctified by these temples are. The ancient tradition of caste was one my nationalist parents tried to shield me from for years, and it was only at age eleven, when asked by a schoolmate in Mumbai what my caste was (in an incident

Sri Padmanabhaswamy Temple

I describe below), that I finally demanded an explanation. But caste as an instrument of discrimination was abhorrent to my liberal sensibilities from a very young age.

❧

CASTE AND HINDUISM

It is difficult to pretend that Hinduism can be exempted from the problems of casteism, since the religion has been cited as legitimizing this form of discrimination in some of its sacred texts. The *Rig Veda* does not mention caste in its original books and it first appears in the Purusha Sukta verse, a later interpolation that describes the sacrifice by the gods of Purusha, the cosmic man, to create all human life: according to this verse, from his mouth emerged the Brahmin, the priests and scholars; his arms were made into the Kshatriyas, the warriors and rulers; his two thighs were the general populace, the farmers, merchants and traders who made up the

Dr Bhimrao Ambedkar

Vaishyas; and from his feet the Sudras, the workers, artisans and servants, were born.

The verse has been challenged, especially by the great constitutionalist and Dalit leader Dr Bhimrao Ambedkar, who considered it a fraudulent attempt to legitimize caste discrimination, but there is little doubt that many Hindus believed that the caste system had religious sanction. Ironically, as I have demonstrated in my 2016 book, *An Era of Darkness*, India had castes, but not a caste system: the rigidities of caste as we understand it today were introduced by the British in their desire to understand, categorize, and classify the people they were ruling, in order to control them all the better. What Devdutt Pattanaik describes as the attempt by the British to 'force-fit' some 3,000 jatis (castes, or some say sub-castes, grouped around hereditary professions) into the four varnas established in the Dharmashastras, has given us a complex 'caste system' whose uneven persistence in Hindu society has been the source of both iniquity and confusion.

The language of the Purusha Sukta verse would seem to rule out any but Brahmin priests in Hindu temples, and yet shudra archakas perform rituals in many Hindu places of worship, and in October 2017 the Travancore Devaswom or temple board appointed thirty-six non-Brahmin priests officially, including six Dalits (the former 'untouchables' who were not even admitted to Kerala's temples till 1936 and who are still denied access to the sanctum sanctorum in many temples where that privilege is reserved only for those who wear the sacred thread). It is conventional wisdom that the caste system confined all learning to a narrow, privileged caste of Brahmins, yet Veda Vyasa, the compiler of the Vedas, was born to a low-caste fisherwoman, and Valmiki, the author of the Ramayana, was a low-caste hunter; both are revered today, even by the Brahmins.

Caste may well have originated in Hinduism's desire to accommodate the different racial, sectarian, and occupational groups it encountered, in a social hierarchy: Dr Radhakrishnan called it 'the answer of Hinduism to the forces pressing on it from outside', an instrument to 'civilize' different tribes it absorbed. To this great scholar, caste 'stands for the ordered complexity, the harmonized multiplicity, the many in one which is the clue to the structure of the universe'. That sounds almost admirable, till one understands that this complexity, in practice, ossified into impermeable social barriers that manifested themselves in degrading forms of social discrimination and economic oppression. It was not always the case: there was a famous 'fuzziness' to the operations of caste in the pre-colonial era, and many famous examples of caste mobility (beyond those of Veda Vyasa and Valmiki). Be that as it may, the workings of caste extended into religious worship as well. Many temples forbade entry of the 'lower' castes and the 'outcastes'; the latter became known as 'untouchables' because of the innumerable social prohibitions and indignities to which they were subject.

There is no excusing such abhorrent practices, and many modern Hindus have grown up rejecting the discriminatory aspects of the caste system, while still observing caste preferences when it comes to arranging the marriages of their children. Their logic is simple: caste is a form of community organization we've had for ever, and we are not about to jettison it. We are comfortable with the affinities it implies, and we would prefer to perpetuate our family by arranging marriages within our caste group. But that doesn't mean we will discriminate against people of other castes, or mistreat them: we are educated people, and we know that's wrong. This may strike many modern Indians as a dubious compromise, but the attitude I have summarized is far more common within the Hindu population than many imagine.

It should also be said that the most impressive of India's movements against caste discrimination, from those of Basava in the twelfth century to Sree Narayana Guru in the nineteenth, came from within Hinduism and retained a Hindu vocabulary and conceptual world, including reverence for Hindu deities. Sree Narayana Guru, forbidden as an Ezhava from worshipping at the Shiva temple, entered a river and unearthed a lingam that he consecrated himself, thereby creating his own Shiva rather than rejecting the god who was denied to him. The fourteenth-century Bhakti saint Chokhamela was a Dalit whose fervour for God continued even though he was not allowed inside the temple. In one of his verses he addresses the deity as he might speak to a man of an upper caste: 'I am so hungry; I have come for your leavings, I am full of hope.' In another verse, he brings a 'bowl for your leftover food'; with no access to the shrine, he seeks to fulfil his devotion by serving the deity,

Sree Narayana Guru

submitting himself completely and eating the scraps left behind. This is alarmingly conformist, yet revealing of the extent to which Chokhamela's abject social condition had no bearing on his spiritual standing nor on the extent of his posthumous sanctification. Among the Lingayat saints, too, there were many of humble origins. While Basava, the founder of the sect, was born a Brahmin, many of his prominent disciples were of humbler origins: as Manu S. Pillai records, Allama Prabhu was a drummer, Siddharama a cowherd, Maccayya a washerman, and Kakkaya, a skinner of dead cows.

Still, social mobility was relatively rare in Hinduism, and the lot of the outcastes was a terrible one. Was this because of the religion or the society that practised it? Arguably, untouchability was a social practice for which it is impossible to find scriptural sanction. To suggest that to be a good Hindu you had to practise caste discrimination is therefore theologically unsound. As the philosopher Jonardon Ganeri has explained, 'Hinduism contains within itself the philosophical resources to sustain an internal critique of reprehensible and unjust social practices that have sometimes emerged in Hindu societies.' As those who are familiar with Adi Shankara's beliefs will testify, the Upanishadic insistence on the unity of being, a divinity available to everyone, the atma residing in everyone, and the idea that all human souls ultimately merge into the same Brahman, for instance, implies the equality of all souls and argues against caste discrimination. So does the Vedantic concept of the welfare of all human beings, irrespective of social or economic distinctions: 'Bahujana sukhaya bahujana hitaya cha'. Adi Shankara himself is said to have met an outcaste Chandala who was ordered by his disciples to move out of the path of the great sage. 'Who are you to ask me to move for you?' the outcaste asked the great rishi. 'Is the Self within me different from the Self within you?' Shankara was so struck by this enunciation of Advaita wisdom by the low-born Chandala that he prostrated himself before the untouchable and proclaimed the Chandala to be his guru.

Manu S. Pillai recounts a legend from the same period: 'The sage Vararuchi, son of Sankaracharya's preceptor, married a pariah woman, and fathered 12 children with her. One became a Brahmin, another a carpenter, and one was even a Muslim. Yet another sibling, when they all met for a feast, brought to the table food that he enjoyed: the udder of a cow, or beef if you will. Of course the story goes on to transform the meat into a plant that everyone then consumed, but the lesson is simply that though they were different in what they did and what they ate, they were all born of the same parents, and children of the same land.'

Still, caste discrimination was widespread and iniquitous. Of course Hindus have long accepted the logic

A pictorial representation of caste in India

of 'reservations' (quotas) in our country as a means of making up for millennia of discrimination based on birth. This is why the Constitution inaugurated the world's oldest and farthest-reaching affirmative action programme, guaranteeing Scheduled Castes and Tribes (Dalits and Adivasis) not only equality of opportunity but guaranteed outcomes, with reserved places in educational institutions, government jobs and even seats in Parliament and the state assemblies. Given the appalling discrimination to which they had been subject for millennia especially those subject to the unspeakable privations of untouchability this seems only fair to most, including the majority of caste Hindus, who have not objected to such reservations.

These reservations are granted to groups listed in Schedules of the Constitution on the basis of their (presumably immutable) caste identities. The addition of the Other Backward Classes (OBC) category in 1989 after the acceptance by the VP Singh government of the recommendations of the Mandal Commission added more people to the numbers benefiting from reservations, but it didn't change the basis on which they benefited: despite the 'C' in 'OBC' referring to 'classes', the OBC lists contained castes and sub-castes just above the Dalits in the social pecking order. People like myself tend to disavow caste loyalties as unworthy relics of a more unequal pre-Independence past, but accept that granting benefits on the basis of caste is unavoidable. As for ourselves, as intellectual heirs of a freedom movement that explicitly rejected caste, and outlawed caste discrimination, we aren't supposed to admit to caste feeling even if, in some cases, it lurks somewhere beneath the surface.

Not with me: I am conscious of my own bias in the opposite direction. The son of a Keralite newspaper executive who dropped his caste name (Nair) at college in response to Mahatma Gandhi's exhortations to do so, moved to London and brought his children up in Westernized Bombay, I am a product of a nationalist generation that was consciously raised to be oblivious of caste.

I still remember my own discovery of caste. I was an eleven-year-old representing the 7th Standard in an inter-class theatrical event at which the 8th Standard's sketch featured the scion of a famous Bollywood dynasty (who are Hindu). The boy would later become a successful screen heart-throb. I had acted, elocuted a humorous poem, and MCed my class's efforts, and the young man was either intrigued or disconcerted by what he had witnessed, for he sought me out the next morning at school.

'Tharoor,' he asked me at the head of the steps near the toilet, 'what caste are you?'

I blinked my nervousness at the Great Man. 'I—I don't know,' I stammered. My father, who never mentioned anyone's religion, let alone caste, had not bothered to enlighten me on such matters.

'You don't know?' the actor's son demanded in astonishment. 'What do you mean, you don't know? Everybody knows their own caste.'

I shamefacedly confessed I didn't.

'You mean you're not a Brahmin or something?'

I couldn't even avow I was a something. The Great Man never spoke to me again in school. But I went home that evening and extracted an explanation from my parents, whose eclectic liberality had left me in such ignorance. They told me, in simplified terms, about the Nairs; and so it is to that schoolboy, celluloid hero of the future, that I owe my first lesson about my genealogical past.

Despite this enforced awareness, I grew up thinking of caste as an irrelevance. The idea of caste as a badge of identity did not bother me too much, because I saw it as one of several such badges, to be donned or taken off according to my convenience: my caste identity was relevant to family holidays in my parents' ancestral villages, but irrelevant to my cosmopolitan schooling, and my parents never mentioned (or asked) the caste or religion of any schoolmate who came home to play with me or attend my birthday parties. I grew up ignorant of caste, married outside my caste, and brought up two children to be utterly indifferent to caste, indeed largely unconscious of it. Until my fifties, when I entered the caste-ridden world of Indian politics, it remained that way. Even after I entered the hothouse world of Indian politics I did not deliberately seek to find out the caste of anyone I met or worked with; I hired a cook without asking his caste (the same with my remaining domestic staff) and have entertained all manner of people in my home without the thought of caste affinity even crossing my mind.

Yet India is a land of multiple identities, and one of the key identities, inescapably, is caste. As has been noted, to some, it's an instrument of political mobilization; as the Yadav (OBC) ascendancy in parts of north India has repeatedly demonstrated, when many Indians cast their vote, they vote their caste. English-speaking urban Indians may scorn such behaviour even while accepting it as part of India's political reality. After all, none of us would object if a Dalit leader advertised her pride in being a Dalit, or called for Dalit solidarity. Yet my obliviousness to caste is itself a confession of privilege; no Dalit, my Dalit friends tell me, can afford to be oblivious of caste. Much of the outrage at caste is, of course, when it's not a member of an oppressed community celebrating its achievements, but members of one of the so-called 'upper castes', someone at the top of the heap, celebrating their privileges, power and prominence.

Caste won't disappear from the Indian landscape: too many political and administrative benefits (and disadvantages) derive from your caste affiliation for that to happen, not to mention that for many Indians, it is still part of their lived reality. But for many Hindus it doesn't pack the same punch it used to. If it becomes more and more one of many interchangeable, mutable forms of identity—one fraternity of many that an Indian can lay claim to—it can cease to matter so much. The majority of Hindus aren't there yet, unfortunately. And politics may not let them get there either. In recent years we have witnessed the unedifying (and unwittingly hilarious) spectacle of castes fighting with each other to be declared backward: the competitive zeal of the Meenas and the Gujjars in Rajasthan to be deemed more backward than each other, and the agitations of privileged and powerful castes like the Marathas, the Patels and the Jats for reservations on the same basis, would be funny if all sides weren't so deadly serious. As an uncle of mine sagely observed, 'In our country now, you can't go forward unless you're a backward.' (That may seem a prejudiced remark, but such views are increasingly held by many whose castes are ineligible for reservations). Caste—ironically entrenched in India by British colonial rule, as I wrote in one of my books, *An Era of Darkness*—has remained an inescapable feature of our lives.

The news that a recent survey has established that 27 per cent of Indians still practise caste untouchability is not, in many ways, news at all. Most Indians have grown up in an India where we have seen such behaviour, though the kind of people who read English-language books probably think of it as something that happens in rural, backward villages rather than urban India.

But this survey also packs a few other surprises. It shows almost every third Hindu (30 per cent) admitted to the practice. That is, they refused to allow Dalits into their kitchen or to use their utensils. But bizarrely enough, data from the survey showed that untouchability was also practised by Sikhs (23 per cent), Muslims (18 per cent) and Christians (5 per cent). These are faiths that pride themselves on their enshrining of equality and the brotherhood of faith. Dr Amit Thorat, the survey's lead researcher, at the National Council of Applied Economic Research (NCAER), was quoted by the *Indian Express* as saying, 'These findings indicate that conversion [to religions other than Hinduism] has not led to the total change of mindset that was hoped... caste identity is sticky baggage, difficult to dislodge in social settings.'

My father's and my response—to be oblivious to caste and indifferent to the caste associations of friends, employees and associates—is no longer enough in today's caste-conscious India. For a long time I assumed this was the modern Indian ideal—the egalitarian spirit in which one judged people not by their caste but (to borrow from Martin Luther King Jr.) by the content of their character or the sum of their abilities. But living in India over the last decade, after thirty-four years based abroad, has taught me I was wrong. As an eighteen-year-old blogger, Tejaswini Tabhane, pointed out recently, 'A Brahmin's caste pride comes with humiliation for other castes'. Caste, she writes, 'is both the base and superstructure of Indian society and that both the relations of power as well as the forces of production are mediated through it. Blindness to caste does not take away the social, political and economical privileges one gets because of one's "accident of birth" in a particular ("upper") caste.' In her words, anyone belonging to a hierarchically privileged caste 'is bound to get the advantages of his caste location, willingly or unwillingly, consciously or unconsciously. Caste governs the distribution of resources and opportunities in Indian society. Caste is very much present in your life even if it is not directly visible to you because your social and economic capital is a production of your caste only.'

I have to concede she is right. And that makes her admonition strike home: 'To be born in a privileged caste is not anyone's fault but to refuse to even acknowledge "unearned benefits" accruing due to one's caste and thereby claiming that the very mechanism that enforces them is absent in one's life is not right.' On the other hand, 'For the people belonging to the marginalized lower strata of this system, caste is about humiliation, deprivation, oppression and imposed identity.'

Caste blindness, in other words, is itself an affectation available only to the privileged; the 'lower' castes cannot afford to be indifferent to caste. Parallels are sought to be drawn to debates over race-blind policies in the West, but these are inexact: race, after all, is visible, whereas caste is not, which makes it genuinely possible to be caste-blind in one's social and personal relations in a way that is not feasible in multi-race contexts (a white person cannot credibly say,

'I didn't realize he was black', least of all when a white employer rejects a black applicant's job application, but an upper-caste Hindu can plausibly claim, 'I didn't know she was a Dalit'). Still, the temper of the times demands consciousness of caste and positive compensatory action for its disabilities, rather than blindness to it. Jawaharlal Nehru had hoped caste would disappear from India's consciousness, as I had allowed it to from mine. In today's India, that will no longer do.

The recent NCAER findings confirming the persistence of the iniquitous practice of caste discrimination across India's religious communities do not exonerate Hindu society. But caste, Swami Vivekananda tells us, has nothing to do with religion: it is a purely social practice, and many Hindus can and should bring up their children to abhor the idea of caste. In the Puranas there is the story of a debate between the rishis Vasistha and Vishwamitra on whether the Vedic religion could be universalized or whether it was intended for the Aryan people alone. The Upanishads broadened the appeal of the ritualistic religion depicted in the Vedas, and sages like Adi Shankara and Ramanuja democratized it further. Indeed, Adi Shankara declared that any human being, merely by virtue of their personhood, could attain the Supreme Consciousness through a study of the scriptures, the Puranas and the epics, meditation (japa), fasting (upavasa) and worship (puja). Caste was never approved of by Adi Shankara. The contemporary rejection of caste draws from a long reformist tradition in Hinduism that embraces all of them, as well as Kabir, Nanak, Shirdi Sai Baba, Sree Narayana Guru and Mahatma Gandhi.

Hindu society may have maintained a distasteful practice, but no one can credibly argue that it is intrinsic to the religion. There is a marvellous story of Utanga, a

Shirdi Sai Baba

childhood friend of Lord Krishna, who had received a boon from Krishna that the Lord would provide him water whenever he needed it on his wanderings. On one occasion, overcome by thirst in a remote place, Utanga called upon his boon. An outcaste hunter soon appeared before him, clad in skins and dirty rags, offering him water from an animal-skin water bag. Utanga, a fastidious Brahmin, turned down his offer. The hunter continued his attempts to persuade him to drink the water but Utanga was haughtily unmoved, berating Lord Krishna in his mind for not having fulfilled his promise. The hunter, his generosity spurned even by a man in need, duly disappeared. Soon Krishna himself materialized before Utanga, informing him that he had sent Indra, the

A painting by Raja Ravi Varma showing
Garuda carrying Lord Vishnu and his consorts

king of the Devas, in the guise of the hunter, to offer him
not just water but amrit, the nectar of immortality. 'Since,
instead of accepting his generosity, you chose to judge him
by external factors like caste, you have forfeited the chance
of immortality,' the Lord informed Utanga.

The Hindu who says that caste discrimination is
incompatible with his dharma is a better Hindu than one

who insists her religion does not permit her to engage a Dalit cook in her house (as a senior government official recently did) or claims her faith will not allow her to serve a Dalit boss (which somehow no menial employee in India has yet done). Still, the battles over temple entry to Dalits occurred within living memory; and other instances of the pernicious effect of caste discrimination in the practice of religion are not hard to find. India's first artist to achieve mass popularity, Raja Ravi Varma, did so in the 1890s by printing lithographs of his paintings of Hindu gods, which enabled Dalits to worship in their homes images of the very deities they were not allowed to pray to in the temples, from which they were barred. As I've pointed out a few pages earlier, the great social reformer Sree Narayana Guru in Kerala installed a Shiva-lingam himself in a temple because Hindus of his Ezhava caste were not allowed into the area's established Shiva temples. So the Hindu religion has undoubtedly been complicit in caste discrimination, and the faith's identification with caste oppression has long been the principal negative held against it. Is a religion responsible for the worst behaviour of its followers? Perhaps not; but Hindus collectively need to continue doing all that they can to wash the stain of caste discrimination off the face of their faith.

chapter four

※

GURUS AND THE 'GOD MARKET'

Another aspect of popular Hinduism that does not reflect
well on it is superstition. Hindus are considered prone to
believing in assorted signs and soothsayers; our fondness for
astrology, for instance, is widely observed. It is true that a
Hindu without a horoscope is like an American without a
credit card, and is subject to many of the same disabilities.
I even have two horoscopes: one cast for me soon after
my birth in London by an expatriate Indian doctor there,
another by the family astrologer at the village in Kerala.
They didn't match, and to this day, it seems, I have been
pursuing two mutually incompatible fates, in the worlds of
public service and authorship.

Still, is it fair to saddle Hinduism with the burden of
being responsible for its astrologers, many of whom are
undoubtedly charlatans? Or should the belief of certain
Hindus in astrology be seen as an emanation of Indian
society rather than of the Hindu faith?

Mata Amritanandamayi

The latter case is undoubtedly strengthened by the Hindu affinity for gurus and godmen, whose claims to religious significance often do not extend much beyond their garb (and their gab). Hindus have flocked to ochre-robed dispensers of spiritual wisdom for centuries. There have been ascetic fakirs like Shirdi Sai Baba, performers of miracles like Sathya Sai Baba, teachers of meditation like Maharishi Mahesh Yogi and practitioners of sexual liberation like 'Bhagwan' Shri Rajneesh (who later transformed himself into the somewhat more austere Osho). The legendary Sathya Sai Baba has multiple millions of followers around the world; I have written elsewhere of the spotless town of Puttaparthi that serves as his spiritual headquarters, and continues to attract devotees years after his death. Among the 'living saints' of Hinduism, Mata Amritanandamayi, the 'hugging saint', is revered as the embodiment of unconditional love. Her ashram and spiritual retreat, Amritapuri in Vallikavu near Kollam, is a beehive of activity, thronged with followers from around the world; like Sathya Sai Baba, she channels the donations of her followers to major social welfare projects, running a university, medical college, hospital and a television studio.

Such revered figures follow in a long-established Hindu tradition. Advaita Vedantist Hindus have traditionally held gurus or teachers in high reverence, since many ancient texts suggest that one should seek a qualified and able guide in the pursuit of one's spiritual quest. Following a guru is thus seen by many Hindus as desirable though not mandatory, a path to an end rather than an end in itself; a guru is a guide towards the fulfilment of self-realization, not a substitute for it. In the Advaita tradition, a competent teacher is vital to help a seeker attain correct knowledge and freedom from false knowledge; he (or occasionally she) serves as a revered instructor, counsellor, and shaper of their disciples' values. Since Hinduism emphasizes anubhava, or the knowledge that comes from experience, as much as philosophical knowledge or jnana, which comes from study and reading, a guru can share his experience as a guide and model to the disciple. The best kind of guru is usually an inspirational teacher, a source of wisdom and instruction, a guide moulding the spiritual evolution of the disciple, an elder who imparts his values and a philosopher who reveals the meaning of life to the attentive seeker. Guru means 'dispeller of darkness'; the exalted place of the guru in Hindu thinking reflects the fact that while a mother merely gives us physical birth, a guru ensures our spiritual rebirth. Not all self-anointed gurus are, however, worthy of the appellation.

India is full of gurus; some are figures of great learning and erudition in the religious texts, some are capable of performing mystical and magical feats beyond rational explanation, and some merely impart a quiet wisdom that their followers find inspirational. Such gurus attract followings in the millions, and many have established ashrams to which their devotees flock, and in which many live either permanently or for regular periods, either conducting religious and spiritual practices, or performing social services in the name of their guru's order. But there are also, in the same domain yet of a different order, charlatans, poseurs and tricksters, in what has been dubbed 'the God Market', who woo the credulous with simplistic ideas of spirituality and amass huge fortunes at the expense of the gullible. These include a female guru who wears red mini-skirts and offers homilies on love, a baba who sits in a tree and dispenses benediction through a touch of his foot, and another who receives the world in his naked glory and whose ultimate blessing comes in the opportunity to grasp his exposed male member. Much of this has nothing to do with Hinduism, except that it is a manifestation of the Hindu's eternal search for spiritual truth, in whatever form it can be found.

Many of the devotees of these godmen are not Hindus. Equally, some of these godmen are not Hindu but count Hindus among their followers. It is important to note that the hold godmen have on their followers is not purely a function of religious devotion; rather it has a lot to do with a sense of drift in Indian society, an aimlessness and hopelessness that requires a religious anchor. Clinching evidence for this proposition came in the person of a godman who is not strictly a Hindu, but a Sikh—the self-styled Baba Gurmeet Ram Rahim Singh Insan, whose name is a compound of Sikh, Hindu and Muslim names with 'Insan' meaning 'Human', and whose jailing in August 2017 created a crisis across two Indian states and the national capital.

The flamboyant, jewellery-bedecked Gurmeet Singh had a reputation for sexually exploiting his female followers, but only two of them had the courage to sue. The case took fifteen years and 200 sittings of the court before he was convicted; during this time, numerous efforts were made by the Baba's devotees to pressure the investigators, the police, the judges and the complainants to withdraw the suit, but they did not give in.

Baba Gurmeet Ram Rahim Singh Insan was always a peculiar godman, eschewing spiritual asceticism for gaudy showmanship and ostentatious living. He liked his hair long, his motorcycles powerful, his cars expensive, his attire sequinned and his women clingy. He performed in popular music videos of his own composition—his biggest hit is called 'Love Charger'—and had a feature film made about himself called *Messenger of God*. This unlikely 'Rockstar Baba', however, amassed a mass following of fanatic worshippers estimated at over ten million.

He or his henchmen kept this flock together in ruthlessly effective ways. A crusading small-town journalist who reported the rape complaint against him was murdered in 2002. The Baba's movement, known as the Dera Sacha Sauda, amassed a significant land bank and real estate assets, and exerted influence over various aspects of life in the states of Punjab and Haryana; its reach extended to the national capital, Delhi.

And yet the Dera Sacha Sauda fulfilled a genuine need in northern Indian society, giving millions an identity and a standing they had not previously known. Sections of people who had long known only oppression found in the dera movement a measure of security, safety and dignity they and their families had not historically enjoyed, as well as (or so the cynics say) a simpler, more 'market-friendly' version of religious faith. The dera movement considerably predates Ram Rahim, and had established itself for valid and even admirable reasons well before he became its best-known exponent.

Dera members are overwhelmingly Sikhs, though there are many Hindus among them. Sikhism is a faith that enjoins equality among its faithful, a message that had in the past inspired conversions of people from the lower Hindu castes, particularly Dalits and the 'Other Backward Classes'. But so deep is the prejudice in Indian society that many converted Sikhs found themselves treated no better by their co-religionists of higher castes, who dominate the official Sikh religious bodies such as the Shiromani Gurdwara Parbandhak Committee (SGPC), which runs the major gurudwaras or Sikh shrines.

Faced with an entrenched status quo, many Sikhs of less privileged backgrounds became disillusioned. Their feelings of anger and helplessness, compounded by poor education and soaring unemployment, led them to alcohol and drugs, the latter often imported from neighbouring Pakistan, which itself has a surfeit of hallucinogens from Afghanistan. Punjab became known as the drug capital of India, a reputation underscored in the searing portrayal of mass drug addiction in the recent hit film *Udta Punjab*.

It is in this context that the Dera Sacha Sauda and its charismatic leader emerged as saviours. For all his bling, Baba Gurmeet Ram Rahim Singh Insan exemplified an alternative life. The dera offers free education to its members and their children, free food for the hungry, and meaningful employment in its enterprises; it keeps the faithful off drugs, and more than jobs, it gives them a sense of meaning and purpose to their lives. In the process, it gives them that most precious and intangible of human needs—it gives them dignity and a sense of belonging.

Politicians played along with the Baba and his dera, and

indeed with several other such religious movements; Dera Sacha Sauda is one of the biggest, but far from the only, of several deras dotting Punjab and Haryana. The deras, after all, helped keep social peace, tamp down discontent, and channel frustrations towards constructive activity. Rather than disapprove of them as dangerous cults, successive governments rushed to embrace them. Their religious nature offered a far safer alternative to drugs and crime. The deras ended addiction, replaced anomie with community and redirected despair to divinity, even if some gurus dressed in flashy jackets and drove around in Range Rovers.

The intense loyalty the deras in turn inspire cannot be underestimated. Their fulfilment of people's basic needs is suffused with the religious fervour that comes along with affiliation to a spiritual guru. And most of them are led by figures less ostentatious and controversial than Gurmeet Ram Rahim Singh Insan. But social and economic insecurity is at the heart of a dera's religious appeal and its fanatic following. Where government and civil society failed, a seeming charlatan with an insatiable lust succeeded, and his success mattered far more than his flaws. People who were willing to lend their wives and daughters to their guru could not understand why the same 'blessing' extended to two girls should land him in jail. As an anonymous posting on social media pointed out, 'a lost man doesn't care if a rapist gives him direction. A hungry man will take food from a murderer's hand'.

The mass upsurge by Dera followers on their guru's conviction revealed their fears that without him and his organization, they might once again slide back into the margins. This explains the intensity of their identification with him, whatever he does. They are literally willing to kill for him or, as they might see it, for themselves.

The rioting and destruction that followed his conviction—

over thirty people killed, hundreds of vehicles burned, several buildings (including two new hotels) set ablaze, train rakes wrecked, roads blocked—paralyzed life across an important swathe of northern India for several days. Many Indians lamented that such blind religious devotion should thrive in their country in the second decade of the twenty-first century. But the violence raises far more troubling questions than that.

The episode shows that India's much-vaunted economic growth and development has shallow roots indeed: that it has failed to deliver caste equality and social justice to the underclasses. It shows official institutions of governance all-too-readily subcontracting their responsibilities to religious orders, and enabling their leaders to live above the law. It shows the fragility of law and order systems, which failed so spectacularly in the face of mass fury. And it shows the hold of religious leaders on the loyalties, and the passions, of vast sections of people who find validation for their lives in such unthinking followership.

Baba Gurmeet Ram Rahim Singh Insan has finally ended up in prison, even if he was flown there in a luxury helicopter with an 'adopted daughter' in devoted attendance, as he nibbled abstractedly at a piece of chocolate, with a police escort that included law-enforcement officials carrying his bags. The Baba may be in jail—but, rather than either the Hindu or Sikh religions, it is Indian society that is still in the dock.

❧

HINDU FATALISM

One unavoidable issue to be dealt with relating to popular notions of Hinduism is that of 'Hindu fatalism'—does not our belief in destiny, in karma and predestination, make us inured to our lot in life and accepting of Fate, rather than seeking to change it?

There is an old story, from our ancient Puranas, the kind of story Hindus have often told to illustrate larger points about themselves.

A man—the quintessential Hindu, one might say—is pursued by a tiger. He runs fast, but his panting heart tells him he cannot run much longer or faster. He spots a tree. Relief! He accelerates and gets to it in one last despairing stride. He climbs the tree. The tiger snarls beneath him, but he feels he has at least escaped its snapping jaws. But no— what's this? The branch on which he is sitting is weak, and bends dangerously. That is not all; wood-mice are gnawing away it. Before long, they will eat through it and the branch will snap and fall.

The man realizes this, sees the tiger below him waiting for him to tumble into its grasp. But as the branch bends, it sags over a well. Aha! Escape? Our hero looks hopefully into the well. Perhaps he can swim! But the well is dry. Worse, there are poisonous snakes writhing and hissing on its bed, waiting for prey.

What is our hero to do? As the branch bends lower, he perceives a solitary blade of grass growing on the wall of the well. On the tip of the blade of grass gleams a drop of honey.

What action does our Puranic man, the archetypal Indian, take in this situation?

He bends with the branch, and licks up the honey.

This story is at least 2,000 years old, but it could be told today. It speaks of what the Orientalists saw as Hindu fatalism, a tendency for us to be resigned to our lot and to accept the world as it is ordained to be. The story speaks of our self-absorption in the face of impossible circumstances, and our willingness to make the best we possibly can out of those impossible circumstances.

Arjuna praying to Lord Krishna during the Kurukshetra war

That is the Hindu answer to the insuperable difficulty. One does not fight against that which one cannot overcome, but seeks instead to find the best way, for oneself, to live with it. In many ways, it explains what Westerners have tended to see as Hindu fatalism, and V. S. Naipaul referred to as a tendency for 'non-doing'.

And yet this is a very partial understanding of Hinduism. The Bhagavad Gita in fact asks Hindus to raise themselves by the self; that is, to use whatever elements Fate has dealt them—the circumstances of their birth, their location, their access to wealth, the opportunities for education and so on—as best they can to move towards self-realization. The fact that circumstances are what they are does not deny the Hindu the freedom of will to seek to change them. The position of the planets at the time of a Hindu's birth may have determined some of his possibilities, charting good phases and bad ones in his life, but then it is up to him to make what he can of them. It is wrong to suggest that everything is willed by Fate for the quiescent Hindu, that his destiny is decreed. The Hindu works with God to fulfil his potential. God is not just above and beyond us; to the Hindu, He is also within us. He struggles with us, suffers with us, strives with us. To that degree, the Hindu knows he makes his own fate, in partnership with God.

Early in my United Nations career, my first boss, a lay preacher in his native Denmark, asked me a pointed question: 'Why should a Hindu be good?' Not, I replied, in order to go to heaven or avoid hell; most Hindus do not believe in the existence of either. If heaven is a place where a soul should sprout white wings and sing the praises of God, it must be rather a boring place, hardly worth aspiring to, and God must be a rather insecure Being. And as for hell, the very notion of hell is incompatible with Hindu cosmology, since it suggests there is a place where God is not, and that, to the Hindu, is impossible to conceive, for God is everywhere or He would not be God.

If Hinduism is, indeed, a manava dharma, an ethical code applicable to the whole of humanity, then it is legitimate for a non-Hindu to ask why indeed should a Hindu be good? First of all, because he is bound by the moral obligation to fulfil his dharma, the right action his religion enjoins upon him always to undertake.

The Hindu is taught that there are six principal obstacles to the performance of dharma: two are Purusharthas gone wrong, kama as lust rather than desire, and lobha as greed and avarice for material possessions (beyond artha which is the legitimate acquisition of wealth and worldly goods for a worthy life). Four other vices are personal failings that are within an individual's capacity to prevent: krodha (hatred), mada (vanity), matsarya (envy) and moha (delusion arising from ignorance or infatuation). These six obstacles are prevented and overcome through the practice of seven essential virtues laid down from the time of Adi Shankara: ahimsa (non-violence), satyam (truth), shivam (piety), sundaram (the cultivation of beauty), vairagyam (detachment), pavitram (purity) and swabhavam (self-control). The rejection of these vices and the practice of these virtues are essential for a Hindu to lead a good life.

My boss was a worldly-wise man; he wanted a more pragmatic reason for why a Hindu should be good. If it was not the promise of a better life in the next world, or a desire to avoid eternal damnation in Hell, what was a Hindu's incentive? I explained that whereas in Christianity the body has a soul, in Hinduism the soul has a body. In other words, we are emanations of a universal soul, the atman, which does not die; it discards its temporal form, the body, from time to time. Since the purpose of the soul is ultimately to reach moksha, to attain union with Brahman and stop the endless cycle of birth and rebirth in various bodies, the incentive for a Hindu to be good lay in the desire to progress towards this goal. An amoral Hindu, one who lived in adharma, would be in disharmony with the world and be set back in his soul's striving for moksha.

I am not sure he was satisfied with my answer, and I am not sure you, the reader, will be. There was, however, a catch in what I was propounding. If the soul is permanent and the body is not, it makes sense that the soul sheds bodies and keeps returning to earth until it has attained moksha; from this flows the doctrine of punarjanmam (reincarnation), the idea that one will be reborn until one has attained that level of self-realization.

The idea of reincarnation, emerging from the endless cycle of birth and rebirth, is basic to Hinduism. If in other faiths the individual is a body which has its own soul, in Hinduism the individual is a soul which happens to be in

The doctrine of punarjanmam

temporary possession of a certain body; the immortal soul occupies a mortal corpus, which it discards at the end of its physical life, only to re-emerge in another form, until it accomplishes true self-realization and moksha, and merges with Brahman. This cycle of birth, death and rebirth is known as Samsara, and it is a belief that addresses one of the central challenges facing every believer in God—if God is all-knowing, all-seeing, all-compassionate and merciful, why does He permit so much suffering, pain, inequality and inequity to bedevil his creations? The Hindu answer is that such suffering is the result of man's own actions in a previous life; our present circumstances are caused or enabled by our past deeds and misdeeds, action and inaction. The soul continues from life-cycle to life-cycle, hopping from body to body as a caterpillar climbs onto a blade of grass and jumps to a new one (the metaphor is Upanishadic, not my own.)

I always considered this deeply unfair: why should a human being, conscious only of himself in his present life, have to suffer for wrongs he does not recollect and misdeeds he has no memory of having committed in previous lives of which he is unaware? Still, I had to accept it was a more coherent explanation than the contradictory ones offered by other faiths, which struggled to reconcile the world's injustices with their theological belief in a merciful God. If you thought of God as, for instance, an old man in a white beard looking down benevolently at you from the heavens, listening to your prayers and interceding when He saw fit, then it was difficult to accept that His benevolence stopped short of your well-being despite your prayers, or that He was indifferent to the cruelty and suffering assailing His creatures. If you stopped thinking of God that way, however, but saw God in everyone and everything, in the bad and the good, in the unfair as well as the just, as an impersonal cosmic force that just *is*—then you can come to terms with the world's tragedies as well as its joys.

The idea of reincarnation is related to that of karma, or action—the accumulated actions of your life. So the very circumstances of your birth—the home, the place, the nation and the opportunities into which you are born—are determined by your soul's actions in its previous incarnation. The time and circumstances of your death, too, are beyond human agency; when you have finished enjoying the benefits earned from (and paying for the misdeeds committed in) your previous life, your time on earth ends and your soul discards your body, to enter another. This is known as prarabdha karma. Then there are your characteristics, tendencies and aptitudes, themselves emerging from the accumulated learnings of your previous lives; this is called sanchita karma and can be changed by your efforts, education and conduct in your present life. Finally there is agami karma, those of our actions which will pave the way for our future (reborn) life. Our evil words or deeds in the present life will mar our soul's prospects in the next, whereas good deeds, right actions and the fulfilment of our dharma without regard to reward, will ensure our rebirth at a higher stage of the progress towards moksha.

To some this suggests another, somewhat simplistic, answer to the question 'Why should a Hindu be good?' Be good so that you are reborn in a better situation in your next life than in the present one; if you are good, you may reappear as a king or a sage, whereas if you are bad, you might come back as an invalid or a mosquito. (Or as Amartya Sen, the Nobel laureate, put it: 'As a Hindu, if you are a good economist in this life, you come back in the next as a physicist. If you are a bad economist in this life, you come back in the next as a sociologist.') Jokes apart, your prarabdha karma is established by what your soul has experienced in its previous foray in a human body: your incentive to be good is to improve its chances of a better time in its next innings.

I was never comfortable with this idea, since it seemed to me to have been devised somewhat self-servingly by the upper castes to ensure social peace. Do not rebel if you are born poor or 'untouchable', the doctrine seemed to imply, since it's merely your soul paying for the sins of your past life; and do not blame us for leading a much better life than you, since we are merely reaping the benefits of our past good deeds.

Behave, conform, accept your lot and serve your

Dr Amartya Sen

betters, the doctrine seemed to suggest, and you will enjoy the rewards next time around. As a philosophy to reconcile people with their lot, and that would help maintain social peace, such a belief-system was of inestimable value. (It also justified human suffering in terms that no other religion's theology could match.) But I found it ethically dubious—and so, no doubt unfairly, looked askance at the idea of reincarnation itself. I was wrong to do so, since the socio-political rationale was irrelevant to the Hindu sages who had advanced the theory of punarjanmam. They were less concerned about issues of socio-political conformism than I was; the rishis' interest lay in the soul's unsteady and imperfect progress towards self-realization and merger with the cosmos. Their doctrine was about the divine soul, not the social circumstances of the body it happened to occupy.

SECTION FOUR

~

GREAT SOULS
OF HINDUISM

Shiva, Parvati and *Ganesh on Mount Kailash*

Tripura Sundari is a Hindu goddess and one of the ten Mahavidyas. She is considered a manifestation of Goddess Parvati. She is the primordial creator along with Lord Shiva. She is depicted here enthroned and surrounded by Brahma, Vishnu, Shiva, Ishvara, Parashiva Murugan and Mahaganapati. Lakshmi and Saraswati are fanning her.

chapter five

GREAT SOULS OF HINDUISM

Much of what I believe as a Hindu comes from an early and intense reading of the writings and lectures of Swami Vivekananda, the magnetic-eyed saint with the majestic mien and marvellous oratorical skills, who did more than anyone else to place Hinduism on the world map in the late nineteenth century. Swami Vivekananda was an inspiration to me right from my formative years. One of the few accomplishments I remember from a hyperactive extra-curricular life at college relates to him. I was asked to deliver, at age eighteen in 1974, the annual Vivekananda Memorial Oration at Delhi University. The honour was given to me because of my fondness for his ideas and a willingness to recite them with something approaching the oratorical flourish for which he was famous; any fantasy of association with him, alas, ends there.

To understand Vivekananda's Hinduism one has to go much farther back in time. His ideas emerged from the Advaita Vedanta School of Hindu philosophy, anchored in the oldest Upanishads and established by Adi Shankara in the eighth century CE, which as we have seen is undoubtedly the most influential of the multiple schools of philosophy and theology that characterize Hinduism.

❧

HINDUISM: THE EARLY DAYS

It is said that the roots of Hinduism can be traced to the Indus Valley Civilization that flourished around 3300 to 1700 BCE (although some sources claim that it is even older). Since the script of that civilization has not yet been satisfactorily deciphered, it is difficult to aver this with any certainty, but the ruins of the Harappan cities seem to suggest a priestly hierarchy and a cult of worship, and Indus Valley seals show a cross-legged figure who seems to represent Shiva. At any rate, the worship of male and female gods clearly existed, as perhaps did a fertility cult, along with the worship of nature, animals and spirits. The doctrines of what we recognize today as Hindu dharma were first established (it is said, by the sage Yajnavalkya) in around 3000 BCE (many scholars dispute the historicity of this date, suggesting instead dates a millennia and a half later, 1500 BCE). They were reified in the four Vedas, composed roughly between 1700 and 500 BCE, laying down many of the mantras and benedictions, rituals and ceremonies of the faith, together with commentaries on these. The faith was then replenished by the sage Veda Vyasa—who is said to have codified the Vedas and is credited as the 'author' of the epic the Mahabharata.

But despite the richness of the epics such as the Mahabharata and Ramayana, the religion of the later Vedas became excessively ritualistic and rigidly hierarchical. Other ideas and practices needed to be accommodated.

Swami Vivekananda

Around 150 BCE, some centuries after Vyasa, Patanjali, a notable scholar of the Sankhya School of Hindu philosophy, compiled the *Yoga Sutras*, a classic text on yoga theory and practice, which laid the foundations of classical yoga.

Patanjali's sutras lay down an eight-fold path, ashtanga yoga, which involves a rigorous set of physical, psychological and moral pursuits, following the strictest discipline, which if progressively followed under the guidance of a suitable teacher would lead the practitioner to ultimate self-realization and pure consciousness. Then the Upanishads emerged, throwing the light of sophisticated (and sometimes abstruse) philosophical enquiry on the faith. Building on the sacred Vedas, these were all foundational texts of Hinduism. The Puranas were composed, and their stories helped integrate the Vedic religion with the folk religions of India, absorbing them in a shared ethic.

Subsequently, Hinduism became paralysed by its own inflexible practices of orthodoxy, ritualism and formality, and the rise of mutually antagonistic sects locked in interminable conflict. Inevitably, reformers arose to challenge it, notably the ascetic Mahavira Jaina (c. 599–527 BCE) and the otherworldly Gautama Buddha (c. 563–483 BCE), whose followers branched out into new religions distinct from the Mimamsa Brahminism practised by mainstream Hindus. Both new faiths flourished for several centuries, as Hinduism descended into esoteric disputes over Sankhya dualism and Charvaka materialism. It was then, in the late eighth century CE, that a youthful South Indian sage rose to heal and rejuvenate a divided religion.

chapter six

ADI SHANKARA

This was Adi Shankara, whose Advaita Vedanta was the philosophically robust response to that era of confusion, integrating diverse thoughts and Hindu practices into a philosophy based on the Vedic dictum of 'One Truth, Many Expositions'. Advaita Vedanta is only one—and arguably the last—of the six schools known as the 'six systems' (Shad Darshanas) of mainstream Hindu philosophy, but it has proved the most enduring. Shankara emphasized the importance of pramanas or methods of reasoning, tempered by anubhava or intuitive experience, which empower the seeker to gain the spiritual knowledge adumbrated by the sacred texts. He focused on selected texts—the Bhagavad Gita, the *Brahma Sutras* and ten of the 108 Upanishads—as the key reference works of Hindu dharma, illuminating them through his bhashyas (commentaries). Reasoning is essential to clarify the truth, according to the Advaita School, and Shankara was a famous debater of his time, challenging and being challenged by those of different philosophical

Adi Shankara and his disciples

persuasions but triumphing always through the power of his reasoning and the force of his arguments. His bhashyas are all written in prose, not verse, with lucidity and sharpness, and employ the Upanishadic question-and-answer format that the West calls 'Socratic'.

Adi Shankara also authored the *Vivekachudamani*, 581 verses spelling out the qualifications required in a student of Vedanta: to be able to discriminate between the real and the unreal; to be able to maintain a spirit of detachment from this world; to have the capacity to control sensory perceptions; and to feel an intense desire to attain self-realization and moksha. The *Vivekachudamani* reviews the entire range of Hindu philosophical thought and argument, from the Upanishads to the Bhagavad Gita. More accessibly, and as part of his effort to popularize the faith, Adi Shankara also authored a hundred stotrams, verses that can be sung as bhajans by the worshipper (or bhakt)—many fairly brief but some quite long, like his most famous bhajan, the Bhaja Govindam. Most of the stotrams relate to the worship of the major Puranic gods, though some are devoted to spiritual themes and others are sung in praise of sacred rivers or the holy city of Kashi (Varanasi). To Adi Shankara, bhakti yoga (the practice of worship) was an important step towards jnana yoga (the cultivation of knowledge). The sage was very conscious of the need to revive the faith of which he was such a master. In Verse 7 of his Bhaja Govindam, he laments the fact that children are interested in play and young men in pretty girls, but the old worry since no one is interested in the Absolute.

Adi Shankara was not merely a philosophical thinker who reconciled the doctrines and traditions of the ancients with a robust interpretation for the future; he was also a practical reformer. He purified the worship of the Goddess, which had become somewhat questionable thanks to dubious practices introduced by the tantrics, and introduced the samayachara form of Devi worship, involving hymns of exquisite beauty like the Soundarya Lahari or the waves of beauty, composed by himself. His ready acceptance of many Buddhist principles and practices so narrowed the gap between the two faiths as to make the absorption of Buddhism by the parent faith inevitable in India.

Adi Shankara's extraordinary travels—which began when he was just eight years old and continued till his death at the age of thirty-two—took him to every corner

The Sringeri Peetham, established by Adi Shankara

of the country, from Rameswaram in the extreme south to Srinagar in the Kashmir Valley in the extreme north, from Dwarka in the west to Kamarupa in Assam in the north-east, and various points in between. He established temples almost everywhere he halted, all of which have remained in continuous use since, and left behind five major mutths headed by successor Shankaracharyas to this day: Jyotirmath near Badrinath (Uttarakhand), Govardhan Mutth in Puri (Odisha), Kalika Mutth in Dwarka (Gujarat), and two in the south, the Sarada Peetham in Sringeri (Karnataka) and the Kanchi Kamakoti Peetham in Kanchipuram (Tamil Nadu). (Most Hindus count only the first four as his major legacies, though the prominence in the twentieth century of the Shankaracharyas of Kanchi has elevated that peetham into a religious seat of equal if not greater significance.) In addition to these 'pontifical' seats, Adi Shankara is credited with the creation and organization of the order of Dasanami Sannyasis, wandering monks who took the message of the faith across the country. Despite Shankara's skill in debate, Advaita nonetheless believes that pure logic cannot alone lead to philosophical truths; knowledge is all very well, but experience and meditative insights are essential too. Shankara's Advaita Vedanta was based on shastra ('scriptures'), pramanas or yukti ('reason') and anubhava ('experiential knowledge'), supplemented by karmas ('spiritual practices') and the purity and steadiness of mind achieved in yoga. None was sufficient in itself: the entire package, as it were, allowed the seeker to gain the knowledge and insights required to attain self-realization.

Shankara also proposed the four 'mahavakyas' or 'great sentences' of his doctrine—'Prajnanam Brahma' (knowledge is Brahman), 'Ayam Atma Brahma' (this atman is Brahman), 'Tattvamasi' (that you are), and 'Aham Brahmasmi' (I am Brahman)—as the guiding principles of Hindu spiritual contemplation, all of which underscored his doctrine that the inner immortal soul, atman, and the great cosmic spirit, Brahman, are really one and the same. Atman and Brahman had been regarded by the 'dualist' Sankhya School of thought as separate entities, but Shankara argued that while they might seem different at the empirical level of reality, this is an illusion. Brahman, the spirit that suffuses the cosmos, is the sole reality; other than Brahman, everything else, including the universe, material objects and individuals, is ever changing, transient and illusory (maya). (As Dr Radhakrishnan was later to explain, maya is not merely illusion, but 'a subjective misperception of the world as ultimately real.') Brahman is Paramarthika Satyam, Absolute Truth, and one's atman or self is identical to it. Realizing this and accepting the true self, pure consciousness, as the only reality (sat), leads to moksha or salvation, defined by some as a state of bliss (ananda) and by others, more modestly, as the endless but not beginning-less absence of pain, the pain all human beings suffer in the course of their ordinary lives. The supreme truth of Brahman is sat-chit-ananda (truth-consciousness-bliss), as Shankara wrote in his *Upadeshasahasri*:

> *I am other than name, form and action.*
> *My nature is ever free!*
> *I am Self, the supreme unconditioned Brahman.*
> *I am pure Awareness, always non-dual.*
> —Adi Shankara, *Upadeshasahasri* 11.7

As I have noted earlier, the *Manduka Upanishad* explains, Om is the bow; one's atman is the arrow, and Brahman the target. The term Advaita ('not-two') refers to the rejection of dualism: as Shankara's follower, the sage Anandagiri, put it, to say that Brahman and atman are separate would be like dividing a fowl in two and saying that one half can be cooked while the other half would lay eggs.

Shankara's Hinduism does not see God as external to the universe. God dwells in the universe, but God is not the universe; He is in it and beyond it. The world is in God, and the two are indivisible. Advaita Vedanta emphasizes jivanmukti, the idea that moksha (salvation or liberation, the realization of the ultimate purpose of each individual) is achievable in the course of our present life. Advaita's adherents seek their spiritual fulfilment in the acquisition of this profound spiritual knowledge and in immersing themselves in the indissoluble union of the true Self (atman or soul) with the highest metaphysical Reality (Brahman).

Shankara also asserted that the realization of self-knowledge required the mind to be purified by an ethical life that observed essential precepts or Yamas such as ahimsa (non-injury, non-violence to others in body, mind and thoughts), satya (respect for truth, abstinence from falsehood), asteya (rejection of theft), aparigraha (abstaining from craving possessions) and a simple life of meditation and reflection. These ideas were to have a profound and lasting impact on Mahtama Gandhi twelve centuries later. (Of ahimsa, Gandhiji wrote: 'Nonviolence is common to all religions, but it has found the highest expression and application in Hinduism.')

From the ancient texts, Advaita Vedanta accepted the idea of the Purusharthas, the four goals of human life. These, as we have seen earlier, are dharma, the right conduct of the individual in accordance with his duties and obligations; artha, the material possessions required to sustain the individual and those dependent upon him; kama, the pursuit of pleasure and comfort, including love and sexual pleasure; and moksha, the individual's ultimate salvation, his liberation from earthly bonds and his realization of union with the divine spirit. This last involves a state of full awareness of the ultimate oneness of the soul, atman, and Brahman; the Hindu realizes the Divine within himself, perceives the Divine in other beings, and accepts that Brahman is in everything, and everything is Brahman.

> *Without beginning and end is he; in the midst*
> *Of chaos is he, and brings forth all things. Creator*
> *Is he, and sole pervader, of manifold forms.*
> *When a man knows God he is freed from all fetters.*
> —*Svetashvatara Upanishad,* V.13.2

Despite such ideas being seen by many as Brahminical and elitist, Advaita Vedanta, by conceiving of Oneness in this manner, lays the philosophical groundwork for the fundamental equality of all human beings. In the same section of his *Upadeshasahasri,* Adi Shankara posits precisely this ethical premise of equality; any bheda (discrimination) based on class or caste or parentage is, Shankara declared, a mistake, a sign of error and of lack of knowledge. Shankara's liberated individual understands and practises the ethics of non-discrimination, since the high-born and the low are all part of the same Oneness. This was all the more significant in a religion on which the pernicious practice of caste discrimination had begun to cast a blight. The Advaita Vedantist recognized all living beings as essentially one, and therefore as essentially equal.

The fully realized self is sat-chit-ananda incarnate, as Shankara himself sings:

Atma Shatakam (The Song of the Self):

I am not the mind, nor the intellect, nor the ego, nor the material of the mind;
I am not the body, nor the changes of the body;
I am not the senses of hearing, taste, smell, or sight,
Nor am I the ether, the earth, the fire, the air;
I am Existence Absolute, Knowledge Absolute, Bliss Absolute—
I am Shiva, I am Shiva. (Shivoham, Shivoham).

I am not the Prâna, nor the five vital airs;
I am not the materials of the body, nor the five sheaths;
Neither am I the organs of action, nor the object of the senses;
I am Existence Absolute, Knowledge Absolute, Bliss Absolute—
I am Shiva, I am Shiva. (Shivoham, Shivoham).

I have neither aversion nor attachment, neither greed nor delusion;
Neither egotism nor envy, neither Dharma nor Moksha;
I am neither desire nor objects of desire;
I am Existence Absolute, Knowledge Absolute, Bliss Absolute—
I am Shiva, I am Shiva. (Shivoham, Shivoham).

I am neither sin nor virtue, neither pleasure nor pain;
Nor temple nor worship, nor pilgrimage nor scriptures,
Neither the act of enjoying, the enjoyable nor the
enjoyer;
I am Existence Absolute, Knowledge Absolute, Bliss
Absolute—
I am Shiva, I am Shiva. (Shivoham, Shivoham).

I have neither death nor fear of death, nor caste;
Nor was I ever born, nor had I parents, friends, and
relations;
I have neither Guru, nor disciple;
I am Existence Absolute, Knowledge Absolute, Bliss
Absolute—
I am Shiva, I am Shiva. (Shivoham, Shivoham).

I am untouched by the senses, I am neither Mukti nor
knowable;
I am without form, without limit, beyond space, beyond
time;
I am in everything; I am the basis of the universe;
everywhere am I.
I am Existence Absolute, Knowledge Absolute, Bliss
Absolute—
I am Shiva, I am Shiva. (Shivoham, Shivoham).

—Adi Shankara, *Nirvana Shatakam*

All of this may seem somewhat abstruse to some, a sort of
Hindu theological primer of no interest to most Hindus,
let alone others. In fact there is far greater complexity to
Advaita Vedanta than my simple summary can even begin
to hint at. The *Kena Upanishad* makes that clear:

I do not think that I know it well. Nor do I know
that I do not know it.

Among us those who know, know it; even they do not know that they do not know.

—Kena Upanishad, II.2

Lord Shiva mounts Nandi, aided by Parvati

However, there was the dawning realization, among many of those who followed in his footsteps in the centuries following Adi Shankara's death in the mountain temple of Kedarnath at the young age of thirty-two, that there was a great need to make his breakthroughs intelligible to the common man. There were other even more compelling reasons for the faith to change and evolve.

THE HINDU WAY

THE IMPACT OF THE BUDDHA, MAHAVIRA AND MUSLIM INVADERS

Though they were eclipsed and even reabsorbed into Hinduism, both Jainism and Buddhism had a lasting impact on the religion they had sought to transform. Buddhist monasticism led to the establishment of the concept of sannyasis in Hinduism—who, inspired by the Buddhists, wear ochre robes, shave their heads and practise celibacy for life. (There was no pre-Buddhist equivalent of this: Hindu priests were grihasthas, married householders, and not sannyasis). Similarly the Buddhist monasteries prompted Sankaracharya to establish mutths, in which sannyasis and lay students could live together and learn in a sort of gurukul. As to Jainism, the acceptance of ahimsa as a basic principle in Hinduism was clearly a response to Mahavira Jaina's emphasis on this doctrine. The adoption of vegetarianism as a superior form of life by a large number of Hindus especially Brahmins is also a Jain contribution to Hinduism.

A statue of the Buddha

Hinduism reasserted itself in response to the rise of
Buddhism and Jainism, largely supplanting or absorbing
these faiths across the country, to the extent that the practice
of Buddhism largely ended (so much so that that until the
1950s, the Buddha in Sarnath sported a Vaishnava namam!),
and the Jains began to be regarded by a section of Hindus
as a sort of Hindu sect (though many Jains disputed this)
rather than as a rival faith. By the tenth century, Hinduism
had reasserted its dominance, swallowed up its reformers,
reformulated its popular doctrines, equipped itself with

a higher philosophy which found acceptance among the intellectuals, accommodated popular forms of idol worship, created major spiritual centres and furnished itself with sannyasis to spread the word. Its supremacy in India seemed incontestable.

But around 1000 CE a new challenge arose from the northwest to the dominance of Hinduism in the subcontinent. The raids into India by Mohammed bin Qasim, who invaded Sind in 712 CE, Mahmud of Ghazni (who attacked India seventeen times between 1000 CE and 1027 CE) and Muhammad Ghori (who launched several bloody raids between the 1180s and the 1220s), among others, took many lives, destroyed much property and left deep scars. Hinduism found itself confronting a dynamic force animated by religious zeal in direct contradistinction to everything the faith stood for. Islam challenged the philosophic basis of Hinduism, questioned its social structure, denied its pantheistic beliefs, expressed contempt for its pluralist doctrines and coveted its treasures. It was a challenge of a very different order from that posed by Buddhism or Jainism. The impact of the Muslim invasions, and the proclivity of some Muslim warlords to attack temples for their treasures and demolish them in the process, as well as the inclination of some of the conquered peoples to adopt the religion of their conquerors, made the need for a renewal and revival of the Hindu faith all the more urgent after the eleventh century CE, when Ghazni's success had rung the alarm bells.

The looting of temples and their subsequent destruction—which occurred repeatedly, in places ranging from historic Somnath on the Gujarat coast to Mathura in the interior—was a direct assault on the Hindus and their faith, and an unmistakeable challenge to which Hinduism had to rise or succumb. For invaders like Mahmud of Ghazni the attacks had twin motives—the fabled wealth of India was mostly

The twenty-four Jain Tirthankaras

hoarded in its temples, which made them attractive targets, but there was also the zeal of the Muslim warrior to smash the seats of idolatry. The Hindus were left with a stark choice—revive or disappear.

Renewal was the Hindu response. This renewal occurred through a number of processes—the simplification and propagation of Brahminical doctrines; the adoption of some practices and beliefs from Buddhism and Jainism; the accommodation of popular folklore, local deities and regional forms of worship into the master faith; the greater emphasis on the worship of gods in easily accessible human form; the use of music, dance and theatre to propagate religious stories; the universal practice of daily worship at home, so that the temple was not the only locus of sustenance for the faith; and eventually, as I describe below, the rise of bhakti worship, in which an almost mystical devotion to a personal god became a hallmark of Hindu religiosity. In addition there was Hinduism's very lack of a central organizational structure: the knowledge of the Vedas was preserved and perpetuated by being passed on from generation to generation within Brahmin families, or by individual sages or gurus to their disciples. Such a diffused pattern of dissemination was much more difficult to eliminate, or to subsume into a new faith. Another vital factor was the early truce between the spiritual and temporal powers in society: in response to the rise of Buddhism and Jainism, Brahmins (the priestly caste) and Kshatriyas (the warrior and ruling class) came to a mutual understanding that their interests would be best served in alliance, rather than in undermining each other.

All of these ensured that not only did India not turn into a fully Muslim country, as so many other Asian countries—from the Maldives to Malaya and Indonesia—were to do, but that Hinduism survived and thrived even in conditions of political dominance by rulers of another faith.

Indeed, the resilience of Hinduism throughout history is little short of remarkable. It has survived innumerable invasions, raids, attacks and outright conquest; each time, where lesser faiths in other countries crumbled before the invader and the majority of the population converted to the conqueror's faith, Hinduism stood strong and bounced back. In the mid-nineteenth century, Karl Marx marvelled at this phenomenon and found it remarkable. Hinduism remained a non-aggressive faith, but it was extraordinarily strong in its own defence. Hinduism took the blows and battled on; and every time the invader withdrew, Hinduism arose again, sometimes bloodied but always unbowed.

chapter eight

❧

RAMANUJA AND THE BHAKTI MOVEMENT

Key to this resilience was doctrinal openness and flexibility of practice. A thousand years ago in southern India, Ramanuja (said to have lived 1017–1137 CE to the age of 120), a great Vaishnava theologian, who headed the monastery at Srirangam, reinvented and revitalized Hinduism, following in Shankara's footsteps with a qualified form of Advaita. His doctrinal contribution was important: his commentaries on the Gita and on the *Brahma Sutras* contested Adi Shankara's interpretations of those scriptures. More important were the religious aspects of Ramanuja's teachings, to the effect that the burdens of karma can be overcome by Divine Grace, attained through the worship of a loving and just God an alternative view to the recondite philosophical constructs of Shankara, and thus a vital contribution to Indian spiritual revival. Through this approach Ramanuja popularized worship and brought organizational energy into the faith, conducting daily pujas and annual temple festivals, allowing image-worship and more inclusive temple-based rituals at the

Ramanuja

Srirangam Mutth he headed and in other nearby temples. Strikingly, he permitted women and worshippers of the lower peasant castes (though not, it should be said, Dalits) to participate in temple worship, a privilege they had been denied. Ramanuja also allowed the chanting of the popular Alvar (or Azhvar) hymns, which were sung in demotic Tamil, the language of the people, rather than in the arcane Sanskrit of official temple liturgy. Ramanuja's reforms spread across southern India to other major Vaishnavite temples and can be seen in many ways as a reinvention of Hinduism, taking Shankara's work to the masses.

Ramanuja's innovations prefigured the popularization of Hinduism in the Bhakti movement, which through prayer and song brought the esoterica of Hindu philosophy in simple language to the ears and the hearts of the common people. In some ways he could be said to be a pioneer of it. The Bhakti movement began in south India and swept northwards, creating a devotional, theistic, popular Hinduism that expressed itself vividly in the cult worship of different gods and goddesses and flourished across much of India between the twelfth and the eighteenth century CE. The movement started in Tamil Nadu between the fourth and the ninth centuries with the Nayanars and the Alvars, several of whom, notably the poetess Andal, were women. They sang in praise of Shiva and Vishnu respectively in Tamil, and as the Bhakti movement spread, brought more vernacular languages into a faith previously dominated by Sanskrit.

Ramananda, a Vaishnava sannyasi from Allahabad, travelled through much of the Indo-Gangetic plain, the land of Aryavarta, in the fourteenth century, preaching the doctrine of Bhakti, urging people to place their trust in, and surrender themselves to, a merciful God. The mysticism of his gospel, its offer of a refuge from the misery of human suffering, its assertion of equality of all before God and its depiction of God as a loving force in the lives of worshippers, gave Ramananda's teachings great appeal. He settled in Varanasi, where among the many disciples he acquired was the remarkable Muslim weaver Kabir, one of a dozen poet-sants (saints), both male and female, who took Ramananda's teachings to the masses.

Bhakti had its stars—poet-saints like Kabir (c. 1440–1510 CE), born a Muslim, who wrote some extraordinarily compelling verses distilling the essence of Hindu philosophy, and who was singing in praise of religious harmony at a time when the West was conducting Inquisitions and burning witches and heretics at the stake; Lalleshwari or

Mirabai

Lalla Rukh (c. 1317–1372 CE), the great Bhakti songstress of Kashmir, who sang passionately of her devotion to Shiva but as emotionally of her refusal to discriminate between Hindu and Muslim; mystic singers like Mirabai (c. 1498–1597 CE), whose songs transported the singer and her audience into a level of ecstasy reminiscent of some of today's evangelical churches; the twelfth-century poet Jayadev, whose *Gita Govindam* revolutionized the worship of Radha and Krishna, and whose ideas were echoed in the lyrics of the blind bard Surdas (c. 1478–1583 CE), the man who helped establish the Vrindavan-Mathura area as Krishna's holy land; and the remarkable writer, poet and saint Tulsidas (c. 1532–1623 CE), author of two of the most popular Hindu texts even today, the *Ramcharitmanas,* retelling the story of Lord Rama, and the Hanuman Chalisa, forty-three devotional verses in praise of the powerful monkey-god. Tulsidas wrote in Avadhi (though initially in Sanskrit); Kabir's verse can still be understood by Hindi speakers today. Verse and song became vehicles for Bhakti ideas throughout India.

Mirabai's husband, the Rana of Udaipur, allegedly disapproved so much of her devotion to Lord Krishna that he tried to poison her; but miraculously the poison turned into honey as she drank it, and she danced in ecstasy before her adored Lord. As one of her hymns declares with the sense of abandonment and ecstatic devotion for which she is known:

> *Tying anklets upon her feet, Mira dances in ecstasy.*
> *People say Mira has gone mad.*
> *Her mother-in-law says she has disgraced the clan,*
> *The Rana sent her a cup of poison,*
> *Which Mira, laughingly, drank.*
> *I have myself become the eternal maid-servant of*
> *My Narayana.*
> *Mira's God is Giridhar, lifter of the mountain.*
> *O Indestructible One, meet me swiftly in your*
> *Eternal embrace.*

Bhakti's creative effulgence was remarkable, and reached its peak, perhaps surprisingly, during the rule of the Muslim Mughal monarchs (1526 to the mid eighteenth century); the movement confirmed Hinduism's resilience in the face of Islamic conquest. But it was also much more than that: the Bhakti movement refreshed and strengthened Hindu society at a time when the state was in Muslim hands. It taught a staunch monotheism, shunned caste distinctions and rules, preached an absolute surrender to God and offered a religious experience that involved the direct realization of God through devotion. To that extent the Bhakti movement's reinterpretation of Hinduism resembled Islam's monotheism and egalitarianism: but its principles

Saint-poet Kabir Das

could also be found in the Upanishads, its personal gods in the Puranas, and its religious doctrine was anchored in that of the Bhagavad Gita, which summons the worshipper to surrender all and take refuge in dharma. The emotional connection of the worshipper to God that Bhakti expressed brought the devotee to a relationship of profound love for the divine, a love that, as the Gita expressed it, combined that of a father and a son, a devoted friend for another and a lover with their beloved.

The remarkable reach of Bhakti ideas ranged from the great poets, philosophers and preachers Narsi Mehta in Gujarat to Vidyapati in Mithila and Chaitanya Deva in Bengal (who founded the Vaishnava movement in Bengal through his kirtanas, devotional songs to Krishna), Jnaneswara, Tukaram, Eknath and Namdev in Maharashtra,

Basavanna in Karnataka and Thyagaraja in Tamil Nadu. The Krishna devotee Shankara Deva, after travelling extensively across India, returned to his native Assam and led a major revival of Hinduism in the north-east of the subcontinent.

In Kashmir in the late tenth century, Acharya Abhinavagupta propounded the doctrines of Kashmiri Shaivism which have profoundly influenced the practice of the faith in that state. Some of the great acharyas from the south, like Ramanuja, in effect established their own sects, restoring strength to the religion while transforming its practice in their areas. Basavanna, also known as Basava or Basaveshwara (c. 1131–1167 CE), with his staunch rejection of the caste system, his emphasis on vegetarianism and his abjuring of temple worship, created a sect, the Lingayats or Veerashaivas, who are hugely influential in modern Karnataka. His challenge to caste was uncompromising. 'Loaded with the burden of the Vedas,' he said dismissively, 'the Brahmin is a veritable donkey.' Though born a Brahmin himself, Basava shed his sacred thread at the age of eighteen and dismissed ideas of caste hierarchy: 'The higher type of man is the man who knows himself.' After all, as he pointed out: 'On the same earth stands the outcaste's hovel and the deity's temple. Whether for ritual or rinsing, is not the water the same?' Members of all castes were the same; the Brahmin and the outcaste were born the same way. Or 'is there anybody in the world,' he asked, 'delivered through the ear?'

Basava established a Hall of Experience (Anubhava Mantapa) where men and women from all castes could meet freely and discuss radical ideas. He shook off the established strictures against inter-dining and inter-marriage with 'untouchables', provoking social and political repression which extinguished his career; but his ideas, compiled in the form of vachanas, survived and have gained in strength to

The world's tallest Basava statue in Basavakalyan, Karnataka

the present day. While the Jain influence is apparent in his establishment of monastery-like mutths, Basava's religious belief was in Vishishta Advaita, in which Shiva is equated with Brahman and the worship of Shiva leads to the Absolute. Another reformer, Madhvacharya (c. 1199–1294 CE), revived ideas of dualism and worship of the saguna Brahman in the form of Lord Krishna. His commentaries on the sacred texts, together with those of Sayana on the Vedas, are amongst the most significant contributions to Hindu philosophy after Adi Shankara's. Madhvacharya upheld dualism; in his theology the atman did not merge with Brahman but dwelt in close proximity to it. He also came closest to a theory of hell in Hinduism, suggesting that some souls were so weighed down by their bad deeds that they were unable to progress to salvation and had to suffer eternal damnation.

It is striking, too, that one offshoot of Bhakti created

a wholly new religion, that of Sikhism. Its founder, Guru Nanak (1469–1539 CE), was also a poet and singer in the Bhakti tradition; the holy book of the Sikhs, the Guru Granth Sahib, includes large numbers of verses by Bhakti poets, most of all by Kabir. In its monotheism, and its emphasis on brotherhood and social equality, Sikhism derived much from Islam too; but its persecution by the later Mughals, notably Aurangzeb, turned Sikhism into a warrior faith, fighting to protect itself and the larger Hindu community. For many years in Sikhism's heartland, Punjab, Hindu families brought up one son as a Sikh, to fight for the faith.

Had Hinduism not acquired the demotic appeal to the masses that Bhakti provided it, many more might have converted to the religion of the rulers. But by offering an individual-centred path to the Divine, and by making spirituality accessible irrespective of one's caste, gender or circumstances of birth, the Bhakti movement revived and rejuvenated the ancient Vedic traditions. Bhakti took Hinduism far away from the formalism of Vedic rituals, the austerity of asceticism, the abstractions of sages; it transformed the quest for moksha to a loving relationship between each individual and his or her personally chosen manifestation of God. Salvation became accessible to the lowest castes, to women and even to those formerly outside the Hindu fold, 'untouchable' Dalits and Muslims. Bhakti brought vigour to the practice of faith by its conduct of shared religious services, collective bhajan-singing, community chanting of the names of the deity being adored, open (indeed sometimes extravagant) emotionalism in expressing love for the Divine, and the holding of festivals and pilgrimages. Much of what we regard as popular Hinduism today can trace its roots to the Bhakti movement.

Even something as basic as temple architecture served to reinforce faith in religion. Familiar legends from Hindu

The Bhakti tradition gave birth to Sikhism

mythology are engraved or painted on the walls and pillars of most temples in the form of sculptures. Any available surface is used; the shikharas and gopurams, the outer walls of the sanctum sanctorum, and where possible on interior surfaces as well. As a result a Hindu temple becomes a permanent advertisement for its faith. Devotees who visit the temple recall and appreciate the visual representation of these tales and legends; this adds to their religious experience and reinforces their conviction.

It is clear from the foregoing that Hinduism has hardly been an unchanging religion. It faced major reform movements and embraced them whole—notably Buddhism, of which Swami Vivekananada said: 'Shakya Muni [the Buddha] came not to destroy, but he was the fulfilment, the logical conclusion, the logical development of the religion of the Hindus...the Buddhist cannot stand without the brain and philosophy of the Hindu, nor the Hindu without the heart of the Buddhist.' The *Matsya Purana* hailed the Buddha as an avatara of Vishnu, as did other texts and temple inscriptions. In Vivekananda's telling, both Buddhism and Sikhism were variants of Hinduism that served to cleanse, purify and ultimately strengthen the mother faith.

The historical evolution of Hinduism testifies to its adaptability. The Vedas gave birth to an excessively ritualistic and formalistic religion; the Upanishads then lightened the practice of Hinduism through a spiritual movement based on philosophical enquiry. When the Upanishadic religion itself became mired in disputes over dogma, Buddhism preached a message of simplicity and morality that contrasted with a Hinduism mired in ritual and abstruse disputation. And then Adi Shankara travelled the length and breadth of the country, leading a moral and religious reawakening. Shankara and Ramanuja restored Hinduism to pre-eminence and popularity as the principal religion of India. Sages like Madhvacharya, Chaitanya, Ramananda and Basava (whose followers, the Lingayats, now want to be classified as a separate religion altogether, like the Sikhs); Kabir, Mirabai, Tulsidas, even Guru Nanak, who founded the Sikh faith, but whom many Hindus, notably Swami Vivekananda himself, see as a Hindu reformer—the names of those who rose to reform, revive and rejuvenate the beliefs of the people in this ancient land are legion. As early as the Gupta period, when Hindu religious revival first occurred in response to the rise of Buddhism, Hinduism came up with creative evidence of its adaptability through its emphasis on the doctrine of avataras. The doctrine is clearly stated in the Bhagavad Gita: 'When religion declines and evil-doers are to be destroyed, I shall be born at different periods,' says Krishna. Some avataras were worshipped as such even in the time of Panini, but it is with

Lord Krishna lifting Mount Govardhana

Krishna that we first have the idea of an avatara of God and not merely a deified human being, a doctrine that was handily adapted to the Buddha himself. Hinduism has never been uniform or unchanging, immovable or unalterable. It is a religion that has abjured the immutable revelation for the growth of human consciousness.

As we have seen, Islam was initially a threat, and the attacks of Muslim invaders on temples and Hindu treasures, as well as the rape and abduction of Hindu women, in a number of episodes in the five centuries from 1000 CE onwards, led to a defensive closing of the ranks and the adoption of protective practices that entrenched restrictions and prohibitions previously unknown in Hindu society. The protection of life, religion and chastity introduced rigidities into Hindu practice: restrictions on entry into temples (to safeguard their treasures from prying eyes), child marriages (to win protection for girls before they were old enough to be abducted by lustful invaders) and even the practice of sati (the burning of a widow on her husband's funeral pyre) were all measures of self-defence during this turbulent period of Indian history, that devolved into pernicious social practices wrongly seen as intrinsic to Hinduism rather than as a reactions to assaults upon it.

But once Muslims went beyond invading and stayed on to rule, won adherents and made their peace with the country, Islamic precepts also played a part in the reshaping of Hinduism: the Bhakti cults and the rise of Sikhism, both strongly influenced by Islamic ideas of equality and brotherhood, testify to that. Although conversion was not uncommon, forced or voluntary, whether of individuals who found it expedient to adopt the religion of the conquerors, or of entire communities (artisan sub-castes in north India, for instance) who were told that failure to convert would result in the loss of patronage for their products by the Muslim ruling classes, it was never universal, except in some pockets of the subcontinent (notably Kashmir, where most of the population, including many Brahmins, converted en masse to Islam, mostly under duress during the reign of Sultan Sikander [1389–1413 CE]). The overwhelming majority of the populace stayed Hindu.

chapter nine

HINDUISM'S RESPONSE TO THE BRITISH

When the British came, with their peculiar blend of curiosity and contempt for the beliefs and practices of the land they had found so absurdly easy to conquer, Hinduism found itself sharing space with a fiercely monotheistic culture that (unlike its precursor, Islam) claimed the trappings of modernity and progress for itself. The British found a Hinduism which, in reaction to Islamic conquest, had in some ways retreated into a shell, adopting practices to shield it from the hostile faith and searching for security in insularity. Thus a civilization which had historically sent envoys around the world, trading with the Roman empire and exporting its religious ideas across Asia, became so self-protective that it forbade travel 'across the black water', and insisted on excommunicating those who violated this proscription, or at least forced them to undergo purificatory rituals before they could be readmitted into the Hindu fold. Most Britons in India sneered at a faith they saw as primitive and mired in superstition. (There were, of course, notable exceptions, but in general the colonial attitude to Hinduism was one of incomprehension and contempt.) The shock of contact inevitably had a catalytic effect, leading to some remarkable reactions on the part of Hindus, including another round of reform.

Some Hindus recoiled in disgust from the British, and retreated into the secure shelter of their faith as they had known it in practice, sealing themselves off from all foreign influence. But a few others looked at their faith in the light of the new intrusion, and were embarrassed by what they saw. The Hinduism they practised seemed, especially if seen through British eyes, mired in superstition and mumbo-jumbo; it was associated with idol worship, with incantations in a dead language, with caste hierarchy and iniquitous social practices. They craved a reformed Hinduism that could hold its own with Western Christianity and even earn the respect of the British.

The most interesting of those who felt this way was Raja Rammohan Roy (1772–1833 CE), an aristocratic Bengali from a prominent and wealthy family, educated in his mother-tongue as well as in Sanskrit, Persian and Arabic before being schooled in English. His view was in direct response to the disadvantageous position that Hinduism found itself in under early British rule. 'The present system of the Hindus is not well calculated to promote their political interests,' he argued shrewdly. 'It is necessary that some change should take place in their religion, at least for the sake of their political advantage and social comfort.'

Accordingly, Roy promoted a rational, ethical, non-hierarchical, and modern Hinduism, committed to ending the worst Hindu social practices of the day and streamlining Hindu theology. He founded a reform movement, the Brahmo Samaj, which was clearly a product of the interaction of his reformist ideas of Hinduism, emerging from a

Raja Rammohan Roy

modernistic reading of Advaita Vedanta, with early-Victorian Christianity. The Brahmos rejected the idolatry that Hinduism had become synonymous with in British eyes and professed belief in a formless God, along with a monotheistic theology based on their reading of the Upanishads and of the Vedanta, Hindu sacred texts that credibly lent themselves well to such a 'modern' interpretation. Brahmos affirmed their belief in the existence of One Supreme God—'a God endowed with a distinct personality and moral attributes equal to His nature, and intelligence befitting the Author and Preserver of the Universe.' Brahmos would worship Him alone, and not necessarily in temples or at specific holy days: 'We can adore Him at any time and at any place, provided that time and that place are calculated to compose and direct the mind towards Him.'

In creating the Brahmo Samaj, Roy was strongly influenced by Unitarianism, whose uncompromising monotheism posited the oneness of God (in opposition to the Trinity of the Father, the Son and the Holy Ghost). Roy's attitude to Hinduism was in many ways comparable to the Unitarians' to Christianity, paring the faith of unnecessary accretions and reducing it to its most basic affirmations of deism. (Today, it is impossible to read of the beliefs of the Unitarian Universalists without being struck by their similarities to the central tenets of Upanishadic Hinduism). Some Hindu scholars refused to consider Roy to be a Hindu at all, seeing in the Brahmo faith a form of Christianity dressed in Indian clothes. Others saw Roy as a staunch reformist within the Hindu faith: he wore a sacred thread all his life. But it would take a Vivekananda, not a Roy, to preach, seven decades later, a robust, modernist and universalist Hinduism, anchored in its own precepts, that could look the rest of the world's religions in the eye and oblige them to blink.

Roy was motivated in large measure by a desire to impress his European acquaintances by proving, as he put it, that 'superstitious practices which deform the Hindu religion have nothing to do with the pure spirit of its dictates'. Accordingly, he combined precept with action. Social reform was crucial to his approach. Roy rejected those Hindu traditions that his education taught him to see as social evils, campaigning against caste discrimination, the denial of equal rights to women, sati, polygamy and child marriage, while arguing that none of these practices had sanction in the scriptures.

Roy passionately believed in modern, British-style education as an indispensable tool to transform society. The East India Company, busily engaged in sending back to England as much money as they could squeeze out of India, had no desire whatsoever to spend funds on creating educational institutions for Indians. So Roy realized an

Indian would have to take up the challenge. In 1817, he set up the Hindu College at Calcutta in collaboration with a Scotsman not affiliated to the East India Company, David Hare, following it up with the Anglo-Hindu school in 1822 and the Vedanta College in 1826. Roy founded the Vedanta College to create an institution where his monotheistic doctrines could be taught alongside a contemporary Western curriculum, in a synthesis of Western and Indian learning. Roy maintained a frenetic pace of institution-building: in 1830, for instance, he helped Rev. Alexander Duff to establish the General Assembly's Institution (now known as Scottish Church College). Not only did Roy donate the land on which the institution was built, he personally recruited the first batch of Indian students to study there. He also campaigned for freedom of the press, which was hemmed in with various restrictions in his time.

Roy died, at the age of sixty-one, on a trip to England undertaken with a view to raising the stipend paid by the British to the Mughal emperor, as well as in the hope of presenting a better account of his country to the British. He is buried in Bristol, amongst the people he had tried to impress, but far from the country he had worked so hard to transform. His influence outlasted him, though the Brahmo Samaj never acquired the prominence or the popularity that he might have hoped for and that he might have been able to give it had he lived a longer life.

Subsequent Brahmo thinkers included Debendranath Tagore, who questioned important Hindu precepts, challenging the authority of the Vedas and belief in reincarnation and karma, and Keshub Chandra Sen, who emphasized personal religious experience over doctrine and sought to make spirituality more accessible to ordinary people. Vivekananda's initial beliefs as a teenager were strongly influenced by these thinkers, whom he met and interacted with in his late teens, and the doctrines of the Brahmo Samaj. (But, as we shall see, he moved from the Brahmos as he learned new ideas at the feet of the mystic Ramakrishna Paramahamsa.)

chapter ten

MYSTICS AND REFORMERS

Brahmoism was not the only response to British Christianity in the colonial era. The brave and determined Ishwar Chandra Vidyasagar in Bengal led a social movement for widow remarriage, setting an example by marrying a widow himself. He also worked for the teaching of Sanskrit to be offered to all castes. The great Sanskrit scholar R. G. Bhandarkar set up the Prarthana Samaj in Bombay with M. G. Ranade to oppose the iniquities of the caste system. Half a century after Roy created the Brahmo Samaj, a dynamic Hindu sage, Swami Dayanand Saraswati (1824–1883), established the Arya Samaj as a pure but reformed version of the Hindu faith.

Unlike Roy, Dayanand asserted the infallible authority of the Vedas, while also affirming belief in one God and rejecting idol-worship as the Brahmos had done, along with other Puranic accretions to the pure Vedic religion. Arguing that idolatry and polytheism, which so attracted the contempt of the Christian missionaries, were not mentioned in the

Vedas, Dayanand Saraswati called on Hindus to terminate these practices. (However he opposed cow-slaughter, a debatable position for one anchoring himself in the Vedas, which is replete with stories of sacrificial offerings of animal, including at least one reference to the slaughter of cows.) He established gurukuls (Vedic schools) as alternatives to English education; these schools emphasized Vedic values and culture, while teaching the Hindu precepts of devotion to, and the pursuit of, truth (satyam). The Arya Samajis saw their faith as Sanatana Dharma, and found their almighty Creator (known as Om, the primordial sound) in the *Yajur Veda*, rather than the Ishvaras of the Puranic age. Like some other Hindus, they saw the text of the Vedas as itself divine, and reciting the Vedas as a sufficient act of worship.

But their belief systems were not purely of ancient origin. The reaction to Christianity in their doctrines is evident not only in the discarding of idol-worship but in the Arya Samaj doctrine that the Vedas are 'revealed' texts, while the other sacred books of the Hindus—the Puranas, the epics and even the Gita—are not. They are equally dismissive of the supposedly revealed texts of other faiths, such as the Bible and the Quran. In this respect the Arya Samaj departed from the principle of acceptance of other faiths as equally valid, the principle that characterizes Swami Vivekananda's Hinduism.

As a reform movement, the Arya Samaj advocated the equality of all human beings and the empowerment of women; it opened its doors to all Hindus irrespective of caste or sect, performing simple marriages according to the prescriptions in the Brahmanas of the *Yajur Veda*. It also created a conversion ritual called shuddhi, complete with formal certification, for non-Hindus wishing to enter the faith, something which had never existed before and which seemed to have been inspired by Christian practices of baptism. In his *The*

Swami Dayanand Saraswati

Discovery of India Jawaharlal Nehru describes the Arya Samaj as thus having introduced religious proselytization to Hinduism. (Non-Hindus marrying Hindus have found that if they wish to adopt their spouse's faith, the only way they can do so is through the Arya Samaj's conversion route.)

These practices, however, have helped the Arya Samaj version of Hinduism appear more familiar to those exposed to the way the Semitic religions conduct their faith. Unsurprisingly the Arya Samaj is strongly rooted in many Hindu expatriate communities, offering the equivalent of Christian 'Sunday school' classes in the principles of the faith to Hindu children in suburban America. Yet it remains little more than a sect in its own homeland, adhered to by a modest minority of Indian Hindus.

Greater local success was obtained by three nineteenth-century reformers (and contemporaries) in southern India, Sree Narayana Guru (1856–1928), Mahatma Ayyankali (1863–1941) and Chattampi Swami (1853–1924), whose lives and impact overlapped. Chattampi Swami, an upper-caste Hindu sage, opposed caste oppression and spoke up for the emancipation of women; Mahatma Ayyankali, from an 'untouchable' community, fought successfully against the iniquitous discriminations that prevented outcastes from using certain roads and public spaces in Travancore. But the greatest impact was that of Sree Narayana Guru, who overcame the disadvantages imposed upon the 'backward caste' Ezhava community by preaching a modern Hinduism of love, equality and universalism. 'One religion, one caste, one God for all mankind', was his dictum. 'Whatever a person's caste, it is enough that a human be good', he famously declared. He backed up his precepts by establishing educational institutions throughout the south and by setting up ashrams and spiritual retreats to advance his ideas. Mahatma Gandhi called on Sree Narayana Guru in 1925, three years before the latter's death; without a common language (the guru did not know English and Gandhiji had no Sanskrit), the two great souls communed largely in silence and through an interpreter, but the more famous man emerged awestruck from the experience. In 1999, Sree Narayana Guru was voted by the readers of the most popular Malayalam-language magazine the greatest Keralite of the twentieth century.

The mystic sage Ramana Maharishi (1879–1950), and the revolutionary-turned spiritual guide Sri Aurobindo (1872–1950), were two other remarkable contemporaries born in the nineteenth century. Ramana Maharishi's intense spirituality, his quest for self-realization, his intuitive grasp of Advaita and Bhakti led to him being widely considered a Jivanmukta, one who had attained self-realization in this life. One can see

Ramana Maharishi

Ramakrishna as the exemplar of bhakti yoga, Vivekananda as the very model of karma yoga, and Ramana Maharishi as that of jnana yoga. His key question to aid the attainment of self-realization was '*Who am I?*' Am I the body, the mind, the senses? Ramana Maharishi did not travel to disseminate a message, perform social service or establish a new order of monks, but the simple example of his spirituality made him an object of great popular veneration. It is said that on the night of his death, a comet passed across the sky behind his mountain abode at Arunachalam.

As for the Cambridge-educated Sri Aurobindo, he began as an extremist political revolutionary, and ended as an other-worldly spiritual giant. During his political phase (essentially 1905 to 1910), Sri Aurobindo evolved a philosophy of spiritual nationalism, writing passionately and evocatively of the divinity of the motherland, personified as a goddess, Bhavani Bharati (a forerunner in some ways of the

Sri Aurobindo

Bharat Mata deified by the Hindutva movement). But during his incarceration in a bomb conspiracy case, Aurobindo realized his spiritual interests outstripped his political ones. He moved to the French enclave of Pondicherry and spent the last four decades of his life (1910–1950) there in spiritual contemplation, writing brilliant exegeses on aspects of Hinduism, including a magisterial commentary on the Gita, and establishing an ashram that thrives to this day. Rather than individual salvation, he was concerned with the spiritual evolution of the human race; his concept of Integral Yoga envisaged a threefold path that involved total surrender to the Divine, the raising of human consciousness to a 'supramental' level, and finally the transformation of the terrestrial human race into a wholly new order of being.

It was said of Sri Aurobindo that he could trace almost every modern Western idea to the ancient Hindu scriptures, and that if one could not find a specific reference upon examination, that was because one was reading the words literally and failing to comprehend that the ancient Hindu sages had elliptical and metaphorical means of conveying the ideas that today we consider modern. The French political scientist (and student of modern Hindu politics) Christophe Jaffrelot has labelled the process of adoption and acceptance of Western ideas, beliefs and values by Indian sages, masked by the claim that these were actually derived from the ancient Hindu texts, as 'strategic syncretism'. Whatever one calls it, it was one more instance of how resilient Hinduism was in the face of Western colonial dominance, and how effectively it adapted to the demands of proving its viability and relevance in the modern era.

❁

chapter eleven

SWAMI VIVEKANANDA

Though Ramana Maharishi and Sri Aurobindo achieved their prominence after his death, Swami Vivekananda (1863–1902), who came of age at the culmination of all the developments I have earlier chronicled, was also heir to the grand, diverse and varied traditions of Hinduism, for he had drunk deeply from the well of a faith whose eclecticism he saw as a strength. As he put it, 'sect after sect arose in India and seemed to shake the religion of the Vedas to its very foundations, but [over the years]...these sects were all sucked in, absorbed and assimilated into the immense body of the mother faith. From the high spiritual flights of the Vedanta philosophy, of which the latest discoveries of science seem like echoes, to the low ideas of idolatry with its multifarious mythology, the agnosticism of the Buddhists and the atheism of the Jains, each and all have a place in the Hindu's religion.'

His initial beliefs were influenced by Brahmo concepts of a formless God and the rejection of idolatry, and anchored

Swami Vivekananda at the Parliament of the World's Religions, 1893

in a rationalized Hindu theology based on the Upanishads and reliant on Advaita Vedanta. But though Brahmoism was an influence, it was by no means the determinant influence; Vivekananda abandoned the Brahmos for the savant who became his guru, the mystic monk Ramakrishna Paramahamsa (1836–1886). Ramakrishna, who was subject to visions, trances and 'intense spiritual rhapsodies' (in the words of Dr Karan Singh), which brought him to purest consciousness, preached a religious universalism in which he urged the thousands who flocked to him to abandon all quarrels over religion and to look for God with a pure heart. He imparted his wisdom in simple parables that won him a devoted following among the masses as well as the elite of his day, as well as deep spiritual attainment that he imparted to his most illustrious devotee. From Ramakrishna, Swami Vivekananda acquired a more profound, as well as broader, familiarity with Hindu doctrines of the oneness of atman and Brahman, of the role of spirituality and the quest for self-realization and liberation, as well as the stories and parables through which these beliefs could be propagated.

Vivekananda explained his sacred texts in terms his Western audience at the Chicago Parliament of the World's Religions could understand: 'The Hindus have received their religion through revelation, the Vedas. They hold that the Vedas are without beginning and without end. It may sound ludicrous to this audience, how a book can be without beginning or end. But by the Vedas no books are meant. They mean the accumulated treasury of spiritual laws discovered by different persons in different times. Just as the law of gravitation existed before its discovery, and would exist if all humanity forgot it, so is it with the laws that govern the spiritual world. The moral, ethical, and spiritual relations between soul and soul and between individual spirits and the Father of all spirits were there before their discovery, and would remain even if we forgot them.'

This led Vivekananda to the ringing affirmation that whereas many Westerners think of the self as a body that possesses a soul, Hinduism sees the self as a soul that possesses a body: 'The Vedas declare,' he said, that 'I am a spirit living in a body: I am not the body. The body will die, but I shall not die.' On the question of the existence of God, again an idea that would make his faith more comprehensible to foreigners, Vivekananda explained: 'At the head of all these laws, in and through every particle of matter and force, stands One, "*by whose command the wind blows, the fire burns, the clouds rain and death stalks upon the earth*".' (The 'One' was a carefully-chosen word; whereas to the Swami it implied the oneness of Brahman and atman, cosmic spirit and soul, it also embraced the idea of the One God of the Semitic faiths.) 'And what is His nature?' Vivekananda went on. 'He is everywhere, the pure and formless One, the Almighty and the All-merciful.

"*Thou art our father, Thou art our mother, Thou art our beloved friend, Thou art the source of all strength; give us strength. Thou art He that beareth the burdens of the universe; help me bear the little burden of this life.*" Thus sang the Rishis of the Veda.'

A certain amount of mysticism inevitably came into the message, as his audience expected: 'The Hindu believes he is a spirit. Him the sword cannot pierce Him the fire cannot burn Him the water cannot melt—Him the air cannot dry. The Hindu believes that every soul is a circle whose circumference is nowhere, but whose centre is located in the body, and that death means the change of this centre from body to body... The Vedas teach that the soul is divine, only held in the bondage of matter; perfection will be reached when this bond will burst and the word they use for it is, therefore, "mukti"—freedom, freedom from the bonds of imperfection, freedom from death and misery.'

But here Vivekananda had a little surprise up his sleeve for the listening Westerners, particularly for those who thought of their God as a distant vision, or an aged and forbidding figure in the clouds with a white beard. 'And how to worship Him?' he asked of his God. 'Through love. He is to be worshipped as the one beloved, dearer than everything in this and the next life. This is the doctrine of love declared in the Vedas, and let us see how it is fully developed and taught by Krishna whom the Hindus believe to have been God incarnate on earth. He taught that a man ought to live in this world like a lotus leaf, which grows in water but is never moistened by water; so a man ought to live in the world—his heart to God and his hands to work.' For Vivekananda this selfless love for God was implicit in the teachings of the Bhagavad Gita. 'It is good to love God for hope of reward in this or the next world, but it is better to love God for love's sake; and the prayer goes: "Lord, I do not want wealth nor children nor learning. If it be Thy will, I shall go from birth to birth; but grant me this, that I may love Thee without the hope of reward—love unselfishly for love's sake."'

To Vivekananda, the answer to the question 'What is Hinduism?' could be reduced to the idea of realization, of the union of atman and Brahman, the moksha taught by Advaita Vedanta: 'The whole object of [Hinduism] is by constant struggle to become perfect, to become divine, to reach God, and see God; and this reaching God, seeing God, becoming perfect even as the Father in Heaven is perfect, constitutes the religion of the Hindus...' He explained: 'There is something beyond even this fine body, which is the Atman of man, which has neither beginning nor end, which knows not what death is...I am already joined—from my very birth, from the very fact of my life—I am in *Yoga* [union] with that infinite life...'

From there, having explained Hinduism in terms that Westerners could grasp, Vivekananda firmly parted from their basic assumptions. He argued that the Hindu religion 'means realization and nothing short of that. "Believe in the doctrine and you are safe" can never be taught to us, for we do not believe in that; you are what you make yourselves...religion is to be realized, not only heard; it is not in learning some doctrine like a parrot.'

This dismissal of Western catechisms enabled Vivekananda to argue robustly that Advaita was science rather than philosophy. Hinduism has always been free of the science versus faith conflicts that have bedevilled other religions. Indeed, in 1896, Vivekananda claimed that Advaita appealed to modern scientists: 'I may make bold to say that the only religion which agrees with, and even goes a little further than modern researchers, both on physical and moral lines, is the Advaita, and that is why it appeals to modern scientists so much. They find that the old dualistic theories are not enough for them, do not satisfy their necessities.

A man must have not only faith, but intellectual faith too.'

He also argued that 'there is no polytheism in India'. The idol worship one saw in India's temples should not be taken literally: 'By the law of association the material image calls up the mental idea and vice versa. This is why the Hindu uses an external symbol when he worships. He will tell you it helps to keep his mind fixed on the Being to whom he prays. He knows as well as you do that the image is not God, is not omnipresent... To the Hindu, man is not travelling from error to truth, but from truth to truth, from lower to higher truth. To him all the religions from the lowest fetishism to the highest absolutism, mean so many attempts of the human soul to grasp and realize the Infinite, each determined by the conditions of its birth and association, and each of these marks a stage of progress.' And he added that it was not very different in the so-called monotheistic faiths: 'The images, crosses, and crescents are simply so many symbols—so many pegs to hang spiritual ideas on. It is not that this help is necessary for everyone, but those that do not need it have no right to say that it is wrong.' Idolatry in India 'is the attempt of undeveloped minds to grasp high spiritual truths'.

The Swami was certainly not seeking to downplay his own faith: far from it, he spoke proudly in 'the name of the most ancient order of monks in the world' and 'the mother of religions'. Vivekananda was contemptuous of what he called 'kitchen religion', the farrago of taboos and restrictions on diet and conduct that had come to constitute Hinduism for some. But he also made no distinction between the actions of Hindus as a people (embodied by their grant of asylum to people fleeing religious oppression, for instance) and their actions as a religious community (visible in their tolerance of other faiths). He spoke proudly of Hindu India offering refuge to Jews fleeing Roman persecution and Zoroastrians escaping Muslim rule in Persia: 'I am proud to belong to a country which has sheltered the persecuted and the refugees of all religions and all countries of the earth.' For him, there was no real distinction between Hindu believers accepting other faiths and Hindus extending asylum to people of other faiths, because Hinduism was as much a civilization as a set of religious beliefs.

In a different speech to the same Chicago convention, Swami Vivekananda set out his philosophy in simple terms: 'Unity in variety is the plan of nature, and the Hindu has recognized it. Every other religion lays down certain fixed dogmas and tries to compel society to adopt them. It places before society only one coat which must fit Jack and John and Henry, all alike. If it does not fit John or Henry, he must go without a coat to cover his body. The Hindus have discovered that the absolute can only be realized, or thought of, or stated through the relative, and the images, crosses, and crescents are simply so many symbols—so many pegs to hang spiritual ideas on. It is not that this help is necessary for everyone, but those that do not need it have no right to say that it is wrong. Nor is it compulsory in Hinduism.'

Vivekananda was also, uncommonly for his time, a believer in gender equality: he related well to women, who numbered among his closest devotees, and worked with them to take his message to the world. It is no wonder then that he began those inspiring speeches to the Parliament of the World's Religions with the words, 'Sisters and brothers of America...' The first time he uttered them, it was reported, the phrase, and his voice, had an electrifying effect upon the audience.

In his book *Raja Yoga* Vivekananda introduced the 'four yogas', his interpretation of Patanjali's *Yoga Sutras*, as a practical means for each individual to work towards realizing the divine force within himself. The four yogas were raja yoga (psychological and mystical practices as well as spiritual exercises), karma yoga (work and the way of action and social service in the quest for the divine), bhakti yoga (devotional worship and expression of love for the divine), and jnana yoga (the path of knowledge and reason in the pursuit of self-realization). The four paths were distinct but could be pursued simultaneously or in parallel. Vivekananda tried to combine all these in himself. Vivekananda pursued his own divinity by discipline and effort, deep study, reading and reflection, and huge physical effort that included walking the length and breadth of India with nothing but a staff, a water pot and his own charisma to sustain him.

He was a profoundly moral figure, with none of the indulgences that modern Indian 'godmen' have become known for: as Adi Shankara preached, he lived by a code of truth, purity, celibacy and unselfishness that anchored his shraddha (faith). Although many of his deeply committed followers were women, he treated them as sisters and daughters, irrespective of their age, and lived the celibate life of a brahmachari, seeing intimate relations as incompatible with his mission of spiritual service. In this he remained essentially a monk, but unlike his preceptor Ramakrishna he was no other-worldly figure: a compelling speaker and a magnetic presence, Swami Vivekananda was focused on human behaviour in the real world he saw around him. He argued that it is an insult to preach religion to a man with an empty stomach, and for many in India, he said, God will only appear as a loaf of bread.

The Vedanta, interpreted in comprehensible contemporary terms, became the vehicle for his preaching. As Vivekananda explained: 'Each soul is potentially divine. The goal is to manifest this Divinity within by controlling nature, external and internal. Do this either by work, or worship, or mental discipline, or philosophy—by one, or more, or all of

Ramakrishna Paramahamsa

these—and be free. This is the whole of religion. Doctrines, or dogmas, or rituals, or books, or temples, or forms, are but secondary details.'

Vivekananda lived up to this precept himself: work, worship, mental discipline and philosophy, he mastered them all. He believed that spiritual realization needed the awakening of the human will; this required him to adopt a path of pursuing spirituality through service. Worldly success was important, but such success could only be the outcome of focused thought and action. It is important to remember that Swami Vivekananda—despite being a spiritual figure, despite being a disciple of the immortal Ramakrishna Paramahamsa, despite being a sannyasi who travelled the length and breadth of India and taught the message of Vedanta and the Gita, the message of religion and spirituality as he understood it—was also very much anchored in the real needs of India, of his people at that time and in the future.

Sri Ramakrishna Temple at Belur Mutth

Of the many angles from which the social problems of India could be analysed, he proceeded from the religious and spiritual perspectives. Therefore, the Swami founded the Ramakrishna Math, based on the twin ideals of self-realization and service to the world, and named for his guru, Sri Ramakrishna Paramahamsa. But since a math (or matham or mutth) is essentially a place of contemplation, Vivekananda laid the foundation of the Ramakrishna Mission, also named for his preceptor, as a philanthropic, volunteer organization to work alongside the religious monastic order to spread his teachings throughout the world. The Mission based its work on the principle of karma yoga, the path of selfless, altruistic service propounded by Vivekananda. Karma yoga preached an ethic of action and doing, not merely of the meditation and reflection that was all that spirituality had hitherto been identified with. Ever since its inception, the Ramakrishna Mission has stayed true to its motto of 'Atmano mokshartham jagat hitaya cha', which translated from Sanskrit means 'For one's own salvation, and for the good of the world'.

Vivekananda undoubtedly revolutionized the traditional image of the Hindu monk, the sannyasi, in India by setting the example and making social service an integral part of the sannyasi's life. Initially, after the passing away of his guru, Sri Ramakrishna, he had thought of going on a pilgrimage to holy places like Varanasi, Ayodhya, Vrindavan, and the ashrams of yogis in the Himalayas. However, after a couple of years spent on such visits, he turned his gaze to the common people for whom the only reality in life was their struggle for survival.

When, around Christmas of 1892, he travelled on foot to Kanyakumari, at the southern tip of India, he meditated on the 'last bit of Indian rock' jutting out into the ocean, on which now stands the Vivekananda Rock Memorial. It was at this juncture in his life that the Swami pondered over his experiences of observing the miseries of the poor in the various parts of the country, which culminated in his 'Vision of One India'. This has now come to be called the 'Kanyakumari resolve of 1892', about which he later wrote:

'At Cape Comorin, sitting in Mother Kumari's temple, I hit upon a plan: we are so many sannyasins wandering about, and teaching the people metaphysics? It is all madness. Did not our Gurudeva once say, "An empty stomach is no good for religion?" That those poor people are leading a life of brutes is simply due to ignorance... Suppose some sannyasins, bent on doing good to others, go from village to village, disseminating education and seeking in various ways to better the condition of all down to the Chandala...can't that bring forth good in time? ... We, as a nation, have lost our individuality, and that is the cause of all mischief in India. We have to give back to the nation its lost individuality and

The Vivekananda Rock Memorial at Kanyakumari

raise the masses...' Vivekananda wanted 'to set in motion a machinery which will bring noblest ideas to the doorstep of even the poorest and the meanest'.

These ideas galvanized his followers, in a country that had long been inured to the tyranny and oppression faced by a majority of the people. And thus began a new epoch in his life. Nationalism—not just in the sense of overthrowing the foreign ruler, but in the sense of national reawakening—became a prominent theme in Vivekananda's thought. He believed that a country's future depended on its people, and his teachings focused on what today we might call human development. Our modern systems of governance have a lot to learn from his teachings. His assessment of the social problems of India was realistic, rather than theoretical, largely owing to the fact that he wandered all over the country for years, with a few followers behind him and a begging bowl in his hand. He connected with the common man to a degree that would be the envy of most modern politicians.

What bothered the Swami, even more than poverty itself, was the gulf between the rich and the poor, between the high-placed and the low-born, and further, the ugly sight of the strong regularly oppressing the weak. 'This is our native land', he often bemoaned, 'where huts and palaces exist side-by-side.' Such was the dichotomy of the times that it seemed inconceivable to him that India could have the unity and brotherhood which are preconditions for national greatness. Born, as it were, a 'disunited mob', we could not combine: in our unity would lie the fulfilment of our nationhood.

But this would mean liberation from ourselves and not just from the British. Vivekananda was searingly honest in his criticism of the social practices that kept India backward. He denounced the oppression of the masses by iniquitous social practices, including caste discrimination. He propagated the idea that 'the divine, the absolute, exists within all human beings regardless of social status'. He also voiced his opposition against the manner in which women were kept in conditions of servile dependence on men, which made them 'good only to weep at the slightest approach of mishap or danger'. He taught us values that actually mandated change in the arrangements of our society. He refused to accept it when religion was cited in favour of iniquitous social practices like child marriage: he was a religious reformer as well as a social reformer. Child marriage, which Rammohan Roy had fought against, still persisted across India, since the British were reluctant to outlaw it. 'A girl of eight is married to a man of thirty and the parents are jubilant over it. And if anyone protests against it, the plea put forward is that our religion is being overturned', he lamented. His devotee Sister Nivedita, born in Britain as

Sister Nivedita

Margaret Noble, started a girls' school in Calcutta to advance his progressive ideas about the education of women. He wanted a fully educated India, an objective we have not yet fulfilled a century and a quarter later.

These practices, and the dissensions which divided Hindu society, pained Swami Vivekananda all the more because they were being adhered to in the name of religion. He preached that 'seeing the divine as the essence of others will promote love and social harmony', but he had no illusions about how prevalent such attitudes were. He was furious about those who claimed their beliefs were superior to anyone else's. 'Ask a man who wants to start a sectarian fight,' he declaimed, "Have you seen God? Have you seen the Atman? If you have not, what right have you to preach

His name—you walking in darkness trying to lead me into the same darkness—the blind leading the blind, and both falling into the ditch?"'

Vivekananda helped create, in his own lifetime, a band of volunteers to work among the poor, the distressed and the marginalized. Many of these were young people, for Swami Vivekananda personified the eternal energy of Indian youth and awakened in many young people a restless quest for truth. One of his more famous exhortations to young Indians came from his lectures in *Raja Yoga*, in which he memorably said, 'Take up one idea. Make that one idea your life—think of it, dream of it, live on that idea. Let the brain, muscles, nerves, every part of your body, be full of that idea, and just leave every other idea alone. This is the way to success, that is the way great spiritual giants are produced'.

A spiritual giant himself, Vivekananda expressed his mission in disarmingly simple terms: 'What I want to propagate is a religion that will be equally acceptable to all minds; it must be equally philosophic, equally emotional, equally mystic and equally conducive to action'. His own teachings, as well as the work done by the Ramakrishna Math and Mission in the century after his passing, have made Swami Vivekananda a modern day apostle of the ideas that underpin the modern Hindu's conception of the world and of our place in it.

But the fact is that he never considered himself detached from the world; his spirituality was anchored in the world. Swami Vivekananda taught us that a true nationalism was rooted in both spiritual yearning and a spirit of social service. 'Arise, awake, and stop not till the goal is reached' was his motto, citing a sloka of the *Katha Upanishad*. And that, to my mind, is the great lesson he leaves to those of us in public life: that we must have values, that we must join the quest for attainment of some knowledge of the Divine, for that is ultimately what all spirituality is about, but that spirituality is meaningless if it is not embedded in a genuine concern for the well-being of ordinary people in our country, and a willingness to act on it.

In multiple speeches around the world and in India, Vivekananda continually reiterated a basic message: that the Hindu recognizes one supreme spirit that suffuses the universe. He worships the one God while recognizing that others see and name Him differently. Ekam sat vipra bahudha vadanti: the Truth is One but sages call It by different names.

chapter twelve

AFTER THE SWAMI,
TOWARDS THE MAHATMA

Two decades after Vivekananda's premature death at the age of thirty-nine, a very different figure, clad not in the saffron or ochre robes of the Hindu sage but in the cap and gown of the Oxford don, rose to explicate the Hindu religion to an audience of academics and theologians. Delivering the prestigious Upton Lectures at the age of thirty-eight, Dr Sarvepalli Radhakrishnan, then the youngest Fellow of All Souls' College, described 'the Hindu view of life' in contemporary terms. For the Hindu, Radhakrishnan explained, God is in the world, though God is not the world, and the world is not God; He is more than the Creator, he preserves, protects, destroys, remakes, and strives continuously, alongside human beings. The *Brihadaranyaka Upanishad* captures this idea beautifully, though Radhakrishnan did not cite it:

He who is abiding in the earth, yet different from the earth;
He who is abiding in the water, yet different from the water;
He who is abiding in the wind, yet different from the wind...

—*Brihadaranyaka Upanishad*, III.7.3–7

In both places, the text uses the same Sanskrit word, 'antara' which means both 'interior to (abiding in)' and 'different from'. There is no dualism between the natural (the reality we see around us) and the supernatural (the cosmic spirit); each is rooted in the other. As Radhakrishnan brilliantly put it: 'The Hindu spirit is that attitude towards life which regards the endless variety of the visible and the temporal world as sustained and supported by the invisible and eternal spirit.'

Like Vivekananda in Chicago, Radhakrishnan had some startling news for his Western audience: the Hindu did not think in terms of good and evil. 'Evil has reference to the distance which good has to traverse. Ugliness is halfway to beauty. Error is a stage on the road to truth.' After all, he added: 'As every soul is unlike all others in the world, the destruction of even the most wicked soul will create a void in God's scheme.' There was no notion of sin in this philosophy, nor of Heaven nor Hell. (And yet the idea of sin is not wholly absent from the Vedas; the notion that sins can be washed away in holy waters goes back to the *Rig Veda*.) Damnation was not God's way, since the sinner was himself part of the universal cosmic spirit. How could there be a hell, since it was impossible for there to be a place where God was not? Vivekananda had said years earlier that Hindus reject the idea of fear and the idea of sin: 'the Aryans threw it aside as a very primitive sort of idea and went further on...[for] a more philosophical and

Dr Sarvepalli Radhakrishnan

transcendental idea.' That idea Radhakrishnan expressed in almost poetic terms: 'The cure for error is not the stake or the cudgel, not force or persecution, but the quiet diffusion of light.'

Radhakrishnan spoke as a professor of philosophy; Vivekananda declaimed as a preacher; but their message was the same, rendering the Hinduism of Advaita Vedanta comprehensible to the modern Western mind. It was, however, the charismatic Swami who had the more lasting impact. Vivekananda's overt respect for all other paths and religions was an integral part of what he preached. Part of his appeal lay in the way he combined ancient wisdom with contemporary insights, in spreading his profound message of interfaith harmony and spirituality married to rationalism.

Vivekananda had quoted the Bhagavad Gita to the effect that 'Whosoever comes to me, through whatsoever form, I reach him; all men are struggling through paths which in the end lead to me.' Vivekananda went on to denounce the fact that 'sectarianism, bigotry, and its horrible descendant, fanaticism, have long possessed this beautiful earth. They have filled the earth with violence, and drenched it often with human blood, destroyed civilization, and sent whole nations to despair'.

His confident belief that the death-knell of these negative forces had been sounded was sadly not to be borne out. But his vision—summarized in the Sanskrit credo 'sarva dharma sambhava'—all religions are equally worthy of respect—is, in fact, the kind of Hinduism practised by the vast majority of India's Hindus, whose instinctive acceptance of other faiths and forms of worship has long been the distinctive hallmark of Indianness, not merely in a narrow religious sense, but in a broader cultural and spiritual sense too.

The efforts of Swami Vivekananda and the other Hindu reformers and thinkers served to reassert their faith in the face of the racist notions of Christian superiority sought to be peddled by the colonial rulers. Far from the religion of superstitious idol-worshippers caricatured by the imperialists, they demonstrated that Hinduism was sophisticated, monotheistic and inclusive. It was a faith that had undergone several reformations and absorbed them all; the incorporation of Buddhist ideas, for instance, had made the Buddha—a figure familiar to, and respected by, many Westerners—a part of the Hindu faith. Hinduism had survived in even more sophisticated and cosmopolitan a form, and it would see off the threat of colonial modernity as well.

And yet, curiously enough, the nature and content of the Vedanta tradition meant that while it enabled Hindus to stand up with self-confidence against imperial rule, it did not generate a narrow Hindu nationalism. If Hinduism, as Advaita Vedanta taught, was an inclusive faith, the nationalism it animated must also be inclusive. Hindus thus agitated against colonial oppression, but they were happy to pursue the goal of swaraj or self-rule through collective action with other Indian religious communities.

❋

MAHATMA GANDHI

The leader who most embodied this approach was Mahatma Gandhi, who called himself a follower of Advaita Vedanta. Swami Vivekananda had preached Advaita Vedanta as an inclusive universal religion; similarly Gandhiji did not conceal his own staunch Hinduism, but presented it as a faith that respected and embraced all other faiths. He was immersed in Hindu beliefs and customs, and profoundly influenced by the Yamas of Adi Shankara, particularly ahimsa and satya to which he gave profound meaning when he applied them to the nationalist cause. But when Gandhiji held prayer-meetings at which Hindu devotional bhajans were chanted, so also were songs, hymns and verses sacred to other religions. He actively promoted syncretism: 'Raghupathi Raghava Raja Ram,' he chanted, 'Ishwara Allah Tero naam'. This practice emerged from his Vedantic belief in the unity of God and all human beings; he believed staunchly that all beings have the same atman and therefore should be treated with equality. His conviction that all paths to God should be seen as equally valid led him to respect the beliefs and practices of other faiths and to refuse to impose his own upon them (as he explained when refusing to advocate a ban on cow slaughter that would affect other communities).

Such behaviour did not endear him to every Hindu. Gandhiji's assassin, Nathuram Godse, denounced 'Gandhiji's betrayal of Hinduism' during his trial. It was an odd charge, since many saw Gandhiji as the quintessential Hindu leader in Indian politics, but it is true that his Hinduism was not particularly religious in the conventional sense. He died with the name of Rama on his lips but there is no evidence that he ever believed in or worshipped a personal god. ('There is an indefinable mysterious power that pervades everything,' he wrote, implying faith in an impersonal, undefinable power: 'I don't regard God as a person.') Gandhiji declared his faith in 'all that goes by the name of Hindu scriptures' but, as the scholar K. P. Shankaran points out, he 'immediately qualified it by saying that he also believed in all other religious texts in a similar way'. He also took Hinduism's eclectic and wide-ranging texts and belief structures literally, making it clear that he retained the right to choose what tenets he believed in, to interpret what they taught him, and to reject anything in them that he could not agree with. His emphasis on the ethics of satya and ahimsa, elevating them above almost any of the other principles of Hinduism, was distinctive: 'Truth for me is God.'

Gandhiji was more a reinterpreter of Hinduism than a reformer of it; by drawing from it to suit his beliefs and purposes, he redefined the traditional vocabulary of Hinduism without ever departing from it. He criticized many of the iniquitous social practices of Hinduism without denouncing the faith from which they had emerged, and unlike his contemporary Ambedkar, who denounced Hinduism's distortions and cruelties and eventually left the faith, Gandhiji always tried to change it from within. According to Prof Shankaran, Gandhiji's rejection of the vocabulary of the European enlightenment and modernity (for the reasons he had explained in his 1909 book, *Hind Swaraj*) forced him to fall back on a vocabulary that he was familiar with, that of the Vaishnava tradition of his parents. Gandhiji's objective was to create an ethical Indian state

The Father of the Nation, Mohandas Karamchand Gandhi

founded on ahimsa and satya, non-violence and truth, principles he found in Advaita philosophy. The national motto of independent India—Satyameva Jayate, truth alone triumphs—is from the *Mundaka Upanishad*, chosen by Mahatma Gandhi as his guiding credo. His own translation of the Bhagavad Gita portrays the text as a philosophy of Anashakti Yoga, meant for votaries of ahimsa. Gandhiji took a text that had traditionally been seen as extolling war and action, and transformed it into a paean to non-violence and truth. It was quite a feat (what some have seen as a creative 'misreading' of the text), that located his Hinduism on a platform of ahimsa and satya, and at the same time anchored his political strategy in the Hindu faith of the masses.

And even while doing so, Gandhiji took care to include Indians of other faiths in his capacious and agglomerative version of Hinduism. Gandhiji noted that there is ample religious literature, both in the astika and nastika religious traditions, that supports a pluralistic approach to religious and cultural diversity. He found support for his Advaitist beliefs not only in the Vedanta but in the Jain concept of 'Anekantavada'—the notion that truth and reality are perceived differently by different people from their own different points of view, and that therefore no single perception can constitute the complete truth—from which he derived the axiom that 'truth is many-sided and relative'. Gandhiji often expressed the view that the spirit of synthesis was the essential hallmark of Indian civilization. This led him to declare once, in response to being classified a Hindu: 'I am a Hindu, a Muslim, a Christian, a Parsi, a Jew'. (To which the Muslim League leader Muhammad Ali Jinnah tartly riposted: 'Only a Hindu could say that.')

As a Hindu, I am proud to lay claim to the legacy of the tradition of thought and action that began with the Vedas and grew under Adi Shankara, flowered through Bhakti, embraced social reformers like Raja Rammohan Roy and Sree Narayana Guru, and has Swami Vivekananda and Mahatma Gandhi as two of its fountainheads.

SECTION FIVE

~

A FAITH FOR
THE TWENTY-FIRST
CENTURY

Kali, the most fearsome form of Shakti

Goddess Durga vanquishing the world of evil

chapter thirteen

HINDUISM TODAY: CURRENT CONTROVERSIES AND CONTESTATIONS

When I was a columnist for *The Hindu*, which despite its name has been a secular, even left-inclined, newspaper throughout its existence, I received a number of letters from readers on the subject of Hindu ethics and dharma, prompted by some of my writings on the subject. One letter, from the retired Director-General of Police of Tripura State, Mr B. J. K. Tampi, made a challenging point. Arguing that dharma 'has a pre-eminently secular meaning of social ethics covering law-abiding conduct,' Mr Tampi sought for dharma its due prominence in Hindu life. 'In fact the four ends of human life,' he went on, 'dharma, artha, kama and moksha, are always mentioned in that order. The purport is that the pursuit of wealth and pleasure should be within the parameters of dharma and moksha (the final emancipation of the soul from rebirth through religious practices).' Mr Tampi adds, citing Swami Ranganathananda (1908–2005, the spiritual teacher who was the thirteenth and most famous head of the

A stamp released in 2008 commemorating
Swami Ranganathananda

Ramakrishna Mission): 'The excessive Indian fear of rebirth has led to the neglect of true worldly dharma for the sake of an other-worldly moksha. It has made men unfit both in the worldly (secular) and spiritual spheres.'

Now I have never met the good Mr Tampi—whose theological learning is all the more impressive in one who served in the practical profession of a policeman—but his analysis gladdens my secular heart. The fact is that, despite having done so much to attract the opprobrium of the Hindutva brigade, I do believe that propagating dharma—and instilling deeply at all levels of society the need to live according to one's dharma—can be the key to bridging the present gap between the religious and the secular in India.

The social scientist T. N. Madan has argued that the increasing secularization of modern Indian life is responsible for the rise of fundamentalism, since 'it is the marginalization of faith, which is what secularism is, that permits the perversion of religion. There are no fundamentalists or revivalists in traditional society.' The implication is that secularism has deprived Indians of their moral underpinnings—the meaning that faith gives to life— and religious extremism has risen as an almost inevitable antithesis to the secular project. The only way out of this dilemma is for Hindus to return to the tolerant, holistic, just, pluralist dharma articulated so effectively by Swami Vivekananda, which embraces both worldly and spiritual duty.

After all, as Mr Tampi points out, the Hindu's secular pursuit of material happiness is not meant to be divorced from his obedience to the ethical and religious tenets of his faith. So the distinction between 'religious' and 'secular' is an artificial one: there is no such compartmentalization in Hinduism. When you conduct your life by performing your duties ethically, are you 'secular' or (since you are fulfilling your dharma while adhering to a moral code) a 'good Hindu'?

There is also a terminological issue here. The secularism avowed by successive Indian governments, as Prof R. S. Misra of Banaras Hindu University has argued, is based on dharma-nirpekshata ('keeping apart from dharma'), which is impossible for any good Hindu to adhere to. Many politicians, and not only from the Hindutva-minded BJP, have argued that Indian governments cannot observe dharma-nirpekshata but should follow the precept of panth-nirpekshata (not favouring any particular sect or faith). In this they are not far removed from my argument—which I have made for several years before my entry into Indian politics—that 'secularism' is a misnomer in the Indian context of profuse religiosity, and what we should be talking about is 'pluralism'. I believe the roots of India's pluralism can be found in the Hindu acceptance of difference, which has become an article of faith for most of Indian society. But many critics of secularism are not terribly enamoured of pluralism either. To Prof Misra, for instance, the problem with dharma-nirpekshata is that an authentically Indian ethic would ensure that secular objectives are infused with dharma.

I find this view persuasive but incomplete. Yes, dharma is essential in the pursuit of material well-being, public order and good governance; but this should not mean turning public policy over to sants and sadhus, nor excluding any section of Indian society (for instance, minorities who reject the Hindu idea of dharma as irrelevant to their lives) from their rightful place in the Indian sun. If we can bring dharma into our national life, it must be to uphold, rather than at the expense of, our pluralist Indianness.

Hinduism has always acknowledged the existence of opposites (and reconciled them): pain and pleasure, success and failure, creation and destruction, life and death are all manifestations of the duality inherent in human existence. These pairings are not contradictory but complementary; they are aspects of the same overarching reality. So also with the secular and the sacred: a Hindu's life must involve both. To acknowledge this would both absorb and deflect the unsavoury aspects of the resurgence of Hinduism in today's India.

❀

THE DIVERSITY OF HINDUISM

It is essential, if one desires to portray a Hindu vision, to come to terms with the diversity within Hinduism itself. The faith is practised differently by people in different parts

*A representation of a Tamil
Smartha Brahmin*

of the country, or worshipping different manifestations of
the Divine, or adhering to different castes or sects. Even
the Brahmins, who are spread throughout the country and
are associated everywhere with learning, priestly functions
and religious erudition, manifest diversity in their social
practices: while the Malayali Brahmins grow their tuft of
hair at the front, most orthodox Tamil Brahmins wear it at
the back; where Iyengar Brahmin women regard white as
the colour of widowhood, the Namboothiri Brahmin bride
wears white at her wedding. As we have seen, Hinduism
is not a totalizing faith. Each Hindu may have a different

conception of her own dharma.

What Swami Vivekananda would have seen as the strength of Hinduism—its extraordinary eclecticism and diversity, its acceptance of a wide range of beliefs and practices, its refusal to confine itself to the dogmas of a single holy book, its fluidity, the impossibility to define it down to a homogenous 'Semitic' creed—is precisely what some modern Hindu ideologues see as its weakness. The Hindutvavadi quest for polarization and unity is also a yearning to make Hinduism what it is not—to 'Semitize' it so that it looks like the faiths of the 'invaders': codified and doctrinaire, with an identifiable God (preferably Rama), a principal holy book (the Gita), a manageable ecclesiastic hierarchy, and of course a unified race and a people to profess it. This is not the lived Hinduism of the vast majority of Hindus.

Whereas Hinduism is an inward-directed faith, focusing on Self-Realization above all and the union of the soul with the Absolute, Hindutva is an outward-directed concept, aimed at creating social and cultural distinctions for a political purpose. Hindutva, therefore, is disconnected from the central assumptions and tenets of my Hinduism. Yet it piggy-backs on the faith, claiming to represent Hinduism, though it does so not as a set of doctrines or precepts but as a cultural marker. Hindutva adopts the Hindu religion not as a way of seeking the Divine but as a badge of worldly political identity.

Speaking for myself, any attempt to reduce my Hinduism—which sits comfortably with the Nehruvian notion of Indianness—to a sectarian notion of Hindutva is a travesty of what Hinduism really is. I too, as a Hindu, can say, when people tell me 'Garv se kaho ki tum Hindu ho', that I am proud to be a Hindu, but in what is it that we are to take pride? I take pride in the openness, the diversity, the range, the lofty metaphysical aspirations of the Vedanta; of the various ways in which Hinduism is practised, eclectically, and of its extraordinary acceptance of differences.

Unfortunately, as I have noted, the votaries of Hindutva seem to take pride in Hinduism the way in which one might support a football team as a badge of identity, rather than as a set of values, principles and beliefs, and so Hinduism becomes reduced in their retelling to little more than a label on a T-shirt, a badge of allegiance rather than a way of relating to the cosmos.

My notion of Indianness and Hinduness is very much caught up in what Dr Radhakrishnan so memorably spoke of as a view of life. That view of life has very little room for intolerance, for dogma, for attacks on others because of what they do or do not believe. I am a Hindu, and I am a nationalist, but I am not a Hindu nationalist. My nationalism is unquestioningly, all-embracingly, Indian. The Hindutva movement does not speak for Hindus like me.

◆

My own faith in religious pluralism is a legacy of my upbringing in 'secular' India. Secularism in India did not mean irreligiousness, which even avowedly atheist parties like the communists or the southern DMK party found unpopular amongst their voters; indeed, in Calcutta's annual Durga Puja, the communist parties compete with each other to put up the most lavish Puja pandals. Rather, secularism meant, in the Indian tradition, a profusion of religions, none of which was privileged by the state. I remember how, in the Calcutta neighbourhood where I lived during my high school years, the wail of the muezzin calling the Islamic faithful to prayer blended with the chant of the mantras and the tinkling of bells at the nearby Shiva temple and the crackling loudspeakers outside the Sikh gurudwara reciting

A Durga Puja pandal

verses from the Guru Granth Sahib. And just around the corner was St Paul's Cathedral.

As we have seen, the irony is that India's secular coexistence was paradoxically made possible by the fact that the overwhelming majority of Indians are Hindus. That acceptance of difference, which I have explored in this book and elsewhere, characterized the Hinduism propagated by Vivekananda and other visionary Hindu seers. This meant that it came naturally to Hindus to coexist with practitioners of other faiths. In a plural society, religious pluralism was merely one more kind of difference everyone accepted, just as we knew that around us were people who spoke different languages, ate different foods, dressed differently and had different shades of skin colour from ours.

❀

Secularism in India, therefore, did not mean separation of religion from state. Instead, secularism in India means a state that was equally indulgent of all religious groups, and favoured none.

Nor did it mean secularity in the French sense, or laïcité. The French concept keeps religion out of governmental institutions like schools and government out of religious institutions in turn, whereas Indian secularism cheerfully embraces financial support to religious schools and the persistence of 'personal law' for different religious communities. The Indian system has created incentives for various religious denominations to start and operate 'minority schools' and colleges with substantial government funding, impart religious education, and be exempt from various regulations and stipulations the Indian government imposes on non-minority institutions. (Critics, especially of the Hindutva variety, do not hesitate to point out that while government schools and colleges may not impart religious instruction, religious sects and charities affiliated to minority communities may open their own schools and receive state financial assistance even as they impart religious indoctrination).

Under the Indian version of secularism, the government's financial largesse is extended to Muslim Wakf Boards, Buddhist monasteries, and certain Christian religious institutions; and under a 1951 Religious and Charitable Endowments Law, state governments are empowered to take over, own and operate Hindu temples, collect revenue from offerings and redistribute that revenue to such purposes as they deem fit, including any non-temple-related ones. This may well be worth re-examination. Still, it came as shock when, in 2016, the BJP government invited a Jain monk to address the Haryana assembly, seating him in an exalted position above the Speaker of the House. Many Hindus saw this as a grave mistake. Religiosity is hardly unknown in our politics—there are several saffron-robed sadhus who have been elected to Parliament and one, Yogi Adityanath, serves as the chief minister of India's biggest state, Uttar Pradesh—but giving an *unelected* religious figure a position of prominence in an elected, representative democratic legislative body was fundamentally wrong, and crossed a line that had hitherto never been breached.

While the Haryana government's actions might have been unconscionable, there is no getting away from the fact that India is not secular in the commonly understood sense of the word. What it is, is pluralist: an overwhelmingly Hindu-majority country running political and governmental institutions that promote the survival, success and perpetuation of religious minorities. It is the idea that rather than distancing itself from religion (the idea of dharma-nirpekshata condemned by the critics of secularism), the state can embrace *all* religions.

My generation grew up in an India where our sense of nationhood lay in the slogan, 'unity in diversity'. We were brought up to take pluralism for granted, and to reject the communalism that had partitioned the nation when the British left. In rejecting the case for Pakistan, Indian nationalism also rejected the very idea that religion should be a determinant of nationhood. We never fell into the insidious trap of agreeing that, since Partition had established a state for Muslims, what remained was a state for Hindus. To accept the idea of India you had to spurn the logic that had divided the country.

In some ways, this kind of Indian secularism has ancient roots in our history. Admired monarchs from Ashoka, in the third century before Christ, to Harsha, in the sixth

Emperor Akbar

century CE, gave their recognition and patronage to different religions. Ashoka's Rock Edict XII forbade people from honouring their own sects at the expense of others, and condemning the beliefs of others. Citizenship and political status in his state were never linked to one's religion. The coexistence of religions is evident from the fact that the Ellora Cave temples, some Jain, some Hindu and some Buddhist, were carved next to each other between the fifth and tenth centuries. While this traditional approach to secular or pluralist practice was not that of the Islamic kingdoms that established themselves from the twelfth century onwards, even Muslim rulers bound to uphold the less welcoming tenets of their faith had to reconcile themselves to ruling an overwhelmingly non-Muslim populace and accommodating prominent Hindus in government and the military. One monarch, the Mughal Emperor Akbar, went so far as to create his own syncretic religion, Din-e-Ilahi, to meld the best features of Islam, Hinduism and the other faiths of which he knew into a new 'national faith'. It did not outlast his reign, but the attempt was extraordinary.

The concept of sarva dharma sambhava accepting the equality of all religions was propounded by great Hindu sages like Ramakrishna and Vivekananda, as we have seen, and upheld by Mahatma Gandhi and the Indian nationalist movement. While it was an axiomatic tenet of the post-Independence India in which I grew up, sarva dharma sambhava has been increasingly rejected by some proponents of Hindutva who spurn the notion of religious universalism in favour of a more robust assertion of Hindu cultural identity and Hindus' political rights. The Hindutva ideologue David Frawley (Pandit Vamadeva Shastri), for instance, warns against sarva dharma sambhava, arguing that only Hindus are asked to practise this belief, which simply leads to confusion and 'does not convince the opponents but deludes the Hindus themselves'. Frawley asks: 'When have Christians or Muslims in India ever been criticized for violating Sarva Dharma Samabhava?... Under the guise of religious tolerance this idea of equality of religions is used to prevent scrutiny of [others'] religious dogmas'.

Yet the lived reality of Indian syncretism is difficult to deny. Hindus who made the arduous uphill trek to the cave temple of Amarnath in northern Kashmir, where an ice lingam, a naturally-formed stalactite, is worshipped, would have known that a third of their offerings went to the family of Adam Malik, a Muslim shepherd who, it was said, found the cave four centuries ago and led a Hindu sadhu to see the astonishing sight. In my novel, *Riot,* I wrote of Syed Salar Masud Ghazi, popularly known as Ghazi Miyan, a

Basilica of Our Lady of Good Health in Velankanni

Muslim warrior who is worshipped as a saint by Hindus in the Bahraich area of Uttar Pradesh. A number of Muslim religious figures such as Nizamuddin Auliya, Moinuddin Chishti, Shah Madar and Shaikh Nasiruddin (alias Chiragh-i-Dilli) are also worshipped by Hindu devotees to this day. Hindu pilgrims, after the steep climb to the shrine of Lord Ayyappa at Sabarimala, first stop at the idol-less shrine dedicated to the Lord's Muslim companion, Vavar Swami. Even the richest Hindu temple, at Tirupati, has a Muslim connection. One legend has it that Lord Balaji's second wife is Muslim, Bibi Nanchira, the daughter of a sultan who was enamoured of the Lord, much to her father's dismay, until Balaji appeared in the Sultan's dreams and informed him that He wished to marry his daughter. The Sultan, overwhelmed, acquiesced and today Balaji's second wife is said to live in the town below, at His feet, while His first wife Padmavati resides on Tirumala hill, at the temple, in His heart.

Such stories are not uncommon in India. A Muslim goddess, Bonbibi, is worshipped in idol form as the protector of the mangrove forests adjoining the Bay of Bengal. The Nawabs of Oudh celebrated the annual Ram Leela and Krishna Leela and both established and patronized the Hanuman festival in Lucknow known as Bada Mangal. In Bengal, Muslim Patua painters specialized in painting the Hindu epics on long pieces of craft paper. Hindus are regular worshippers at Christian shrines like the Basilica of Our Lady of Good Health in Velankanni or Mount Mary Church in Mumbai; and in Kerala's Ambalappuzha, an image of St Thomas used to be carried in procession to the Krishna temple on festive occasions, alongside those of Krishna and associated Hindu divinities.

Stories abound of the two communities habitually working together in pre-colonial times on issues that benefited principally one: for instance, Hindus helping Muslims to rebuild a shrine, or Muslims doing the same when a Hindu temple had to be reconstructed. Devout Hindus were sometimes given Muslim names and were often fluent scholars in Persian; Muslims served in the army of the Maratha (Hindu) warrior king Shivaji, as did Hindu Rajputs in the forces of the fiercely Islamist Aurangzeb. The Vijayanagara army included Muslim cavalry contingents. At the village level, many historians argue that Hindus and Muslims shared a wide spectrum of customs and beliefs, at times even jointly worshipping the same saint or holy spot. As I have mentioned earlier, in Kerala's famous pilgrimage site of Sabarimala, after an arduous climb to the hilltop shrine of Lord Ayyappa, the devotee first encounters a shrine to his Muslim disciple, Vavar Swami. In keeping with Muslim practice, there is no idol therein, merely a symbolic stone slab, a sword (Vavar was a warrior) and a green cloth, the colour of Islam. Muslim divines manage the shrine. (In another astonishing example, astonishing since it is both anachronistic and syncretistic, a temple in South Arcot, Tamil Nadu, hosts a deity of Muttaal Raavuttan, a Muslim chieftain—complete with beard, kumkum and toddy pot—who protects Draupadi in the Mahabharata. Note, of course, that Islam did not exist when the Mahabharata was composed, but in post-Islamic retellings, a Muslim chieftain has entered the plot!)

Indians of all religious communities had long lived intertwined lives, and even religious practices were rarely exclusionary: thus Muslim musicians played and sang Hindu devotional songs, Hindus thronged Sufi shrines and worshipped Muslim saints there, and Muslim artisans in Benares made the traditional masks for the Hindu Ram-Leela performances. Northern India celebrated what was called a 'Ganga-Jamuni tehzeeb', a syncretic culture that melded the cultural practices of both faiths. Romila Thapar has recounted how deeply devotional poetry was written by some poets who were born Muslim but worshipped Hindu deities, notably Sayyad Ibrahim, popularly known as Raskhan, whose dohas and bhajans dedicated to Lord Krishna were widely recited in the sixteenth century. The Mughal court, she points out, became the most impressive patron of the translation of many Sanskrit religious texts into Persian, including the epic Mahabharata (translated as the *Razmnamah*) and the Bhagavad Gita, with Brahmin priests collaborating on the translations with Persian scholars.

To Gyanendra Pandey, such tales, as well as parables of Hindu generals in Mughal courts, or of Hindu and Muslim ministers in the Sikh ruler Ranjit Singh's entourage, suggests there was 'fuzziness' about self-conscious identities and a lack of self-definition on the basis of religion (or even of caste), within both the Hindu and Muslim populations. These stories do not suggest mutually incompatible or hostile ideologies.

The reality of syncretism runs deep into social practice. Muslim artisans create the masks for the major Hindu festival of Dussehra in the holy city of Varanasi; the Ram Leela could not be performed without their work. Muslim Patachitra painters sing and paint pats (scrolls) about Hindu divinities. And among the most famous exponents of Hindu devotional music are the Muslim Dagar brothers—not to mention the Baul singers, a legacy of the Bhakti tradition, who sing Sufi-inspired folk songs in praise of a universal God. Muslim sociologists and anthropologists have argued that Islam in rural India is more Indian than Islamic, in the sense that the faith as practised by the ordinary Muslim villagers reflects the considerable degree of cultural assimilation that has occurred between Hindus and Muslims in their daily lives. The late Muslim reformist scholar Asghar Ali Engineer once wrote that 'rural Islam... [is] almost indistinguishable from Hinduism except in the form of worship.... The degree may vary from one area to another; but cultural integration between the Hindus and Muslims is a fact which no one, except victims of misinformation, can deny.'

One of the most striking images of India that went around the internet in recent years was a photograph of a Muslim couple on Janmashtami day setting out on their scooter, the man with a beard and skullcap, the woman in all-encompassing burqa, taking their child to act in a school performance—and this Muslim boy was dressed as Krishna, complete with kiritam, peacock feather, blue-hued skin and flute.

This is the lived 'Hinduism' that has made India what it is. India's is a civilization that, over millennia, has offered refuge and, more important, religious and cultural freedom, to Jews, Parsis, Muslims and several varieties of Christians. Christianity arrived on Indian soil, or so legend has it, with

THE HINDU WAY

St Thomas the Apostle ('Doubting Thomas'), who is said to have come to the Kerala coast some time before 52 CE and was welcomed on shore by a flute-playing Jewish girl. He made many converts, so there are Indians today whose ancestors were Christian well before any European discovered Christianity (and before the forebears of many of today's Hindu chauvinists were even conscious of themselves as Hindus). One of the oldest mosques in the world outside the Arabian peninsula is also in Kerala, in Kodungalloor. The India where the muezzin's prayer and the pujari's mantra co-exist is an India of which we can all be proud.

But as this book is about Hinduism, what sticks in my craw is the claim of the perpetrators of communal violence that they are acting in defence of my faith. Hinduism believes that there are various ways of reaching the ultimate truth. To me, the fact that adherents of this faith, in a particular perversion of its tenets, have chosen to take human life and destroy somebody else's sacred place in its name, to kill others because of the absence of a foreskin or lack of a mark on the forehead, this ultimately makes me, as a Hindu, deeply sorrowful and, in a very fundamental way, ashamed.

As I have shown throughout this book, how, after all, can such a religion lend itself to 'fundamentalism'? That devotees of this supremely tolerant faith have assaulted Muslims and Christians in its name is particularly galling. As we have seen, Hinduism has survived the Aryans, the Mughals, the British; it has taken from each—language, art, food, learning—and outlasted them all. Muslim invaders destroyed Hindu temples, putting mosques in their place, but this did not make India a Muslim land, nor did Hinduism suffer a fatal blow. Survival is the best revenge, rather than reprisal; undoing the wrongs of a different era through new wrongs in a different context only compounds the original sin ('an eye for an eye,' as Mahatma Gandhi famously said, 'makes the whole world blind'). Large, eclectic, agglomerative, the Hinduism that I know understands that faith is a matter of hearts and minds, not bricks and stone. 'Build Ram in your hearts' is what Hinduism has always enjoined: if Ram is in your heart, it would matter very little where else He is, or is not. How does it matter, then, what bricks or stones Ram can also be found in?

Living with people of various kinds of faith, Hindus developed their tradition of acceptance of difference, but also understood that in both principle and practice, religion and politics should be divorced. Our founding fathers, the majority of whom were Hindus, decided that India was not a Hindu Pakistan—and the vast majority of Indians took pride in that assertion. Where Pakistan reserved its top constitutional positions only for Muslims, and stamped 'non-Muslim' on the passports of its minority citizens in confirmation of their second-class status, Indians revelled in the prominence enjoyed by its various minorities in public life. Neither politics nor governance—and certainly not culture, sport or entertainment—was based on religious principles, and success in no field required a litmus test of faith.

Throughout the decades after Independence, the political culture of the country reflected these 'secular' assumptions and attitudes. Though the Indian population was 80 per cent Hindu and the country had been partitioned as a result of a demand for a separate Muslim homeland, three of India's eleven presidents were Muslims; so were innumerable governors, cabinet ministers, chief ministers of states, ambassadors, generals, and Supreme Court justices. During the war with Pakistan in 1971, when the Pakistani leadership was foolish enough to proclaim a jihad against the Hindu unbelievers, the Indian Air Force in the northern sector was commanded by a Muslim (Air Marshal, later Air

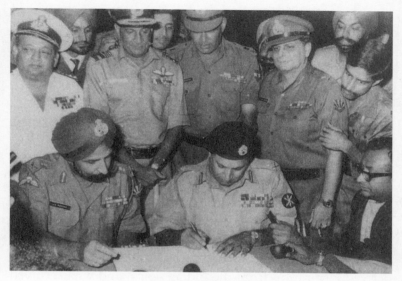

*Lt Gen Niazi signing the Instrument of
Surrender under the gaze of Lt Gen Aurora*

Chief Marshal, I. H. Latif); the army commander was a
Parsi (General, later Field Marshal, S. H. F. J. Manekshaw),
the general officer commanding the forces that marched
into Bangladesh was a Sikh (General J. S. Aurora), and the
general flown in to negotiate the surrender of the Pakistani
forces in East Bengal was Jewish (Major-General J. F. R.
Jacob). They led the armed forces of an overwhelmingly
Hindu country.

That is 'Hindu India'.

So the idea of India is of one land embracing many. As I
have written before, it is the idea that a nation may endure
differences of caste, creed, colour, culture, cuisine, conviction,
costume and custom, and still rally around a consensus. That
consensus is around the simple principle that in a diverse
democracy you don't really need to agree—except on the
ground rules of how you will disagree. The reason India
has survived all the stresses and strains that have beset it

for over seventy years, and that led so many to predict its imminent disintegration, is that it maintained consensus on how to manage without consensus.

Nationalism is by definition indivisible, whereas religion and culture take on multiple manifestations. Culture, of course, contributes to national identity; yet culture alone cannot mould the nationalism of a country, leave alone that of a plural land like India. In India during colonial rule, the reassertion of Hindu culture was a nationalist project, which witnessed the revival of dance forms like Bharata Natyam and traditional classical music as well as modern literature in Indian languages, modern art (from Raja Ravi Varma who borrowed Western styles for Indian subjects, to the Bengal School and painters like M. F. Husain who derived inspiration from the Indian epics) and what evolved into the gaudy cinema of Bollywood.

One of the amusing, but nonetheless important, sidelights of the development of Hindutva theory has been the controversy about the origins of the Aryans. The Hindutva approach inevitably had implications for the commonly accepted narratives about India, including the idea that the Indo-Aryan people had migrated to northern India from the Central Asian steppes some time before 1500 BCE and authored the foundational texts of Hinduism, the Vedas. The RSS ideologue M. S. Golwalkar believed that was impossible; Hinduism, he was convinced, was an indigenous faith that sprang up on Indian soil, and so the Indo-Aryans could not possibly have come from elsewhere. His and V. D.] Savarkar's idea of India being the punyabhumi of the Hindus required the Aryans to be indigenous to India, in contrast to India's Muslims, whose faith clearly originated in the Arabian peninsula. A veritable cottage industry was born of RSS-inclined historians debunking the Aryan migration theory, insisting that the Aryans, as the founders of Hinduism, belonged all along to India.

Some less-ideological scholars point out that the *Rig Veda* does not speak of any other land but northern India or Aryavarta. In her *Sacred Plants of India,* Dr Nanditha Krishna shows how every plant and animal mentioned in the *Rig Veda* originates from this area. This leads some to the conclusion that the Aryans could not have come from anywhere else. But the same textual and vegetal evidence could also suggest that while the Aryans came from elsewhere, they only composed the Vedas after having created a settled civilization in the Indo-Gangetic plains, which is why their allusions are all to India.

Unfortunately for the Hindutva ideologues, who seemed to be winning the historical battle, recent genetic research—published in a paper (in a peer-reviewed journal called *BMC Evolutionary Biology*) by Prof Martin P. Richards and fifteen other scientists, titled 'A Genetic Chronology for the Indian Subcontinent Points to Heavily Sex-biased Dispersals'—has confirmed that there were indeed significant migrations from the Central Asian steppes into the Indian subcontinent, starting from around 2000–1500 BCE. DNA studies show that the Indo-Aryan ethno-linguistic group has a higher signature of Central Asian genes than the corresponding Dravidian speakers; and given that Indo-Aryan languages have close affinities with the larger Indo-European linguistic family, it appears beyond dispute that a common proto-language was involved. The implications for the Savarkar-Golwalkar theory, though, are subversive, since they suggest that Hinduism or the Vedic religion may itself have originated with invaders from outside India, making it as 'un-Indian' in its origins as Islam or Christianity. The conclusions are sufficiently tentative to fall short of conclusive; one critical analysis concludes that 'it is difficult to deduce the direction of haplogroup R1a migration either into India or out of

The Vaikuntha Perumal Temple in Kanchipuram

India, although the genetic data certainly show that there was migration between the regions'. The Hindutvavadis continue to insist the Indo-Aryans and their faith are indigenous to India, but DNA evidence may prove impossible to refute. Much of the dispute seems to centre not around whether there were infusions from abroad but as to whether they occurred 12,000 years ago or 4,000–3,500 years ago. If the first hypothesis is right, the resulting population was indigenous well before they composed the Vedas; the latter suggests a shorter gap between their arrival in India and the emergence of Hinduism.

To me this seems a distinction without a difference, but then I am much more comfortable with the idea that migrations into the subcontinent have been a permanent feature of Indian history than the Hindutva brigade is. In fact the Hindu Pallava kingdom even imported a monarch from Southeast Asia, when King Parameshwaravarman died without an heir in c. 731 CE. A Pallava princess had been given in marriage to the Cham dynasty generations earlier and it was presumed one of her descendants could carry on the royal lineage. Accordingly, a delegation of nobles was sent to the Cambodia–Vietnam region and returned with a fourteen-year-old boy, who ruled for sixty-four years as King Nandivarman II (reigned c. 731–795 CE) and built a number of magnificent temples, including the famous Vaikuntha Perumal in Kanchipuram. Hinduism has been strengthened by its imports too.

❀

HINDUISM AND THE BATTLES OVER CULTURE

In recent years Hindu culture has become contested terrain, with attacks on the artist M. F. Husain on the grounds that he had insulted Hinduism by depicting goddesses in the nude, assaults on film-makers portraying 'Hindu heroines', and the banning of books that some Hindu activists claimed offended them. Ironically such actions rested upon contestable interpretations of Hinduism itself—and have been conducted in the name of a faith which proudly includes no concept of heresy. Thus Hindutva mobs attacked and vandalized the invaluable Bhandarkar Oriental Research Institute's library in Pune to protest its co-operation with the research work of the historian James Laine, whose book allegedly cast aspersions on the parentage of the Hindu warrior hero Shivaji. The courts offer a less dramatic form of censorship, since Hindutva activists can invoke Section 295(a) of the Indian Penal Code, which criminalizes insults to religious sentiments, though the intent was only to outlaw inflammatory writings published with deliberate and malicious intent. Under this provision, serious scholars like Wendy Doniger, who has authored several learned and brilliant studies of Hinduism, have been sued, and publishers, intimidated by the forces arrayed against them and reluctant to spend what it would take to defend their authors' freedoms, have usually caved in. One of Doniger's books on Hinduism was not only withdrawn from the marketplace by its publishers, but all existing copies pulped in order not to give offence to the Hindutvavadis.

The destruction and pulping of books, and the burning of libraries, is possible because the colonial-era law criminalizes even accurate statements about Indian religion and history if these statements offend the sentiments of any community in India. Still, to see such actions being carried out in the name of the Hindu faith is profoundly disquieting. In the Hindu culture that I grew up with, books are revered. If I so much as accidentally touched a fallen book or even a magazine or newspaper with my foot, I was brought up to bend down, touch it again with my fingertips in apology and apply my fingers to my eyes and forehead to beg forgiveness from the Goddess Saraswati for my transgression, a practice I still perform in my seventh decade. This respect for the printed word can be found among Hindus of every part of the country. How can people who claim to be Hindu not just disrespect but actually destroy books?

It is time all Indians, but especially Hindus, woke up to what is being done to our heritage in our name. To reduce the soaring majesty of an inclusive, free-ranging, eclectic and humane faith to the petit-bourgeois morality of narrow-minded bigots is a far greater betrayal of our culture than anything an artist can paint.

For where, in the Hindutva brigade's definition of 'Bharatiya sanskriti', do the erotic sculptures of Khajuraho belong? Should their explicitly detailed couplings not be pulled down, as Fashion TV's cable signals were during the last BJP government? What about the *Kama Sutra*, the tradition of the devadasis, the eros of the Krishna Leela—are they all un-Indian now?

When the late, great Nobel Prize-winning Mexican poet Octavio Paz wrote his final ode to our civilization, *In Light of India*, he devoted an entire section to Sanskrit erotic poetry, basing himself, among other things, on the Buddhist monk Vidyakara's immortal eleventh-century compilation of 1,728 kavya, many of which are exquisitely profane. Are poets like Ladahachandra or Bhavakadevi, who a thousand years ago wrote verse after verse describing and praising the female breast, to be expelled from the Hindutva canon of 'Bharatiya sanskriti'? Should we tell future Octavio Pazes seeking to appreciate the attainments of our culture that the Mahabharata on TV is 'Bharatiya sanskriti', but a classical portrayal of the erotic longings of the gopis for Krishna is not?

That Mahabharata on TV, which broke a viewership record set by its predecessor Ramayana on TV, has much to answer for. It would be unwise to underestimate the significant role of Ramananda Sagar's *Ramayana* serial on Doordarshan in promoting Hindutva revival through a cardboard depiction of Rama as a Bollywood B-film hero, complete with crude special effects, melodramatic dialogue and theatrical acting. Encouraged by its success, B. R. Chopra offered similar treatment to the Mahabharata; both epics became the most widely-watched shows on television, attracting some 92 per cent of all television viewers to their weekly telecasts. A nation glued to its television sets in an era where there was only one channel, the public broadcaster Doordarshan, found itself alternately unified and exalted by seeing its collective national myths rendered simply and accessibly on the small screen. One of the many ironies of contemporary India is how a secular government and a materialistic Bollywood combined to produce the religious underpinnings for the rise of Hindu cultural nationalism in India.

(This has actually continued into the present day. There has been a proliferation of television channels, but several show hugely popular 'serials', the Indian version of soap operas, which embody and propagate conservative 'Hindu' values. Many Bollywood superstars are themselves Muslim, including five who sport the surname Khan, and they have all portrayed devout Hindu heroes and danced to devotional songs before Hindu idols. The portrayal of sympathetic Muslim characters in popular cinema, like the brave and patriotic Pathan in *Zanjeer* (1972) or the lovable Akbar in *Amar Akbar Anthony* (1977) has declined, subliminally reinforcing the notion of India as a land of Hindu ethos rather than pluralist culture.)

Hindutva hypocrisy is also much in evidence on the subject of alcohol, deemed to be un-Hindu and officially banned in the prime minister's own home state of Gujarat (though, reportedly, widely available, at a price, under the table). Wide and frequent are the calls for Prohibition, and rare indeed the figure in Indian public life who would be willing to be photographed with a drink in his hand. And yet alcohol has a hoary history in Hindu literature. Soma, or Som-Ras, was the favourite beverage of the Vedic deities and was offered in most of the sacrifices performed in honour of Rig Vedic gods like Indra, Agni, Varun, and others. The Vedic gods were no teetotallers, and drinking was an essential feature of these sacrifices: for instance, in one ritual (performed at the beginning of the Vajapeya sacrifice), the historian D. N. Jha describes a collective drinking ritual in which a sacrificer offered five cups to Indra as well as seventeen cups of soma and seventeen cups of sura to thirty-four gods. A large variety of some fifty intoxicating drinks are mentioned in ancient Hindu texts. Jha tells us that the use of alcohol by men was quite common, though sometimes discouraged among Brahmins, and instances of drinking among women were not rare. Sanskrit literature, including the plays of Kalidasa, and Buddhist Jataka texts, frequently mention alcoholic drinks. Ancient Hindus were far less puritanical than those who claim to be custodians of their legacy today. The prohibitionist instincts of the Hindutva revivalists find their sternest rebuke in the divine hedonism of their most ancient gods.

But the disapproval of alcohol as a sinful Western indulgence is of a piece with the assault on any cultural practice deemed to be insufficiently Hindu by the self-appointed guardians of Bharatiya sanskriti or Indian culture. After years of attacking couples holding hands on 14 February, trashing stores selling Valentine's Day greeting cards and shouting slogans outside cafes with canoodling couples, Hindutva activists changed tactics recently. The Hindu Mahasabha has announced that it would send squads out to catch any unmarried couples out for a tryst on Valentine's Day and promptly cart them off to a temple to be married. (And, if the Hindutvavadi MP and Godse admirer Sakshi Maharaj has his way, they will be lectured on the virtues of producing between four and ten children forthwith, in order to give his fantasies a voting majority.)

The changing face of intolerance might be amusing if it weren't for the fact that all involved are deadly serious. The nativists argue that Valentine's Day is an imported celebration, which it is (but so is Christmas, or Id-ul-Nabi, or International Women's Day, for that matter, and they don't have the nerve to attack those). They also argue that it is un-Indian because it celebrates romantic love, and there they're completely wrong. In fact historians tell us that in ancient times, there was a well-established Hindu tradition of adoration for Kamadeva, the lord of love, which was

Temple sculpture in Khajuraho

only abandoned after the Muslim invasions in medieval times. But then no one in the Hindu Mahasabha has any real idea of Hindu tradition—their idea of Indian values is not just primitive and narrow-minded, it is also profoundly anti-historical.

In fact what young people today call 'PDA' or 'public display of affection' was widely prevalent in ancient India. As late as the eleventh century, Hindu sexual freedoms were commented upon by shocked travellers from the Muslim world. Today's young celebrants of Valentine's Day are actually upholding India's ancient pre-Muslim culture, albeit in a much milder form than is on display, for instance, in Khajuraho. How ironic that they should incur the disapproval of the self-appointed custodians of Hindu culture!

So young Hindus in the mood for love steered clear of the officious busybodies of the Hindutva brigades, though the police made no effort to stop the thugs when they intruded on a young Valentine's Day couple (and the Uttar Pradesh government headed by the mahant Yogi Adityanath even authorized 'anti-Romeo squads' to curb young lovers). Would it have been better if the BJP government, with its fondness for rebaptizing government schemes with new Sanskrit appellations, gave serious thought to just calling Valentine's Day *Kamadeva Divas*, to link it to ancient Hindu culture? The Hindutvavadis might find it more difficult to object.

But it's in the 'self-appointed' part that the real problem lies. All this is being done in the name of a notion of Indian culture whose assertion is based on a denial of our real past. India's culture has always been a capacious one, expanding to include new and varied influences, from the Greek invasions to the British. The central battle in contemporary Indian civilization is that between those who, to borrow from Walt Whitman, acknowledge that as a result of our own historical experience, we are vast, we contain multitudes, and those who have presumptuously taken it upon themselves to define—in increasingly narrower terms—what is 'truly' Indian.

It may not seem to matter very much what some lumpen elements think of a Bollywood film, or of Valentine's Day, for that matter. But it is precisely this kind of narrow-mindedness that also led to the notorious 'pulping' of Wendy Doniger's erudite study of Hinduism. If these intolerant bullies are allowed to get away with their lawless acts of intolerance and intimidation, we are allowing them to do violence to something profoundly vital to our survival as a civilization.

Pluralist and democratic India must, by definition, tolerate plural expressions of its many identities. To allow the self-appointed arbiters of Bharatiya sanskriti to impose their hypocrisy and double standards on the rest of us is to permit them to define Indianness down until it ceases to be Indian.

But I am not optimistic about the prospects for any

such development. My late father, Chandran Tharoor, used to tell me more than five decades ago that India is not just the world's largest democracy, it is also the world's largest hypocrisy. The wisdom and accuracy of his perception was again on display when my two attempts to introduce a Private Member's Bill to amend Section 377 of the Indian Penal Code (which criminalizes homosexuality) were comprehensively defeated in the Lok Sabha by homophobic bigotry in the name of Hindutva.

Here was the spectacle of a parliamentary democracy refusing to entertain debate—the ruling party using its brute majority to defeat a motion without even a discussion. How can a deliberative legislature in what claims to be the temple of democracy dismiss an issue out of hand without even hearing the arguments in its favour or against it?

And to add to the hypocrisy, nowhere in over two thousand years of recorded Hindu texts is there any evidence that the Indian ethos was intolerant of sexual difference or gender orientation. Ours is a culture that embraces Shikhandi in the Mahabharata, the homoerotic sculptures (mixed in with the rest) in Khajuraho, and the very concept of the Ardhanarishwara, the half-man half-woman embodiment of divinity. No historical records reveal the persecution or prosecution of sexual deviancy in India. Now we have the spectacle of the party of Hindutva, the self-appointed guardians of Bharatiya Sanskriti, betraying a Hindu history of tolerance in order to uphold (without debate) an iniquitous law from the British colonial era. It is a new low in the annals of Indian democracy and a triumph for Indian hypocrisy.

In proposing to amend Section 377, I had explained that we shouldn't have a law on the books that can be used to oppress and harass innocent people conducting their personal lives in private. What two people do to express their love and desire for each other should be strictly between them.

The government has no place in India's bedrooms.

But equally important, I had tried to explain (though alas, I was not allowed to do so in Parliament) that my Bill was not about sex but about freedom. Section 377 violates the constitutional rights of dignity, privacy, equality and non-discrimination (Articles 14, 15 and 21) guaranteed to all Indian citizens. It is a British relic, drafted in 1860 and based on outdated Victorian morals rather than authentically Indian values. It has no place in twenty-first century India.

To add to the ironies, within half an hour of the defeat of my amendment, I was rising in the same Lok Sabha to speak in favour of the Rights of Transgender Persons Bill, which had already been passed earlier in the Rajya Sabha. The passage of this progressive bill would have the indirect effect of nullifying the application of Section 377 to transgenders, while leaving it on the books to be used to harass and oppress homosexuals and straight people. How's that for both democracy and hypocrisy taken to their extreme?

Ironically, the problem was not solved by Hindu-majority public opinion but by the one source of hope that remained for a progressive outcome in keeping with the long-established Hindu tradition—a secular institution, the judiciary. The Supreme Court struck down Section 377 in September 2018 on legal rather than scriptural grounds; but it is ironic that where a Hindutva-inclined majority renders our elected legislature a bastion of illiberalism, it is the unelected judiciary that remains the last repository of hope for the timeless values of our civilization.

❦

Indian politics, in all its manifestations, continues to both amaze and appal. The latest example of both lies in a uniquely Indian phenomenon, one which has begun to flourish under the current government—cow vigilantism.

Many orthodox Hindus, particularly in the northern Indian states irreverently dubbed 'the cow belt', not only do not eat beef, but worship the cow as Gaumata, the mother of all, a provider of nourishment and sustenance. Several Indian states have passed laws outlawing cow slaughter; some go farther and neither permit the possession nor the consumption of beef. These are, for the most part, barely enforced; the police have better things to do than to check people's kitchens.

But following the BJP's victory in the 2014 and 2019 elections, a wave of Hindu triumphalism has swept the land. In its wake have come new laws to protect cows and vociferous demands for their strict enforcement. Gaurakshak or cow protection societies have been revived, and many have taken it upon themselves to compel compliance. In the process, not only have they taken the law into their own hands, but they have perpetrated grave crimes, including murder, in the name of the cow. For example, seventy cases of cow-related violence were reported in an eight-year period from 2010 to 2017, of which 97 per cent (68 out of 70) occurred during the first three years of BJP rule and a majority of these occurred in BJP-ruled states. 136 people were injured in these attacks and 28 killed: 86 per cent of the victims were, of course, Muslim. The trend continues unabated.

Muslims have not been the only targets of the cow vigilantes. In addition, the lynch-mobs have linked their cause to another staple of Indian society—violence against Dalits. Many Dalits still make a living performing tasks that other Hindus are unwilling to take on. Upper-caste Hindus may worship the cow, but cows, alas, are not immortal, and when they die (ideally of natural causes), their carcasses need to be disposed of. This task has traditionally been left to Dalits, who for centuries and more have skinned the animal to sell its hide to tanners and leather-makers, disposed of its meat to Muslim butchers in the few states where it is legal, and buried or cremated the rest. It is a distasteful task to many caste Hindus, and most are happy to let willing Dalits do it. In turn, dead cows have become a source of livelihood for many Dalits and Muslims.

But several recent incidents have shaken the foundations of this arrangement. Four Dalit youths caught skinning a cow were stripped, tied and beaten with iron rods in the state of Gujarat by cow vigilantes who accused them of killing the animal (they had not). Two Dalit women were assaulted in BJP-ruled Madhya Pradesh for carrying cow meat (which turned out, upon inspection, to be buffalo meat and therefore not illegal).

Such incidents have heightened the sense of vulnerability felt by many who do not necessarily share the reverence the vigilantes feel for cows. Yet, for the first time, India has a central government that refuses to disapprove of cow vigilantism. The Minister for Social Justice in the first Modi government, whose principal responsibility is to promote the welfare of India's Dalits, regretted not the vigilantes' violence but the fact that they had perpetrated it on the basis of ill-founded rumours. In other words, their mission was so transcendently just that their misbehaviour could be condoned if their targets really had killed or eaten a cow.

The atmosphere of cow fundamentalism enforced by the vigilantes has caused immense economic complications. Many farmers look after their cows with respect, but once they are too old to produce milk, they find it unaffordable

*Matsya (the fish avatar of Vishnu) saves
the saptarishi (seven sages) and Manu*

to maintain them and quietly sell their cows to butchers
(or to those who could transport them across state lines to
states where cows could legally be slaughtered). With this
option now foreclosed in the present climate, many farmers
are being driven into debt by the expense of maintaining
unproductive and uneconomic cattle. Several, unable to
tend them or to sell them, simply let them loose. And the
country's population of stray cows is proving increasingly
unsustainable.

It is not a coincidence that 63 per cent of atrocities
against Dalits because of cow vigilantism occur in just
four states—U.P., Bihar, M.P. and Rajasthan, in order of
magnitude. The rise of Hindu chauvinism, unchecked by
government, has given rein to assorted petty bigotries.

Goddess Saraswati appears before Sage
Yajnavalkya

There are signs of an incipient Dalit backlash against the injustice of being obliged to do unpleasant work to make a living and then being assaulted for doing it. After the Gujarat incident one group of Dalits in the state has flatly refused to continue with its traditional profession of disposing of dead cows. 'If the cow is your mother,' they asked upper-caste Hindus, 'why don't you bury her?'

The irony is that, as a commentator on the Dharmashastras points out, though the cow was sacred in Vedic times, it was this that allowed for beef to be consumed. There are references in the Rig Veda, in the Dharmashastric literature, the *Taittiriya Brahmana* ('Verily, the cow is food') and the *Vajasaneyi Samhita* that support the contention of beef being eaten at the time. The historian D. N. Jha has pointed out dozens of examples to prove that the *Rig Veda* is full of allusions to the slaughter and consumption of cows. Ancient lawgivers, Manu included, appear to grant sanction for the slaughter and consumption of cow meat. The great sage and law-giver Yajnavalkya is quoted as saying, on the subject of whether beef should be eaten: 'I, for one, eat it, provided that it is tender'.

Ambedkar theorized that the worship of the cow emerged from the struggle between Buddhism and Brahmanism; by making the cow a sacred animal and beef-eating a sacrilege, he argued, Brahmanism sought to establish its supremacy over Buddhism. Be that as it may, the ruling dispensation's relentless drive to promote its ideology of Hindutva has latched on to the cow as its current instrument of choice. Cow protection has become the façade for a broader agenda, and is being resisted precisely for that reason.

There is no doubt about the veneration of the cow across India, and the respect for it as a source of milk and nourishment for all and, after its death, of meat and nourishment for some. Calls during the Constituent Assembly deliberations to ban cow slaughter, opposed by a vocal minority, were finally reduced to a 'directive principle' anchored in economics and not religion: Article 48 of the Constitution says that 'the State shall endeavour to organise agriculture and animal husbandry on modern and scientific lines and shall, in particular, take steps for preserving and improving the breeds, and prohibiting the slaughter, of cows and calves and other milch and draught cattle.' So this 'endeavour' (stopping well short of a ban) was related specifically to the needs of agriculture and animal husbandry, not of worship.

Mahatma Gandhi himself said that though he did not eat meat and was personally opposed to cow slaughter, in a multi-religious country like India he could not justify imposing his Hindu views on the many who did not share his faith. Many Hindus feel the same way; I am vegetarian myself, and abhor the idea of consuming the corpses of animals, but I do not judge those who, for cultural or other personal reasons, do so. I only ask that animals be treated decently and without cruelty, and that even their slaughter, for purposes of consumption, be conducted humanely and with minimal pain and suffering for the poor creatures.

For most of India's existence, the default approach has essentially been 'live and let live'—make your own choice about beef, and let others do the same. Like many Hindus, I have never considered it my business what others eat. Indians have generally felt free to be themselves, within our dynamic and diverse society. It is that freedom that the BJP's followers are challenging today.

The Hindutvavadis, emboldened by the BJP's absolute majority, seek to impose their particular view of what India should be, regardless of whom it hurts. This is why the reaction has been so visceral, even from non-beef eaters like myself. Our resistance is to the way India is being changed into something it never was—an intolerant majoritarian society.

❈

THE QUESTION OF CONVERSION

A final issue that has erupted in the past, has been simmering for a while and is waiting to explode is the issue of conversions of Hindus to other faiths, notably Islam and Christianity. In the case of Islam, the issue has been complicated by allegations of 'love jihad', the alleged entrapment of unwary Hindu girls by Muslim men with the sole intent of conversion to their faith. In the case of

Christianity, the existence of missionary societies with an avowed intent of harvesting souls for the Lord has created suspicion among Hindu groups. Some states have already outlawed conversions without the specific permission of the government; the use of inducements or threats to convert is already illegal across much of the country.

Hindu leaders known for their liberality have tended to be less accommodative on the question of conversions. Swami Vivekananda memorably told his American listeners a century and a quarter ago: 'Christian brethren of America, you are so fond of sending out missionaries to save the souls of heathens. I ask you: what have you done and are doing to save their bodies from starvation? In India, there are 300 million men and women living on an average of a little more than 50 cents a month. I have seen them living for years upon wild flowers. During the terrible famines, thousands died from hunger but the missionaries did nothing. They come and offer life but only on condition that the Hindus become Christians, abandoning the faith of their fathers and forefathers. Is it right? There are hundreds of asylums, but if the Muslims or the Hindus go there, they are kicked out. There are thousands of asylums erected by Hindus where anybody is received. There are hundreds of churches that have been erected with the assistance of the Hindus, but no Hindu temples for which a Christian has given a penny.'

To Vivekananda, it was a case of misplaced priorities. 'Brethren of America, you erect churches all through India, but the crying evil in the East is not religion', he declared. 'They have religion enough, but it is bread that the suffering millions of burning India cry out for with parched throats. What they want is bread, but they are given a stone. It is an insult to a starving people to offer them religion; it is an insult to a starving man to teach him metaphysics. Therefore, if you wish to illustrate the meaning of "brotherhood", treat the Hindus more kindly, even though they are Hindus and are faithful to their religion. Send missionaries to them to teach them how better to earn a piece of bread and not to teach them metaphysical nonsense.'

And he recalled the non-proselytizing instincts of his own faith: 'Do I wish that the Christian would become Hindu? God forbid. Do I wish that the Hindu or Buddhist would become Christian? God forbid... The Christian is not to become a Hindu or a Buddhist, nor a Hindu or a Buddhist to become a Christian. But each must assimilate the spirit of the others and yet preserve their individuality and grow according to their own law of growth.'

Similarly, Mahatma Gandhi considered religious conversion harmful. He wrote, 'If I had power and could legislate, I should certainly stop all proselytizing... In Hindu households the advent of a missionary has meant the disruption of the family coming in the wake of change of dress, manners, language, food and drink.'

At the same time, Hindus like myself accept that every individual's spiritual needs are different, and if some wish to find salvation through another faith, that is surely their prerogative. Certainly, episodes of anti-missionary violence in Odisha and Gujarat some years ago do not speak well of those who perpetrate it: a self-confident faith like Hinduism, secure in its own broad-minded liberality, has no need of goonda violence in its defence. When, at the time of such violence, specifically the brutal murder in 1999 of Australian missionary Graham Staines, and his two sons in Odisha, I wrote a column passionately denouncing it, I was gratified by the large number of readers (including several describing themselves as believing Hindus) who were as outraged as I was at the anti-Christian thuggery that had been perpetrated in the name of Hinduism. Killers of children have no right to claim the mantle of Hinduism, even if they insist they are acting on behalf of their faith; it is as simple as that. Murder does not have a religion—even when it claims a religious excuse.

Of course, it is easy enough to condemn anti-Christian violence because it *is* violence, and because it represents a threat to law and order as well as to that nebulous idea we call India's 'image'. But an argument that several readers made needs to be faced squarely. In the words of one correspondent: could the violence 'be a reaction to provocations from those religions that believe that only their path is the right path and the rest of humanity are infidels?' He went on to critique 'the aggressive strategy being pursued by some interests in the US to get people in India converted en masse to Christianity, not necessarily by fair means.' In his view, 'aggressive evangelism directed against India by powerful church organizations in America enjoying enormous money power, has only one focused objective—to get India into the Christian fold, as they have succeeded, to a considerable extent, in South Korea and are now in the process of conquering Mongolia.' Arguing that 'mass conversions of illiterates and semi-literates—and they also happen to be poor, extremely poor' is exploitative, he concluded: 'powerful organizations from abroad with enormous money power indulging in mass conversion' are 'a destabilizing factor provoking retaliation'.

Such concerns, which are widely shared, including by people in responsible positions in government, must be heeded; but at the same time I cannot accept any justification for the thugs' actions, nor am I prepared to see behind the violence an 'understandable' Hindu resistance to Christian zealotry. Put simply, no non-violent activity, however provocative, can ever legitimize violence. We must reject and denounce assaults and killings, whatever they may claim to be reacting to. Our democracy will not long survive if we condone people resorting to violence in pursuit of their ends, however genuine and heartfelt their grievances may be. The whole point about our system of governance is that it allows all Indians to resolve their concerns through legitimate means, including seeking legal redress or political change—but not violence.

Staines himself had devoted his life to the care of leprosy patients; his widow continued this work after his murder, and was awarded a Padma Shri, a major national honour, by the UPA government of the time. But let us assume, for the purposes of argument, that Christian missionaries are indeed using a variety of inducements (development assistance, healthcare, education, sanitation, even chicanery—though there is only anecdotal evidence of missionary 'trickery') to win converts for their faith. So what? If a citizen of India feels that his faith has not helped him to find peace of mind and material fulfilment, why should he not have the option of trying a different item on the spiritual menu? Surely freedom of belief is any Indian's fundamental right under our democratic constitution, however ill-founded his belief might be. And if Hindu zealots suspect that his conversion was fraudulently obtained, why do they not offer counter-inducements rather than violence? Instead of destroying churches, perhaps a Hindu-financed sewage system or pathshala might reopen the blinkered eyes of the credulous.

Freedom of conscience is not a negotiable right. An India where an individual is not free to change his or her faith would be inconceivable. Some have been citing Gandhiji's criticism of conversions, but his view was based on an eclectic, all-embracing view of religiousness that is a far cry from the narrow bigotry of those who today quote him in opposing conversions. Gandhiji's point was that there was no need to convert from any religion to any other because all religions essentially believed the same thing.

The fact is that many faiths do tend to see theirs as the only true path to salvation, and their religious leaders feel a duty to spread the light of a supposedly superior understanding of God to those less fortunate. As Gandhians or as rationalists we are free to decry their views, but the Indian Constitution gives each Indian the right to 'propagate' his religion—and to challenge that right would, in the most fundamental sense, be unconstitutional.

So let each religion do its thing, and let each Indian be free to choose. At the same time, let conversion be an issue of individual conscience and not mass delusion. I would have no difficulty in considering, in principle, the idea of a democratically-elected legislature deciding that the constitutionally-protected right to convert to another faith can only be exercised by an individual, rather than by an entire clan, tribe or village. An end to ceremonies of mass conversion (often suspected to be achieved by inducements) might not be a bad thing: let each individual who believes he or she has seen the light go through an individual act of conversion—one in which he or she must affirm that they know what they are giving up and what they are entering into.

Of course, the debate is not merely a religious one—it is profoundly political. The devotees of Hindutva let me know in no uncertain terms what they thought of me when I expressed such views in three columns in the *Times of India* in September and October 2008. But I reject their presumption that they speak for all or even most Hindus. Hinduism, we are repeatedly told, is a tolerant faith. The central tenet of tolerance is that the tolerant society accepts that which it does not understand and even that which it does not like, so long as it is not sought to be imposed upon the unwilling. Of course, it is true that, while Hinduism as

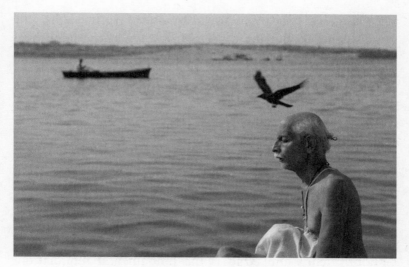

A devotee meditating near the Ganga in Varanasi

a faith might privilege tolerance, this does not necessarily mean that all Hindus behave tolerantly. But one cannot simultaneously extol the tolerance of Hinduism and attack Christian homes and places of worship.

In one of those columns I argued that the premise behind much of the criticism of conversions is troubling because it seems to accord legitimacy to the argument that conversions are inherently anti-national. I made the point that India is founded on the rejection of the very idea that religion should be a determinant of nationhood, and cautioned that the distinction between Hindu nationalism and Indian nationalism could be all too easily blurred. Your Indianness has nothing to do with which God you choose to worship, or not.

In any case, as we have discussed, Hinduism teaches: ekam sat vipra bahudha vadanti. Why, then, are any of my co-religionists unhappy about some tribal Hindus becoming Christian? If a Hindu decides he wishes to be a Christian, how does it matter that he has found a different way of stretching his hands out towards God? Truth is one, the Hindu believes; but there are many ways of attaining it.

As we have seen, Hinduism has never claimed a monopoly on spiritual wisdom; that is what has made it so attractive to seekers from around the world. Its eclecticism is its strength. So the rejection of other forms of worship, other ways of seeking the Truth, is profoundly un-Hindu, as well as being un-Indian. Worse, the version of Indianness propagated by the opponents of conversion—the presumption that to be Hindu is more authentically Indian, and that to lapse from Hinduism is to dilute one's identification with the motherland—resembles nothing so much as the arguments for the creation of Pakistan, of which the nationalism of Gandhi, Nehru and Azad is the fundamental repudiation. In many Muslim countries it is illegal for a Muslim to convert to any other faith; in some, such apostasy is even punishable by death. India has no room for such practices. There is no such thing as a Hindu heresy. Yet, ironically, it is the most chauvinist of the Hindutva brigade who want to emulate this Muslim convention.

The Hindutvavadis are therefore being untrue both to Hinduism and to Indian nationalism. The nationalist movement rejected the belief that religion was the most important element in shaping political identity. In India, our system recognizes the diversity of our people and guarantees that religious affiliation will be neither a handicap nor an advantage. By challenging that right, the advocates of Hindutva are undermining the very basis for Indian citizenship and the constitutional basis of the Indian state.

To say that conversions are somehow inherently wrong would accord legitimacy to the rhetoric of the Bajrang Dal and its cohorts—who declare openly that conversions from Hinduism to any other faith are anti-national. Implicit is the idea that to be Hindu is somehow more natural, more authentically Indian, than to be anything else, and that to lapse from Hinduism is to dilute one's identification with the motherland.

As a Hindu, I reject that notion utterly. To suggest that an Indian Hindu becoming Christian is an anti-national act not only insults the millions of patriotic Indians who trace their Christianity to more distant forebears, including the Kerala Christians whose families converted to the faith of Saint Thomas centuries before the ancestors of many of today's Hindu chauvinists even learned to think of themselves as Hindu. It is an insult, too, to the national leaders, freedom fighters, educationists, scientists, military men, journalists and sportsmen of the Christian faith who have brought so much glory to the country through their actions and sacrifices. It is, indeed, an insult to the very idea of India. Nothing could be more anti-national than that.

One reader, Raju Rajagopal, writing 'as a fellow Hindu', expressed himself trenchantly in describing 'terrorism' and 'communal riots' as 'two sides of the same coin, which systematically feed on each other.' The only difference, he added, is 'that the first kind of terrorism is being unleashed by a fanatical few who swear no allegiance to the idea of India, whereas the second kind of terror is being unleashed by those who claim to love India more dearly than you and I, who are part of the electoral politics of India, and who know the exact consequences of their actions: creating deep fissures between communities, whose horrific consequences the world has witnessed once too often in recent decades.'

That is the real problem here. Nehru had warned that the communalism of the majority was especially dangerous because it could present itself as nationalist. Yet Hindu nationalism is not Indian nationalism. And it has nothing to do with genuine Hinduism either. A reader bearing a Christian name wrote to tell me that when his brother was getting married to a Hindu girl, the Hindu priest made a point of saying to him before the ceremony words to the effect of: 'When I say god, I don't mean a particular god.' As this reader commented: 'It's at moments like that that I can't help but feel proud to be Indian and to be moved by its religiosity—even though I'm an atheist.'

The real alternatives in our country are between those who believe in an India where differences arising from your birth, language, social status, mode of worship or dietary preferences shouldn't determine your Indianness, and those who define Indianness along one or more of these divisions. In other words the really important debate is not about conversions, but between the unifiers and the dividers— between those who think all Indians are 'us', whichever God they choose to worship, and those who think that Indians can be divided into 'us' and 'them'.

It is time for all Hindus to say: stop the politics of division. We are *all* Indians.

A FAITH FOR THE TWENTY-FIRST CENTURY

If Hindutva is resisted by the vast majority of liberal Hindus, it is hardly paradoxical to suggest that Hinduism, India's ancient homegrown faith, can help strengthen Indianness in ways that the proponents of Hindutva have not understood. In one sense Hinduism is almost the ideal faith for the twenty-first century: a faith without apostasy, where there are no heretics to cast out because there has never been any such thing as a Hindu heresy. A faith that is eclectic and non-doctrinaire, responds ideally to the incertitudes of a post-modern world.

So it was hard for a Hindu, proud of his faith's and his country's liberal traditions, not to be mortified, in 2015, when a visiting US president, Barack Obama, felt obliged to deliver a speech in New Delhi urging the government to live up to India's own values—and did it again in a post-presidential visit in 2017.

Barack Obama with Narendra Modi

'India will succeed so long as it is not split along the lines of religious faith,' Mr Obama said in 2015 in an implicit rebuke to the Hindutva brigades. The president was, of course, polite, couching his praise of religious diversity as a mutual strength of both India and the US, and speaking of his own challenges as a politician with the middle name of Hussein in a country increasingly hostile to Muslims. Many Obama critics in the US had alleged that he was a Muslim, not a Christian, the president acknowledged. 'There have been times when my faith has been questioned by people who don't know me...they said that I adhered to a different religion, as if that were somehow a bad thing,' he said.

The president could hardly have been unaware, of course, that India's Hindutva-leaning prime minister had had a long track record of implying that belonging to a different religion than his own is indeed a bad thing—and that he depends for his political success on the support of people who have variously wanted all non-Hindus to convert 'back' to the

THE HINDU WAY

mother faith or be driven out of the country. And he did it again on a visit to New Delhi in December 2017: 'A country shouldn't be divided into sectarian lines and that is something I have told Prime Minister Modi in person as well as to people in America,' Obama declared. 'For a country like India where there is a Muslim population that is successful, integrated and considers itself as Indian, which is not the case in some other countries, this should be nourished and cultivated.'

Of course Indians don't need an American visitor to tell them to uphold the ideal of freedom of religion, when our history is one of coexistence, the acceptance of religious diversity is deeply embedded in our culture and our Constitution reflects our pluralism. It's a great pity that a foreign leader is obliged to recognize that some Indians do not share the values on which India is built and which are reified in our Constitution. As I have long argued, Indian democracy is all about the management of diversity, and if we don't respect our diversity we will no longer be the India that Mahatma Gandhi fought to free.

❦

TOLERANCE AND ACCEPTANCE

As a believing Hindu, I cannot agree with the Hindutvavadis. Indeed, I am ashamed of what they are doing while claiming to be acting in the name of my faith. The violence is particularly sickening: few things shocked many Hindus more than reports of a lynching in mid-2019 of a Muslim man who was beaten to death by a mob demanding he chant 'Jai Shri Ram!' Such incidents have, at different times, led hundreds of thousands of Hindus across India to protest with placards screaming, 'Not In My Name'. As I have explained throughout this book, and would like to reiterate, I have always prided myself on belonging to a religion of astonishing breadth and range of belief; a religion that acknowledges all ways of worshipping God as equally valid—indeed, the only major religion in the world that does not claim to be the only true religion. As I have often asked: How dare a bunch of goondas shrink the soaring majesty of the Vedas and the Upanishads to the petty bigotry of their brand of identity politics? Why should any Hindu allow them to diminish Hinduism to the raucous self-glorification of the football hooligan, to take a religion of awe-inspiring tolerance and reduce it to a chauvinist rampage?

Hinduism, with its openness, its respect for variety, its acceptance of all other faiths, is one religion which has always been able to assert itself without threatening others. But this is not the Hindutva that destroyed the Babri Masjid, nor that spewed in hate-filled diatribes by communal politicians. It is, instead, the Hinduism of Swami Vivekananda, whom I have quoted at such length in this book. It is important to parse some of Swami Vivekananda's most significant assertions. The first is his assertion that Hinduism stands for 'both tolerance and universal acceptance. We believe not only in universal toleration, but we accept all religions as true.' He had quoted a hymn I have already cited, to the effect that as different streams originating in different places all flow into the same sea, so do all paths lead to the same divinity. He repeatedly asserted the wisdom of the Advaita belief that Truth is One even if the sages call It by different names. Vivekananda's vision—summarized in the credo 'sarva dharma sambhava'—is, in fact, the kind of Hinduism practised by the vast majority of Hindus, whose instinctive acceptance of other faiths and forms of worship has long been the vital hallmark of our culture.

Of course it is true that, while Hinduism as a faith might

Maratha warrior-king Shivaji

privilege tolerance, this does not necessarily mean that all Hindus behave tolerantly. Nor should we assume that, even when religion is used as a mobilizing identity, all those so mobilized act in accordance with the tenets of their religion. Nonetheless it is ironic that even the Maratha warrior-king Shivaji, after whom the bigoted Shiv Sena is named, exemplified the Hindu respect for other faiths. In the account of a critic, the Mughal historian Khafi Khan, Shivaji made it a rule that his followers should do no harm to mosques, the Quran or to women. 'Whenever a copy of the sacred Quran came into his hands,' Khafi Khan wrote, Shivaji 'treated it with respect, and gave it to some of his Mussalman followers'. Other sources confirm Shivaji's standing orders to his troops that if they came across a Quran or a Bible they should preserve it safely until it could be passed on to a Muslim or Christian.

It is this doctrine of universal acceptance that has been increasingly called into question by the acolytes of Hindutva. Vivekananda had given his fellow Hindus a character certificate many of them no longer deserve. 'The Hindus have their faults,' Vivekananda added, but '...they are always for punishing their own bodies, and never for cutting the throats of their neighbours. If the Hindu fanatic burns himself on the pyre, he never lights the fire of Inquisition.' These words have a tragic echo over 125 years later in an India in which Hindu fanaticism is rising, and adopting a form that Vivekananda would not have recognized as Hindu.

The economist Amartya Sen made a related point in regretting the neglect by the votaries of Hindutva of the great achievements of Hindu civilization in favour of its more dubious features. As Sen wrote about Hindu militants: 'Not for them the sophistication of the Upanishads or Gita, or of Brahmagupta or Sankara, or of Kalidasa or Sudraka; they prefer the adoration of Rama's idol and Hanuman's image. Their nationalism also ignores the rationalist traditions of India, a country in which some of the earliest steps in algebra, geometry, and astronomy were taken, where the decimal system emerged, where early philosophy—secular as well as religious—achieved exceptional sophistication, where people invented games like chess, pioneered sex education, and began the first systematic study of political economy. The Hindu militant chooses instead to present India—explicitly or implicitly— as a country of unquestioning idolaters, delirious fanatics, belligerent devotees, and religious murderers.'

To discriminate against another, to attack another, to kill another, to destroy another's place of worship, is not part of the Hindu dharma so magnificently preached by

Vivekananda, nor the Hinduism propagated in twenty-first-century India by popular spiritual leaders like Sri Sri Ravi Shankar (founder of the Art of Living) and Sadhguru Jaggi Vasudev (founder of the Isha Foundation), who preach a humane, practical faith using techniques of meditation and yoga as well as spiritual advice anchored in the ancient texts. Why, then, are the voices of Hindu religious leaders not being raised in defence of these fundamentals of Hinduism against those who would violently pervert it?

I reject the presumption that the purveyors of hatred speak for all or even most Hindus. The Hindutva ideology is in fact a malign distortion of Hinduism. It is striking that leaders of now-defunct twentieth-century political parties like the Liberal Party and the pro-free enterprise Swatantra Party were unabashed in their avowal of their Hinduism; the Liberal leader Srinivasa Sastry wrote learned disquisitions on the Ramayana, and the founder of Swatantra, C. Rajagopalachari ('Rajaji'), was a Sanskrit scholar whose translations of the Itihasas and lectures on aspects of Hinduism are still widely read, decades after his death. Neither would have recognized the intolerance and bigotry of Hindutva as in any way representative of the faith they held dear. Many leaders in the Congress Party are similarly comfortable in their Hindu beliefs while rejecting the political construct of Hindutva. It suits the purveyors of Hindutva to imply that the choice is between their belligerent interpretation of Hinduism and the godless Westernization of the 'pseudo-seculars'. Rajaji and Sastry proved that you could wear your Hinduism on your sleeve and still be a political liberal. But that choice is elided by the identification of Hindutva with political Hinduism, as if such a conflation is the only possible approach open to practising Hindus.

I reject that idea. I not only consider myself both a Hindu and a liberal, but find that liberalism is the political ideology that most corresponds to the wide-ranging and open-minded nature of my faith.

◆

The misuse of Hinduism for sectarian minority-bashing is especially sad since Hinduism provides the basis for a shared sense of common culture within India that has little to do with religion. Bestselling authors like Amish Tripathi have achieved spectacular success by reinventing characters from Hindu mythology and the epics in stories accessible to modern readers, without surrendering to the prevalent chauvinism and bigotry of the Hindutva reassertion. Hindu festivals, from Holi to Diwali and of course Kerala's Onam, have already gone beyond their religious origins to unite Indians of all faiths as a shared experience (the revelry of Holi, the celebratory gift-giving of Onam, and the lights, firecrackers, mithais and social gambling of Diwali, have made all three into 'secular' occasions). Festivals—utsavas, melas, leelas—all 'Hindu' in origin, have become occasions for the mingling of ordinary Indians of all backgrounds; indeed, for generations now, Muslim artisans in the Hindu holy city of Varanasi have made the traditional masks for the annual Ram Leela, as I have noted earlier. Religion lies at the heart of Indian culture, but not necessarily as a source of division; religious myths like the Ramayana and the Mahabharata provide a common idiom, a shared matrix of reference, to all Indians, and it was not surprising that when Doordarshan broadcast a fifty-two-episode serialization of the Mahabharata, the script was written by a Muslim, Dr Rahi Masoom Raza. Hinduism and Islam are intertwined in India; both religions, after all, have shared the same history in the same space, and theirs is a cohabitation of necessity as well as fact.

Onam celebrations in Kerala

To some degree, India's other minorities have found it comfortable to take on elements of Hindu culture as proof of their own integration into the national mainstream. The tennis-playing brothers Anand, Vijay and Ashok Amritraj all bear Hindu names, but they are Christian, the sons of Robert and Maggie Amritraj, and they played with prominent crosses dangling from their necks, which they were fond of kissing in supplication or gratitude at tense moments on court. But giving their children Hindu names must have seemed, to Robert and Maggie, more nationalist in these post-colonial times, and quite unrelated to which god they were brought up to worship. I would not wish to make too much of this, because Muslim Indians still feel obliged to adopt Arab names in deference to the roots of their faith, but the Amritraj case (repeated in many other Christian families I know) is merely an example of Hinduism serving as a framework for the voluntary cultural assimilation of minority

Yesudas

groups, without either compulsion or conversion becoming an issue. Keralites almost unanimously consider the Christian singer Yesudas (whose very name is derived from Jesus!) to be the greatest-ever singer of Malayalam devotional songs and bhajans; for decades his songs were played at and around the Guruvayur Temple while, as a Christian, the singer himself was not allowed in. (In September 2017 it was, however, announced that were he to make a formal request, he would be permitted entry as a confirmed bhakt of Lord Krishna.)

❦

HINDUISM AS CULTURE

It is possible to a great extent to speak of Hinduism as culture rather than as religion. The inauguration of a public project, the laying of a foundation stone or the launching of a ship usually start with the ritual smashing of a coconut, an auspicious practice in Hinduism but one which most Indians of other faiths cheerfully accept in much the same spirit as a teetotaller acknowledges the role of champagne in a Western celebration. Interestingly, similar Hindu customs have survived in now-Muslim Java and now-Buddhist

Thailand. Islamic Indonesians still cherish the Ramayana legend, now shorn (for them) of its religious associations. Javanese Muslims bear Sanskrit names. Hindu culture can easily be embraced by non-Hindus if it is separated from religious faith and treated as a heritage to which all may lay claim. I have often argued that the Mahabharata and the Ramayana should be taught in our schools just as the *Odyssey* and the *Iliad* are in Western ones, not as religious texts but as towering accomplishments of our culture and the source of so many legends and cultural references.

Amartya Sen is right to stress that Hinduism is not simply the Hindutva of Ayodhya or Gujarat; it has left all Indians a religious, philosophical, spiritual and historical legacy that gives meaning to the civilizational content of secular Indian nationalism. In building an Indian nation that takes account of the country's true Hindu heritage, we have to return to the pluralism of the national movement. This must involve turning away from the strident calls for Hindutva that would privilege a doctrinaire view of Hinduism at the expense of the minorities, because such calls are a denial of the essence of the Hinduism of Vivekananda. I say this not as a godless secularist, but as a proud Hindu who is mortified at what his own faith is being reduced to in the hands of bigots— petty men who know little about the beliefs, the traditions and the history of the faith in whose 'defence' they claim to act. They have distorted a pluralist religious philosophy in the process of instrumentalizing it as a political ideology.

The way in which history and cultural memory informs contemporary attitudes varies from family to family. My mother's prosperous Nair family in Palakkad, for instance, lived in mortal terror of imminent attack by Tipu Sultan and lost most of its wealth in a foolish attempt to protect it from him by burying their treasures in an unknown location—they never found them again! But despite the stories that have been wryly and ruefully told and retold and passed down the generations over the two centuries since, my family and I never extended our dislike of Tipu and his marauders to a rejection of 'Muslims' as a whole, and certainly not to any Muslims of today. While we have no illusions about past attacks on temples by Muslim raiders, we did not bring up our children to use the past to justify bigotry in the present. One can appreciate history and leave it where it belongs.

Indians today have to find real answers to the dilemmas of running a plural nation. Nationalists often define their nation in terms of a cohesive group of people, held together by a common enemy. The common enemy of Indians is an internal one, but not the one identified by the Hindutvavadis and their ilk. The common enemy lies in the forces of sectarian division that would, if unchecked, tear the country apart—or transform it into something that most self-respecting Hindus would refuse to recognize.

In many ways, the fundamental conflict of our times is the clash between, no, not civilizations, but doctrines—religious and ethnic fundamentalism on the one hand, secular consumerist capitalism on the other. The clash is taking place amidst a paradox. Thanks to globalization, the world has been coming together into a single international market, just as it is simultaneously being torn apart by civil war, terrorism and the breakup of nations. Today there is a backlash, or more accurately two kinds of backlash: one a widely-seen current of economic anti-globalization, as the 'losers' rebel against the elites who have been exporting their jobs to faraway lands, and the other what one can call cultural anti-globalization, whose proponents seek the comforts of traditional identity. In many places in the West the two backlashes overlap, but in a country like India they do not; India's government seeks to be part of globalization while rejecting the cultural diversity it implies. The Hindutva

THE HINDU WAY

movement in India is part of this latter backlash against cosmopolitanism, multiculturalism and secularism in the name of cultural rootedness, religious or ethnic identity and nationalist authenticity.

In India this claim to authenticity and rootedness has taken on a majoritarian Hindu colouring under the BJP. It has sought to reduce Indians to a singular identity framed around their religious affiliation. Every one of us, as I have pointed out in my 1997 book *India: From Midnight to the Millennium,* has many identities. Sometimes religion obliges us to deny the truth about our own complexity by obliterating the multiplicity inherent in our identities. Religious fundamentalism, in particular, does so because it embodies a passion for pure belonging, a yearning intensified by the threatening tidal wave of globalization as well as by the specificities of the devotees' politics. And it feeds on the inevitable sense among its adherents of being wounded, whether real or imagined. In this way, Hindutva reassertion draws from the same wellsprings as Islamist fanaticism and white-nationalist Christian fundamentalism.

What is to be done? We cannot delegitimize religion, and indeed there is something precious and valuable in a faith that allows a human being to see himself at one with others stretching their hands out towards God around the world. But can we separate religion from identity? Can we dream of a world in which religion has an honoured place but where the need for spirituality will no longer be associated with the need to belong? If we want religion to stop feeding fanaticism, terror and ethnic wars, we must find other ways of satisfying the need for identity. If identity can relate principally to citizenship rather than faith, to a land rather than a doctrine, and if that identity is one that can live in harmony with other identities, then we might still escape the worst horrors that the doomsayers

Bharat Mata

(like Samuel Huntington, who two decades ago foretold a
'clash of civilizations') can conceive. A domestic 'clash of
civilizations' would destroy India, which has survived and
thrived as a civilizational medley.

Thanks in many ways to the eclectic inclusiveness of
Hinduism, everything in India exists in countless variants.
There was no single standard, no fixed stereotype, no 'one
way'. This pluralism emerged from the very nature of the
country; it was made inevitable by India's geography and
reaffirmed by its history. There was simply too much of
both to permit a single, exclusionist nationalism. When the

Hindutvavadis demanded that all Indians declare 'Bharat Mata ki Jai' as a litmus test of their nationalism, many of us insisted that no Indian should be obliged to mouth a slogan he did not believe in his heart. If some Muslims, for instance, felt that their religion did not allow them to hail their motherland as a goddess, the Constitution of India gave them the right not to. Hindutva wrongly seeks to deny them this right.

We were brought up to take this for granted, and to reject the sectarianism that had partitioned the nation when the British left. I was raised unaware of my own caste and unconscious of the religious loyalties of my schoolmates and friends. Of course knowledge of these details came in time, but too late for any of it to matter, even less to influence my attitude or conduct. We were Indians: we were brought up (and constantly exhorted) to believe in an idea of nationhood transcending communal divisions. This may sound like the lofty obliviousness of the privileged, but such beliefs were not held only by the elites: they were a reflection of how most Indians lived, even in the villages of India. Independent India was born out of a nationalist struggle in which acceptance of each other which we, perhaps unwisely, called secularism was fundamental to the nationalist consensus.

It is true that Hindu zealotry—which ought to be a contradiction in terms—is partly a reaction to other chauvinisms. As I have pointed out, the unreflective avowal by many Hindus of their own secularism has provoked the scorn of some Hindus, who despise the secularists as deracinated 'Macaulayputras' (sons of Macaulay) or 'Babur ke aulad' (sons of Babur). They see such Hindus as cut off from their own culture and heritage, and challenge them to rediscover their authentic roots, as defined by the Hindutvavadis.

But Hinduism is no monolith; its strength is found within each Hindu, not in the collectivity. Defining a 'Hindu' cause may well be a political reaction to the definition of non-Hindu causes: the Hindutva idea originated around the same time as the rise of a separate Muslim consciousness in the polity in the early twentieth century, and the resentments that spilled over into the destruction of the Babri Masjid in the century's last decade were largely articulated in opposition to the imagined 'appeasement' of India's minorities. The rage of the Hindu mobs is the rage of those who feel themselves supplanted in this competition of identities, who think that they are taking their country back from usurpers of long ago. They want revenge against history, but they do not realize that history is its own revenge.

The Hindutva project seeks to reinvent Hindu identity with a new belief structure and a new vocabulary. They seek to make Hinduism more like the Semitic religions they resent but wish to emulate: to pick fewer sacred books, notably the Gita, and exalt them would produce a less 'baggy', tighter version of the faith; to focus on fewer gods, notably Shiva, Rama and Krishna, with Ganesh and various forms of Devi thrown in, would provide a sharper sense of Hindu divinity; to standardize religious practices around specific familiar festivals, rituals and gatherings, would provide a greater sense of community. Their associated efforts include a desire to control and restrict what Hindus eat, so their rejection of beef (even though several castes did eat it in the past) would itself become a marker of identity; to promote Hindi as a national language (though it is quite foreign to nearly half the country) so as to ensure that the vocabulary of Hindudom can be more easily transmitted; to mouth the same slogans ('Bharat Mata ki Jai!' and 'Jai Shri Ram!') and chant the

A puja alcove in a home

same songs ('Vande Mataram' is a must), even though some Muslims are uncomfortable with both, in order to promote conformity. This invented Hinduism has much more to do with an era of political and cultural insecurity and a faltering new sense of aspiration than with the Vedas, the Puranas or the Bhakti movement: it denies the lived history of Hinduism even while claiming to speak in its name.

The central challenge of India is the challenge of accommodating the aspirations of different groups in the national dream. The ethos of Hinduism—inclusionist, flexible, agglomerative—helped the nation meet this challenge. The doctrine of Hindutva prefers uniformity to accommodation. The battle for India's soul will be between two Hinduisms, the 'secularist' Indianism of the nationalist movement and the particularist fanaticism of the Ayodhya mob. It is a battle that continues to rage as I write these words.

◆

The inevitable backlash to my writings about Hindutva excesses, from the Babri Masjid demolition to the Gujarat horrors, has largely taken the form of belligerent emails and assorted social media fulminations from the less reflective of the Hindutva brigade. I have been excoriated as 'anti-Hindu' and described by several as a 'well-known leftist', which will no doubt amuse those of my friends who knew me in college thirty years ago as one of the very few supporters of Rajaji's conservative Swatantra Party in those consensually socialist times. And from time to time a Hindutvavadi, reminding me of the religion that has been mine from birth, succumbed to the temptation to urge me predictably to heed that well-worn slogan: 'Garv se kaho ki hum Hindu hain.'

All right, let us take him up on that. I am indeed proud that I am a Hindu. But of what is it that I am, and am not, proud?

I am not proud of my co-religionists attacking and destroying Muslim homes and shops. I am not proud of Hindus raping Muslim girls, or slitting the wombs of Muslim mothers. I am not proud of Hindu vegetarians who have roasted human beings alive and rejoiced over the corpses. I am not proud of those who reduce the lofty metaphysical speculations of the Upanishads to the petty bigotry of their own sense of identity, which they assert in order to exclude, not embrace, others.

I am proud that India's pluralism is paradoxically sustained by the fact that the overwhelming majority of Indians are Hindus, because Hinduism has taught them to live amidst a variety of other identities.

I am proud of those Hindus, like the Shankaracharya of Kanchi, who say that Hindus and Muslims must live like Rama and Lakshmana in India. I am not proud of those Hindus, like 'Sadhvi' Rithambhara, who say that Muslims are like sour lemons curdling the milk of Hindu India.

I am not proud of those who suggest that only a Hindu, and only a certain kind of Hindu, can be an authentic Indian. I am not proud of those Hindus who say that people of other religions live in India only on their sufferance, and not because they belong on our soil. I am proud of those Hindus who realize that an India that denies itself to some of us could end up being denied to all of us.

I am proud of those Hindus who utterly reject Hindu communalism, conscious that the communalism of the majority is especially dangerous because it can present itself as nationalist. I am proud of those Hindus who respect the distinction between Hindu nationalism and Indian nationalism. Obviously, majorities are never seen as 'separatist', since separatism is by definition pursued by a minority. But majority communalism is in fact an extreme form of separatism, because it seeks to separate other Indians, integral parts of our country, from India itself. I am proud of those Hindus who recognize that the saffron and the green both belong equally on the Indian flag.

The reduction of non-Hindus to second-class status in their own homeland is unthinkable. As I have pointed out here, and in my other writings, it would be a second partition: and a partition in the Indian soul would be as bad as a partition in the Indian soil. For Hindus like myself, the only possible idea of India is that of a nation greater than the sum of its parts. That is the only India that will allow us to call ourselves not Brahmins, not Bengalis, not Hindus, not Hindi-speakers, but simply Indians.

How about another slogan for Hindus like me? *Garv se kaho ki hum Indian hain.*

◆

There is an old Puranic story about Truth. It seems a brash young warrior sought the hand of a beautiful princess.

Her father, the king, thought he was a bit too cocksure and callow. He decreed that the warrior could only marry the princess after he had found Truth.

So the warrior set out into the world on a quest for Truth. He went to temples and monasteries, to mountain tops where sages meditated, to remote forests where ascetics scourged themselves, but nowhere could he find Truth.

Despairing one day and seeking shelter from a thunderstorm, he took refuge in a musty cave. There was an old crone there, a hag with matted hair and warts on her face, the skin hanging loose from her bony limbs, her teeth yellow and rotting, her breath malodorous. But as he spoke to her, with each question she answered, he realized he had come to the end of his journey: she was Truth.

They spoke all night, and when the storm cleared, the warrior told her he had fulfilled his quest. Armed with his knowledge of Truth, he could go back to the palace and claim his bride.

'Now that I have found Truth,' he said, 'what shall I tell them at the palace about you?'

The wizened old creature smiled. 'Tell them,' she said, 'tell them that I am young and beautiful.'

So Truth exists, but is not always true. That subtle insight is typical of the wisdom of the ancient Hindus. It gives the lie to the petty bigotries, the glib certitudes, the righteous fanaticism of today's Hindutvavadis.

The tragedy for many Hindus is that the Hindutvavadis, often ironically referred to by their critics as bhakts (the 'devout'), are betraying daily the values of the very faith to which they claim to be committed. Since the original Bhakti movement began in Tamil Nadu in the sixth century, Hindu thought has stressed the personal nature of religion and emphasized the inclusive philosophy and all-embracing syncretism of the faith that Adi Shankara and Vivekananda taught to the world as Hinduism. The traditional Hindu texts, starting with the Vedas, were imbued with a sense of philosophical wonder, raising questions about creation, the nature of being and the meaning of life, and treating nothing as too sacred to interrogate. It is an act of treason to Hinduism to take this faith of mystery and doubt and reduce it to brazen certitudes, to shun diversity and extol dogma and to claim that it is the only authentic Hinduism.

The political project of Hindutva is nothing less than an assault on the religion; but where Hinduism has for millennia proved its resilience to external attacks, it is now revealing its vulnerability to attack from within. That is why Hindutva politics must be resisted; in presenting a view of Hinduism that is at odds with everything Hinduism has sought to stand for, it seeks to refashion Hinduism as something it has never been. Indeed, as the economist and public intellectual Kaushik Basu has argued, it reveals the insecurity of the Hindutvavadis that they want to remake their country and religion in the very image of the countries and religions they claim to detest.

Hinduism attaches importance to pramana (instruments of warranted inference) in the pursuit of jnana, or knowledge. As long as you can demonstrate the validity or rigour of your pramana, you are entitled to the specific belief structure you wish to adhere to. It is this feature, unlike other traditions that rely on revelation as claims to truth, that ensures Hinduism is more open to diversity of belief. My friend Keerthik Sasidharan suggested to me, in twenty-first-century terms, that Hinduism is analogous to an open-source operating system on top of which others can build applications to be deployed in the receptive hardware of human brains. All Hinduism demands before the formation of any belief is analytical and logical consistency. Even the existence of God is subject to this test.

The Jagannath Temple at Puri

The Nietzschean formulation that God created Man and Man returned the compliment is anticipated more than a millennium ago in this verse by Udayanacharya, the tenth-century logician, addressed to the deity Jagannath of Puri:

You're so drunk on wealth and power
that you ignore my presence.
Just wait: when the Buddhists come,
your whole existence depends on me.

(Yet it should be said that Udayanacharya is the very sage credited with so roundly trouncing Buddhists in debate that Buddhism never dared to challenge Hinduism in India thereafter.)

❀

When I became India's first and only official candidate for the post of United Nations Secretary General in 2006, I was asked by some journalists about the role my Hindu faith played in my worldview. I conceded that it was true that faith can influence one's conduct in one's career and life. For some, it is merely a question of faith in themselves; for others, including me, that sense of faith emerges from a faith in something larger than ourselves. Faith is, at some level, what gives you the courage to take the risks you must take, and enables you to make peace with yourself when you suffer the inevitable setbacks and calumnies that are the lot of those who try to make a difference in the world. So I had no difficulty in saying openly that I am a believing Hindu. But I was also quick to explain what that phrase means to me. I'm not a 'Hindu fundamentalist'. As I have explained in this book, and said often in the past, the fundamental thing about Hinduism is that it is a religion without fundamentals. My faith in global diversity emerges from my Hindu beliefs as well, since we have an extraordinary diversity of religious practices within Hinduism, a faith with no single sacred book but many. Mine is a faith that allows each believer to reach out his or her hands to his or her notion of the godhead. I was brought up in the belief that all ways of worship are equally valid. I relished pointing out that my father prayed devoutly every day, but never used to oblige me to join him. In the Hindu way, he wanted me to find my own truth. And that was precisely the manner in which I brought up my own sons.

Finding my own truth gave me a truth that admits of the possibility that there might be other truths. I therefore bring to the world an attitude that is open, accommodating and tolerant of others' beliefs. Mine is not a faith for those

The author with Kofi Annan and Sir Brian Urquhart

who seek unquestioning dogmas, but there is no better belief-system for an era of doubt and uncertainty than a religion that cheerfully accommodates both.

The misuse of religion for political purposes is of course a sad, sometimes tragic, aspect of our contemporary reality. As UN Secretary General Kofi Annan had once said, the problem is never with the faith, but with the faithful. All faiths strive sincerely to animate the divine spark in each of us, but some of their followers, alas, use their faith as a club to beat others with, rather than a platform to raise themselves to the heavens. Since Hinduism believes that there are various ways of reaching the ultimate truth, as a Hindu I fully accepted the belief systems of others as equal to my own. That is why I cannot and do not accept the Hindutvavadi fanatics' interpretation of the values and principles of my faith.

But what does it mean to me to be a practising Hindu? As I have mentioned already, I have never been a frequent visitor to temples, though I do believe in praying everyday, even if it is only for a couple of minutes. Many Hindus who can afford the space have a place for puja within their homes; at minimum, a picture, a little statue, or several. I too had a little puja alcove at my home in Manhattan, and somewhat larger ones now in my homes in Delhi and Thiruvananthapuram, where I try to reach out to the divine spirit. Yet, I believe in the Upanishadic doctrine that the Divine is essentially unknowable and unattainable by ordinary mortals. All prayer is an attempt to reach out to that which we cannot touch. While I do occasionally visit temples, and I appreciate how important they are to my mother and most other devout Hindus, I believe that one does not need any intermediaries between oneself and one's notion of the Divine. If God is in your heart, it matters little where else He resides.

So I take pride in the openness, the diversity, the range, the sublime philosophical aspirations of the Vedanta. I cherish the diversity, the lack of compulsion, and the richness of the various ways in which Hinduism is practised eclectically. And I admire the civilizational heritage of tolerance that makes Hindu societies open their arms to people of every other faith, to come and practise their beliefs in peace amidst Hindus. It is remarkable, for instance, that the only country on earth where the Jewish people have lived for centuries and never experienced a single episode of anti-Semitism is India. That is the Hinduism in which I gladly take pride.

Hinduism's suitability for the modern world lies in many ways in its recognition of uncertainty and its pragmatic non-dogmatism. The religion of 'maybe He does not know' is a faith for the non-dogmatic, one which looks beyond the blacks and whites, the grim certitudes of lesser mortals, to the acknowledgement of the scope for doubt, for different points of view on the great questions of life and death.

Vivekananda's immortal 'We believe not only in universal toleration but we accept all religions as true' is a prescription for peace and coexistence among competing dogmatisms in a world full of too many dogmas. This is why it was perhaps the ideal faith for a candidate for United Nations Secretary General to profess. (And when I lost the race, my faith offered me consolation too, in the Bhagavad Gita's dictum that one did what was one's dharma to do, regardless of the consequences.)

Hinduism does not see the world in terms of absolutes. Blacks and whites are largely absent from its ethos. It sees competing notions of good and evil, duty and betrayal, everywhere, and seeks wisdom in finding the right approach suited for each specific circumstance. Vivekananda used to tell a parable of the frog in the well: 'I am a Hindu. I am sitting in my own little well and thinking that the whole world is my little well. The Christians sit in their little well and think the whole world is their well. The Muslims sit in their little well and think that is the whole world.' To Vivekananda, the world was one where each frog had much to learn from the others, if he would only look beyond his well.

Hinduism is not a totalizing belief system; it offers a way of coping with the complexity of the world. It acknowledges that the truth is plural, that there is no one correct answer to the big questions of creation, or of the meaning of life. In its reverence for sages and rishis, it admits that knowledge may come from an exchange between two or more views, neither of which necessarily possesses a monopoly on the truth. The greatest truth, to the Hindu, is that which accepts the existence of other truths.

Hinduism sees life as an evolving dynamic, not a contest that can ever be settled once and for all. It is open to negotiation on ways of being and believing; it permits

Arjuna seeking Krishna's advice during the battle of Kurukshetra

negotiation even with God. It offers rites and rituals, but leaves it up to each individual to choose which ones he wishes to adhere to. Each Hindu must find his own truth. Each individual achieves his own salvation and self-fulfilment.

At the same time Hinduism is also anchored in the real world. A superficial view of Hinduism sees its other-worldly 'timelessness'. But in fact the religion is anchored not in a world-denying spirituality, as Raimon Panikkar points out; in his words, it is not the timeless, but the 'time-full', which wins Vedic approbation. Time is depicted in hymns in the *Atharva Veda* as perpetually replenishing itself from a full vessel which, in spite of all efforts, can never be emptied. Since time transcends time, it is without beginning or end, without limit; and in that sense it is like God. 'Time am I, world-destroying,' says Krishna in the Bhagavad Gita, stressing 'I am imperishable Time'. As a verse in the *Maitreya Upanishad* puts it:

From time all beings emerge
From time they advance and grow
In time, too, they come to rest.
Time is embodied and also bodiless.

The harm religion does when it is passionately self-righteous—wars, crusades, communal violence, jihad—is arguably greater than the benefits religion produces when it does well (teaching morality, answering prayers, providing balm to troubled souls). In its long history, Hinduism has never launched an apocalyptic war of religion or tried to impose one correct answer on all of life. Hindus like to speak of theirs as a religion of peace, but then so do other faiths. Still, the Hindu scriptures are replete with hymns to peace, and are infused with the idea that human beings must seek peace within themselves and peace with all other human beings. Many Vedic mantras set out to achieve these ends; of these the Shanti Mantra is the most famous, and prays for peace in heaven, on earth and in the human heart. The words 'Om Shantih! Shantih! Shantihi!' are uttered three times at the end of every sacred action or after the recitation of a sacred text—three times because the Hindu seeks peace in all three realms. Humans cannot enjoy personal peace in the absence of peace on earth, but equally there cannot be peace in the world if there is no peace in the inner hearts of the human beings in the world. A verse of the *Yajur Veda* (XXXVI, 17) chants:

To the heavens be peace, to the sky and the earth,
To the waters be peace, to plants and all trees,
To the Gods be peace, to Brahman be peace,
To all men be peace, again and again—peace also to me!

The speaker of the Sixteenth Lok Sabha, the Lower House of the Indian Parliament, the first in that office from the BJP, introduced the practice of uttering 'Om Shantih! Shantih! Shantihi!' after the otherwise ritualistic reading of obituary notices during each session. Though this implied the introduction of religious language into a secular Parliament, her words were echoed by many MPs, and not only those of her party. While as a liberal I was initially dismayed by her doing this, I soon came around to the view that as long as no one was obliged to follow her, calling for peace was hardly objectionable. A Hindu could be overtly Hindu, I felt, if in the process she was being all-embracing in her expression of her faith, while not imposing it on others.

Hinduism is a life-affirming religion of joy and play (leela). It sees the world as suffused with radiance rather than darkness; as the Bhagavad Gita says, 'That splendour which is from the sun, which illumines this whole world, which is in the moon and in fire—know that splendour is also mine.' In turn this refulgence is Man's, since he is enjoined by the Upanishads to see all beings in himself and himself in all things; he therefore radiates in his person the splendour of the Universe. Yes, the Hindu scriptures acknowledge the existence of human sorrow and suffering, but see them as part of an awakening to the transcendent. The Vedas do not ask why we suffer; they take human sorrow as a given, an infliction to be dealt with and overcome. The Upanishads are more questioning of suffering; they use a word, dukha, sadness and existential distress, a word not found in the Vedas. Ideally one must be detached from such suffering, as the Gita teaches, and by eliminating sorrow in oneself through self-realization, help remove it from others. This seems impossible for most ordinary people, and so the easier solution is to take refuge in the Lord.

Similarly, the Hindu scriptures speculate about the mystery of what lies beyond human life, but they are not obsessed with death; as Raimon Panikkar brilliantly put it, 'they seem to describe an existential attitude that takes cognizance of the phenomenon of death but denies to it any character of ultimacy... It is by integrating the fact of death into life, by reabsorbing, as it were, death into life...by finding a ground that is common to both death and life, that we can find the proper Vedic perspective.' This notion of the continuity between life and death is a particularly Hindu idea, with death, as it were, inbuilt into life. Panikkar again: 'The beyond is the unfathomable ocean which makes the beaches on this side worth walking and playing on.'

Hindus believe that, at most, religion can create a platform upon which the beautiful things in life can be attained. Destiny, knowledge, reflection and prayer may equip you to achieve fulfilment. The Hindu is a seeker, but the holy grail he seeks is within himself. Hinduism urges you to explore your own mind and heart to discover the truths about life. The model of the ideal questing Hindu may be found in a description of the sage Narada in the Valmiki Ramayana: 'Dedicated to self-learning, fully in control of the senses, seeker of the truth'. Yoga, meditation, prayer, social service are all means to that end, but not the only ones. You have to work hard yourself to achieve those things that are worth achieving. The doctrine of karma yoga preached by both Vivekananda and Mahatma Gandhi is a doctrine of action, not of passivity or fatalism. There is no lassitude in the pursuit of the Purusharthas.

The wise Hindu can hold two or more opposing ideas together in her mind at the same time. That is the way the world is. For the Hindu texts uniquely operate from a platform of scepticism, not a springboard of certitude. The *Rig Veda* verse that says 'maybe He does not know' about the Creator is not an invention of post-modernism, but the wisdom of a timeless text that has lasted for three and a half millennia and will always be valid.

Most faiths prioritize one identity, one narrative and one holy book. Hinduism recognizes that everyone has multiple identities, accepts diverse narratives and respects several sacred books. Indeed, the folk Hinduism of multiple beliefs cannot be forced into the Abrahamic framework of One Book, One Deity and one way of doing things. The more the Hindu grapples with the great questions, the more she understands how much is beyond our understanding.

Yet the Hindu lives in reality, in the here and now, conscious that on the way to renunciation and liberation from the world, there are worldly duties and responsibilities to family, community and nation that must be performed without regard to their rewards. Hindus do not shelter from the besieging forces of life behind the safety of their doctrinal battlements, the omniscience of their dogmas, the fatwas or encyclicals of their priests. They are unafraid to face the cross currents, acknowledging how little they know. Indeed Hindus are not awed by the complexity of the world, because they accept the world is complex, and much passes their understanding.

❧

A RELIGION FOR THE 21ST CENTURY

In the twenty-first century, Hinduism has many of the attributes of a universal religion—a religion that is personal and individualistic, privileges the individual and does not subordinate one to a collectivity; a religion that grants and respects complete freedom to the believer to find his or her own answers to the true meaning of life; a religion that offers a wide range of choice in religious practice, even in regard to the nature and form of the formless God; a religion that places great emphasis on one's mind, and values one's capacity for reflection, intellectual enquiry, and self-study; a religion that distances itself from dogma and holy writ, that is minimally prescriptive and yet offers an abundance of options, spiritual and philosophical texts and social and cultural practices to choose from. In a world where resistance to authority is growing, Hinduism imposes no authorities; in a world of networked individuals, Hinduism proposes no institutional hierarchies; in a world of open-source information-sharing, Hinduism accepts all paths as equally valid; in a world of rapid transformations and accelerating change, Hinduism is adaptable and flexible, which is why it has survived for nearly 4,000 years.

In 1926, Prof Clement Webb suggested that Hinduism, with its tradition of openness, tolerance and acceptance of the Divine in the most diverse forms imaginable, 'could perhaps more easily than any other faith develop, without loss of continuity with its past, into a universal religion...' This remains true almost a century later. Universalism comes easily to Hinduism. Hindus respect the environment because it embodies the unity of all creation, and in this, too, theirs is a faith for the twenty-first century.

Dr Karan Singh, the former maharaja of Kashmir and Indian politician who is also a superbly readable scholar of Hindu philosophy, identifies five major principles in Hinduism that lend relevance and validity to the faith in today's world. At the risk of inadequate paraphrase, these are, according to him: the recognition of the unity of all mankind, epitomized in the Rig Vedic phrase 'vasudhaiva kutumbakam', the world is one family; the harmony of all religions, epitomized in that Rig Vedic statement that was Swami Vivekananda's favourite, 'ekam sat, vipra bahuda vadanti'; the divinity inherent in each individual, transcending the social stratifications and

Dr Karan Singh (centre) addressing a press conference

hierarchies that have all too often distorted this principle in Hindu society; the creative synthesis of practical action and contemplative knowledge, science and religion, meditation and social service, in the faith; and finally, the cosmic vision of Hindu philosophy, incorporating the infinite galaxies of which the Earth is just a tiny speck. In Dr Singh's own words: 'Such is the grandeur and mystery of the Atman that it can move towards a comprehension of the unutterable mystery of existence. We, who are children of the past and the future, of earth and heaven, of light and darkness, of the human and the divine, at once evanescent and eternal, of the world and beyond it, within time and in eternity, yet have the capacity to comprehend our condition, to rise above our terrestrial limitations, and finally, to transcend the throbbing abyss of space and time itself.' This, Dr Singh says, is the message of Hinduism, and it is a message that can and should resonate throughout the world.

Yet such a universal creed can only be the Hinduism described in this book, rather than the petty intolerant

Hindutva being propagated by bigots in a travesty of the majesty of their faith. Swami Vivekananda had, as usual, put it best: 'If there is ever to be a universal religion, it must be one which will have no location in place or time; which will be infinite like the God it will preach, and whose sun will shine upon the followers of Krishna and of Christ, on saints and sinners alike; which will not be Brahminic or Buddhistic, Christian or Mohammedan, but the sum total of all these...and still have infinite space for development; which in its catholicity will embrace in infinite arms, and find a place for every human being from the lowest grovelling savage, not far removed from the brute, to the highest man towering by the virtues of his head and heart almost above humanity, making society stand in awe of him and doubt his human nature. It will be a religion which will have no place for persecution or intolerance in its polity, which will recognize divinity in every man and woman, and whose whole scope, whose whole force, will be centered in aiding humanity to realize its own true, divine nature. Offer such a religion and all the nations will follow you.'

I am a Hindu who is proud to offer such a religion to the world. I do so conscious that Hinduism does not seek to proselytize, only to offer itself as an example that others may or may not choose to follow. It does not share with the Abrahamic faiths a desire to universalize itself; yet its tenets and values are universally applicable. But first it must be revived and reasserted, in its glorious liberalism, its openness and acceptance, its eclecticism and universalism, in the land of its own birth. As the Hindu hymn (from the *Brihadaranyaka Upanishad*) says, in words that resonate with meaning for every human being on the planet:

Asato ma sad gamaya!
Tamaso ma jyotir gamaya!
Mrityor ma amritam gamaya!

Lead me from Untruth to Truth,
Lead me from darkness to light
Lead me from death to immortality.

NOTES

PROLOGUE

xv   **English-speaking, twenty-first-century reader can understand:** I have throughout eschewed the scholarly Romanized spellings of Sanskrit words favoured by the classic texts for simple versions that approximate the way the words are pronounced. This has led me to invent one spelling, 'mutth', for the Hindu monastery more frequently spelt 'mutt' or 'math', both of which might confuse or mislead the average English-speaker.

CHAPTER ONE: MY HINDUISM

10–11   *Then there was neither...He does not know*: Derived from Nanditha Krishna, *Hinduism and Nature*, New Delhi: Penguin Books, 2017, p. 5–6.

13–14   'there is no heaven...his own father?': Debiprasad Chattopadhyaya and M. K. Gangopadhyaya (eds.), *Cārvaka/Lokāyata: An Anthology of Source Materials and Some Recent Studies*, Indian Council of Philosophical Research, 1990, p. 352.

14   'Its freedom from dogma': Mahatma Gandhi, *Hindu Dharma*, Ahmedabad: Navajivan Publishing House, 1950, p. 6.

15   'a Hindu is he who believes that the Vedas': Quoted in Sri Swami Sivananda, *All About Hinduism*, The Divine Life Society, 1947.

15   V. D. Savarkar, asserted in the 1920s that one could be a Hindu: '[A]

man can be as truly a Hindu as any without believing in the Vedas as an independent religious authority', V. D. Savarkar, *Hindutva: Who is a Hindu?* (originally published under the title *Essentials of Hindutva*), Bombay: Veer Savarkar Prakashan, 1923, p. 81.

15 **'Being a Hindu means all things to all men':** Quoted in Jawaharlal Nehru, *The Discovery of India*, 1946.

16 **'Is it a museum of beliefs...?':** Sarvepalli Radhakrishnan, *The Hindu Way of Life*, London: G. Allen & Unwin Ltd., 1927.

17 **'I am proud to belong to a religion':** Swami Vivekananda, *The Complete Works of Swami Vivekananda*, Chennai: Manonmani Publishers, 2015.

17–18 **'As the different streams having their sources':** Ibid.

18 **'I challenge the world...':** Ibid.

20 **In the beginning everything was Brahman:** Adapted from Friedrich Max Müller, *The Upanishads: Part II*, Oxford: Clarendon Press, 1884.

21 *O Father of the Earth...with our oblation?:* Raimon Panikkar, *The Vedic Experience: Mantramañjari: An Anthology Of The Vedas For Modern Man*, Berkeley: University of California Press, 1977.

30 **Characters depicted in the epics as animals:** I am indebted to Dr Nanditha Krishna for this insight.

36 **what some scholars call the 'inferior deities':** Robert L. Brown, *Ganesh: Studies of an Indian God*, New York: SUNY Press, 1991, p. 21.

41 **a photograph of a spout emerging from the back of a temple:** 'Milk-drinking deities unleash mass hysteria', quoted in *Great Mysteries of the 20th Century*, Reader's Digest, 1999.

CHAPTER TWO: THE HINDU WAY

49 **'Whosoever follows any faith...his faith I shall reinforce':** Shakunthala Jagannathan's translation.

50 **'They pretended not [that] their law was universal':** François Bernier, *Travels in the Mogul Empire*, Manchester: Archibald Constable & Company, 1670.

50 **'God is more than the law that':** S. Radhakrishnan, *The Hindu View of Life*, London: Allen & Unwin, 1926.

51 **'May Vishnu...grant our prayers.':** Diana L. Eck, *Encountering God: A Spiritual Journey from Bozeman to Banares*, Boston: Beacon Press, 1993, p. 76.

52 An 'intelligent Hindu peasant': Herbert Risley, *The People of India*, Simla: Thacker, Spink & Co, 1915, p. 244.

56 Who sends the mind to wander afar...not what people here adore: Juan Mascaro, *The Upanishads*, London: Penguin Books, 1965.

59 Venkatachalapathi temple...the richest temple in the country: The temple's riches are truly staggering. Donations from the public, the value of the thousands of kilos of hair they donate to the Lord through tonsuring their heads at the temple, the price of entry tickets, the specific fees paid for particular rituals and offerings, the sale of prasadam (usually in the form of the famous—and patented—Tirupati laddoo) and the cash deposited in the donation-urns or hundis within the temple itself, amount to an estimated ₹2,500 to ₹3,000 crore annually. Tirupati's budget for 2015–2016 was ₹2,530.10 crore or $392 million, compared to the Vatican's budget of $274 million in the same year. Since Lord Balaji is a particular favourite of those who pray for wealth, their gratitude for answered prayers is also munificent.

61 Indra is said to have drunk three lakes of soma: 'In Tvastar's dwelling Indra drank the Soma, a hundredworth of juice pressed from the mortar', translated by Ralph T. H. Griffith.

64 'Hinduism appears to be very much like India': Rutvij Merchant, 'Answering the ultimate question: who is a Hindu?', *Firstpost*, 24 September 2014.

73 In that period we see enormous evolution: See notes to pp. 245–246.

75 *A profusion of arguments!*: K. Balasubramania Iyer, *Yaksha Prasna*, Bombay: Bhavan's Book Company, 1989.

76 he was not portrayed as a god, but as an ideal man: I am indebted to Dr Nanditha Krishna for this insight.

79 While the Ramayana (composed from around the 200 CE...): Since the precise dates are impossible to establish, some authorities prefer a later date for the commencement of their composition.

85–86 'We are told quite frankly...emerge unscathed.': Upinder Singh, *Political Violence in Ancient India*, Cambridge, MA: Harvard University Press, 2017, p. 236.

98 The *Mundaka Upanishad* (II.2.3) offers a marvellous metaphor: 'Having taken the bow furnished by the *Upanishads*, the great weapon—and fixed in it the arrow rendered pointed by constant meditation and having drawn it with the mind fixed on the *Brahman*,

hit, good looking youth! at that mark—the immortal *Brahman*.'
www.wisdomlib.org

98–99   *How does the wind not cease to blow*: Raimon Panikkar, *The Vedic Experience*, p. 66.

CHAPTER THREE: QUESTIONING HINDU CUSTOMS

106   **Dr Radhakrishnan called it 'the answer of Hinduism'**: Radhakrishnan, *The Hindu Way of Life*, London: Allen & Unwin, 1927.

108   **Allama Prabhu was a drummer**: Manu S. Pillai, 'Women, Lingayats and "the Hindus"', *LiveMint*, 25 September 2017.

109   **'The sage Vararuchi'**: Manu S. Pillai, 'The Kerala of the past and present', *LiveMint*, 2 September 2017.

114   **27 per cent of Indians still practise caste untouchability**: Seema Chishti, 'Biggest caste survey: One in four Indians admit to practising untouchability', *Indian Express*, 29 November 2014.

114   **also practised by Sikhs (23 per cent), Muslims (18 per cent) and Christians (5 per cent)**: A scholar friend finds the figure for Christians surprisingly low. In Tamil Nadu, she tells me, many churches have separate pews and burial grounds for different castes, and some even make Dalits sit outside the church.

114   **'These findings indicate that conversion'**: Amit Thorat, 'Mapping Exclusion', *Indian Express*, 3 December 2014.

115   **As an eighteen-year-old blogger**: Tejaswini Tabhane, 'No Mr Tharoor, I Don't Want to Enter Your Kitchen', *www.roundtableindia. co.in*, 16 September 2017.

CHAPTER SIX: ADI SHANKARA

148   *I am other than name, form and action*: Michael Comans, *The Method of Early Advaita Vedānta: A Study of Gauḍapāda, Śaṅkara, Sureśvara, and Padmapāda*, Delhi: Motilal Banarsidass, 2000.

149   *Without beginning and end is he*: Raimon Panikkar, *The Vedic Experience: Mantramañjarī: An Anthology Of The Vedas For Modern Man*, Berkeley: University of California Press, 1977.

150–51   *I am not the mind... (Shivoham, Shivoham)*: Adapted from Swami Vivekananda, *The Complete Works of Swami Vivekananda*, Chennai: Manonmani Publishers, 2015.

151–52   *I do not think that I know*: Friedrich Max Müller, *The Upanishads*, Oxford: Clarendon Press, 1884.

CHAPTER EIGHT: RAMANUJA AND THE BHAKTI MOVEMENT

162 *Tying anklets upon her feet, Mira dances in ecstasy*: Dr Karan Singh, *Essays on Hinduism,* New Delhi: Ratna Sagar, 1987, p. 25.

164 'Loaded with the burden of the Vedas': Karigoudar Ishwara, *Speaking of Basava: Lingayat Religion and Culture in South Asia*, Boulder, Colorado: Westview Press, 1992, p. 212.

164 'On the same earth stands the outcaste's': Manu S. Pillai, 'Basava and the emergence of Lingayat identity', *LiveMint*, 28 July 2017.

164 'is there anybody in the world': Ibid.

170 Islamic precepts also played a part in the reshaping of Hinduism: In turn Sufism shows the influence of Hindu mysticism on Islam, but that is another story.

170 Brahmins, converted en masse to Islam: The period of Muslim conversions in the north saw the migration of several communities of Hindus southwards, bringing their religion and skills to other parts of India.

CHAPTER NINE: HINDUISM'S RESPONSE TO THE BRITISH

172 'The present system of the Hindus': Gauri Shankar Bhatt, 'Brahmo Samaj, Arya Samaj, and the Church-Sect Typology', *Review of Religious Research*, 10, 1968, p. 24.

CHAPTER TEN: MYSTICS AND REFORMERS

178 replete with stories of sacrificial offerings: See notes to pp. 245–246.

183 Christophe Jaffrelot has labelled the process: Christophe Jaffrelot, 'Hindu Nationalism: Strategic Syncretism in Ideology Building', *Economic and Political Weekly*, Vol. 28 No. 12/13, 20–27 March 1993.

CHAPTER TWELVE: AFTER THE SWAMI, TOWARDS THE MAHATMA

201 *He who is abiding in the earth*: Raimon Panikkar, *The Vedic Experience: Mantramañjarī: An Anthology Of The Vedas For Modern Man*, Berkeley: University of California Press, 1977.

201 'The Hindu spirit is that attitude': S. Radhakrishnan, *The Hindu View of Life*, London: Allen & Unwin, 1926.

201 'Evil has reference to the distance': Ibid.

202 'The cure for error': Ibid.

205 as the scholar K. P. Shankaran points out: K. P. Shankaran, 'In Good

Faith: Gandhi's radical Hinduism', *Indian Express*, 4 December 2017.

206 **what some have seen as a creative 'misreading' of the text:** Ibid.

CHAPTER THIRTEEN: HINDUISM TODAY: CURRENT CONTROVERSIES AND CONTESTATIONS ·

212 **The social scientist T. N. Madan has argued:** T. N. Madan, 'Secularism in its place', *The Journal of Asian Studies*, Vol. 46, No. 4, November 1987, pp. 747-759.

222 **The Hindutva ideologue David Frawley...warns against sarva dharma sambhava:** Vamadev Shastri, 'Sarva Dharma Sambhava: Unity or Confusion of Religions?', www.hinduhumanrights.info, 18 August 2013.

231 **there were indeed significant migrations from the Central Asian steppes:** K. Thangaraj and G. Chaubey, 'Too early to settle the Aryan migration debate', *The Hindu*, 13 July 2017.

231 **'it is difficult to deduce the direction...migration between the regions':** Ibid. Also see Michael Danino, 'Aryans and the Indus Valley Civilization: Archaeological, Skeletal and Molecular Evidence' in *A Companion to South Asia in the Past* edited by Gwen Robbins Schug and Subhash R. Walimbe, Oxford: John Wiley & Sons, 2016; and Danino's response ('The problematics of genetics and the Aryan issue', *The Hindu*, 29 June 2017) to Tony Joseph, 'How genetics is settling the Aryan migration debate', *The Hindu*, 16 June 2017.

232 **the Hindu Pallava kingdom even imported a monarch:** P. L. Kessler, 'South East Asia–Cambodia', www.historyfiles.co.uk.

236 **historian D. N. Jha describes a collective drinking ritual:** D. N. Jha, 'What the Gods Drank', *Indian Express*, 29 July 2017.

238–39 **Yogi Adityanath even authorized 'anti-Romeo squads':** 'UP CM Yogi Adityanath's anti-Romeo squads: "Moral policing", "Taliban-like", international media has its say', *Indian Express*, 3 April 2017.

242 **seventy cases of cow-related violence were reported:** Alison Saldanha, 'Cow-Related Hate Crimes Peaked in 2017, 86% of Those Killed Muslim', *thewire.in*, 8 December 2017 and Suhasini Raj and Rod Nordland, 'Forced to chant Hindu slogans, Muslim man is beaten to death in India', *New York Times*, 25 June 2019.

243 **Four Dalit youths caught skinning a cow:** '4 Dalits stripped, beaten up for skinning dead cow', *Times of India*, 13 July 2016.

243 **Two Dalit women were assaulted in BJP-ruled Madhya Pradesh:**
Siddharth Ranjan Das, 'Muslim Women Beaten Over Beef Rumour,
Spectators Film Attack, Cops Watch', www.NDTV.com, 27 July
2016.

243 **The Minister for Social Justice in the first Modi government:** Amulya
Gopalakrishnan, 'We Are All Gau Rakshaks: Whether or not we
care about cows, we certainly don't mind vigilantism', *Times of
India*, 1 August 2016.

244 **the country's population of cows is proving increasingly unsustainable:**
Venkitesh Ramakrishnan, 'The Cow Menace', *Frontline*, 10
November 2017.

245 **though the cow was sacred in Vedic times, it was this that allowed
for beef to be consumed:** 'It was not that the cow was not sacred
in Vedic times, it was because of her sacredness that it is ordained
in the *Vajasaneyi Samhita* that beef should be eaten.' From
Dharma Shastra Vichar (Marathi) by Panduranga Vaman Kane,
quoted in B. R. Ambedkar, *The Untouchables: Who Were They
and Why They Became Untouchables?*, 1948. Accessed via www.
ambedkarintellectuals.in on 15 June 2019.

245 **references in the Rig Veda, in the Dharmashastric literature:** D. N.
Jha, *The Myth of the Holy Cow*, London: Verso Books, 2004, pg
139. 'The Vedas mention about 250 animals out of which at least
50 were deemed fit for sacrifice, by implication for divine as well as
human consumption. The *Taittiriya Brahmana* categorically tells us,
"Verily the cow is food" (atho annam vai gauh) and Yajnavalkya's
insistence on eating the tender (amsala) flesh of the cow is well
known.'

246 **'I, for one, eat it, provided that it is tender':** 'Nevertheless
Yagnavalkya said, "I, for one, eat it, provided that it is tender."' in
*The Satapatha Brahmana According to the Text of the Madhyandina
School* translated by Julius Eggeling, Oxford: Clarendon Press, 1885,
p. 11.

CHAPTER FOURTEEN: A FAITH FOR THE TWENTY-FIRST CENTURY

258 **'There have been times when my faith has been questioned':** Suhasini
Haider, 'India will succeed if it is not splintered along religious lines:
Barack Obama', *The Hindu*, 28 January 2015.

259 **Muslim man who was beaten to death by a mob:** 'Muslim man

lynched by mob, forced to chant Jai Shri Ram, dies', *India Today*, 24 June 2019.

261 'Whenever a copy of the sacred Quran...Shivaji treated it with respect': Percival Spear, Vincent Smith (trans.), *The Oxford History of India*, 4th edition, London: Oxford University Press, p. 412.

262 'The Hindus have their faults,' Vivekananda added: Makarand R. Paranjape (ed.), *Swami Vivekananda: A Contemporary Reader*, New Delhi: Routledge, 2015.

262 'Not for them the sophistication of the Upanishads': Amartya Sen, 'Threats to Secular India', *Social Scientist*, Volume 21, 1993.

278 *You're so drunk on wealth and power*: http://prekshaa.in/story-verse-udayanacharya-nyaya-tarka-vaisheshika-shastra-buddhism-puri-jagannath/

284 *To the heavens be peace*: Raimon Panikkar, *The Vedic Experience*.

IMAGE CREDITS

Every effort has been made to trace copyright holders and provide complete and correct attribution for the images used inside the book. Any errors or omissions in the list below that are brought to our notice will be remedied in future editions of this book.

Colour inserts: Section One (Ganesha and his two wives, chromolithograph by Raja Ravi Varma © Wellcome Collection; Saraswati, oleograph by Raja Ravi Varma, via Wikimedia Commons). Section Two (A calm and serene Lord Krishna; Krishna and Arjuna on battlefield, both via Flickr © Infinite Eyes). Section Three (Hindu deity Kartikeya or Murugan; Matsya, Lord Vishnu's fish avatar, both by Raja Ravi Varma via Wikimedia Commons). Section Four (Lord Shiva and consort Parvati with sons Kartikeya and Ganesha, via Flickr © Infinite Eyes; Tripura Sundari via Wikimedia Commons © Arjunkrishna90). Section Five (Kali trampling Shiva, chromolithograph by Raja Ravi Varma © Wellcome Collection; Shri Shri Durga, ca. 1885–95, Calcutta, Purchase, Peter Louis and Chandru Ramchandani Gift, 2018 © The Metropolitan Museum of Art, New York).

Pages viii (Brahma on Hamsa, Pahari, circa 1700 © Museum of Fine Arts, Boston); xiii (from The Sundhya or the Daily Prayers of Brahmins by Sophie Charlotte Belnos, 1851, in the collection of the New York Public Library); xv (Hindu trinity, calendar art); 17 (© The J. Paul Getty Museum); 24 (Gift of R. H. Ellsworth Ltd., in honor of Susan Dillon, 1987 © The Metropolitan Museum of Art, New York); 54 (Gift of Florence and

Ravi Varma); 146 (© Calvinkrishy); 156 (Miniature painting of 24 Jain Tirthankaras from Jaipur, circa 1850); 159; 163; 165 (© Sscheral); 167 (Guru Nanak, from *The Oxford Student's History of India* by Vincent A. Smith, 1921); 173; 181; 182; 185; 192; 193; 195 (© Gan13166); 197; 202 (Photograph of Sarvepalli Radhakrishnan presented to First Lady Jacqueline Kennedy in 1962, © The John F. Kennedy Presidential Library and Museum); 206; 212 (© India Post, Government of India, from www.postagestamps.gov.in/); 215 (© Etienne Alexander Rodriques); 218 (© Subhrajyoti07); 221; 223 (© BrownyCat); 229 (© Indian Navy, from www.indiannavy.nic.in); 232 (© Ssriram mt); 238 (© Leon petrosyan); 244; 245 (© Ramanarayanadatta astir); 258 (© Pete Souza); 261; 265 (© Bina R); 266 (© E P Sajeevan); 270 (© Akhand hind fauj); 273 (© Matthieu Moy); 278 (© Henry Dixon); 289 (© Ministry of Human Resource Development, India).

Hindu Mythology: Vedic and Purnanic by W. J. Wilkins, published by Thacker, Spink & Co: Calcutta and Simla, 1913: pages iii, v, xviii.

The Ramayana of Valmiki, published by The Christian Society of India: London and Madras, 1896: page 35.

FURTHER READING

Agrawala, Vasudev Sharan, *Padmavat: Malik Muhammad Jayasi krit Mahakavya (Mool Aur Sanjeevani Vyakhya)*, Jhansi: Sahitya Sadan, 1955.

Ananthamurthy, U. R., *Hindutva or Hind Swaraj*, New Delhi: HarperCollins, 2016.

Andersen, Walter K. and Damle, Shridhar D., *The Brotherhood in Saffron: The Rashtriya Swayamsevak Sangh and Hindu Revivalism*, New Delhi: Vistaar Publications, 1987.

Basham, A. L., *The Wonder That Was India*, London: Picador, 2004.

Chinmayananda, Swami, *The Holy Geeta*, Mumbai: Chinmaya Mission Trust, 1992.

Coomaraswamy, Ananda, *A New Approach to the Vedas: An Essay in Translation and Exegesis*, New Delhi: South Asia Books, 1994.

Deshpande, C. R., *Transmission of the Mahabharata Tradition*, Simla: Indian Institute of Advanced Study, 1978.

Doniger, Wendy, *On Hinduism*, New Delhi: Aleph Book Company, 2013.

———, *The Hindus: An Alternative History*, New Delhi: Penguin Books, 2009.

Eck, Diana, *India: A Sacred Geography*, New York: Harmony Books, 2013.

Elst, Koenraad, *Bharatiya Janata Party Vis-a-vis Hindu Resurgence*, New Delhi: Voice of India, 1997.

Embree, Ainslie T., *Sources of Indian Tradition, Vol. 1: From the Beginning to 1800*, New York: Columbia University Press, 1958.

Gambhirananda, Swami, trans., *Eight Upanishads with the Commentary of Sankaracarya*, Second Revised Edition, Volumes I and II, Kolkata: Advaita Ashrama, 1989 and reprinted 2006.

Ganeri, Jonardon, *Artha: Meaning (Foundations of Philosophy in India)*, New

Delhi: Oxford University Press, 2011.

Golwalkar, M. S., *Bunch of Thoughts*, Fourth Impression, Bangalore: Vikram Prakashan, 1968.

————, *We, or Our Nation Defined*, Third Edition, Nagpur: Bharat Publications, 1945.

Guru, Nataraja, *The Word of the Guru: The Life and Teaching of Guru Narayana*, New Delhi: DK Printworld, 2003.

Jaffrelot, Christophe, *Hindu Nationalism: A Reader*, Princeton: Princeton University Press, 2007.

————, *The Hindu Nationalist Movement and Indian Politics: 1925 to the 1990s*, London: C. Hurst & Co. Publishers, 1996.

Jagannathan, Shakunthala, *Hinduism*, Bombay: Vakil, Feffer and Simons, 1984.

Jha, D. N., *The Myth of the Holy Cow*, New Delhi: Navayana Books, 2009.

————, 'What the gods drank', *Indian Express*, 29 July 2017.

Khan, Ansar Hussain, *The Rediscovery of India: A New Subcontinent*, Hyderabad: Orient Longman, 1995.

Krishna, Nanditha and Jagannathan, Shakunthala, *Ganesha: The Auspicious... The Beginning*, Bombay: Vakil, Feffer And Simons, 1992.

Kumaran, Murkkoth, *The Biography of Sree Narayana Guru*, Sivagiri: Sivagiri Madom, 2011.

Lannoy, Richard, *The Speaking Tree: A Study of Indian Culture and Society*, New York & London: Oxford University Press, 1971.

Mandeville, John, *The Travels of Sir John Mandeville*, Moseley, C. (trans.), London: Penguin Books, 2005.

Mascaro, Juan, *The Upanishads*, London: Penguin Books, 1965.

Menon, Ramesh, *Bhagavata Purana*, New Delhi: Rupa Publications, 2007.

Nehru, Jawaharlal, *The Discovery of India*, Calcutta: The Signet Press, 1946.

Pandey, Gyanendra, 'Which of Us are Hindus?' in *Hindus and Others: The Question of Identity in India Today*, New Delhi: Viking, 1993.

Panikkar, Raimon, *The Vedic Experience: Mantramañjari: An Anthology of the Vedas for Modern Man*, Berkeley: University of California Press, 1977.

Parthasarathy, Swami A., *Vedanta Treatise: The Eternities*, Bombay: Vakil & Sons, 1978.

Prakashan, Bharat, *Shri Guruji: The Man and His Mission, On the Occasion of His 51st Birthday*. Delhi: Bharat Prakashan, 1955.

Prasad, Swami Muni Narayana, *The Philosophy of Narayana Guru*, New Delhi: DK Printworld, 2003.

Radhakrishnan, S., *The Hindu View of Life*, London: George Allen & Unwin Ltd., 1927.

Ramachandran, R., *A History of Hinduism: From the Origins to the Present* (unpublished manuscript), 2017.

Saraswati, Swami Satyananda, *Four Chapters on Freedom: Commentary on the Yoga Sutras of Patanjali*, Munger: Yoga Publications Trust, 1976.

Savarkar, V. D., *Essentials of Hindutva* (available only on PDF) & *Hindutva: Who Is a Hindu?*, 1928, reprint Gorakhpur: Gita Press, 1993.

———, *Hindutva: Who is a Hindu?*, Bombay: Veer Savarkar Prakashan, 1923.

Sen, K. M., *Hinduism*, London: Penguin Books, 1978.

Singh, Dr Karan, *Essays on Hinduism*, Delhi: Ratna Sagar, 1989.

Singh, Upinder, *The Idea of Ancient India: Essays on Religion, Politics, and Archaeology*, New Delhi: Sage Publications, 2016.

Swami, Shri Purohit, *The Geeta: The Gospel of Lord Shri Krishna*, London: Faber and Faber, 1935.

Thapar, Romila: *The Penguin History of Early India from the Origins to* AD *1300*, New Delhi: Penguin Books, 2003.

Tharoor, Shashi, *India: From Midnight to the Millenium and Beyond*, New Delhi: Penguin Books, 2012.

———, *An Era of Darkness: The British Empire in India*, New Delhi: Aleph Book Company, 2016.

———, *India Shastra: Reflections on the Nation in our Time*, New Delhi: Aleph Book Company, 2015.

———, *The Great Indian Novel*, New Delhi: Penguin Books, 1989.

The Life of Swami Vivekananda by his Eastern and Western Disciples, 2 vols., Kolkata: Advaita Ashrama Trust, 1999.

Viswanathan, Ed, *Am I a Hindu?*, New Delhi: Rupa Publications, 1993.

Vivekananda, Swami, *The Complete Works of Swami Vivekananda*, Chennai: Manonmani Publishers, 2015.

Zaehner, R. C., *Hinduism*, London: Oxford University Press, 1962.